APEX

FULL SEND BOOK ONE

NOVA KANE

First edition
Cover Models - S1krrafa & AP_m0t0
Cover Design & Formatting - BeholdenBookCovers
Character Art - @Giulia_fw.arts
Editing - Renee Polkinghorne & Lori Rivera

LOOK TWICE, SAVE A LIFE

IN MEMORY OF THOSE WE'VE LOST

Chris Cane, Cristian Sales, Nelson Webber, MarioS1K, Yesenia Acosta, Dakarai Griffin, John Guate Sr, Andrew Wade, Hendrix, Kris Monette, Eric Gonzalas, Eric Draga, Michael Burroughs, Dylan Brackett, Gabriella Meek, Brandon Carter, Robert Mendenhall Jr, Tony Valentino, Ryan Wallach, Shawn Conley, Lucas Cowden, Travis Dalton, Shawn Vowels, Nate Allen, Reece Alvarez, Dawon Anderson, Theo Angelakos, Shaun Arnold, Jay Holley, Kyle Aronowitz, Audrey Oefinger, Steven Baggett, Martin Baltimore, Brandon Barody, Herbie Bartels, Rhenky 'Primo' Beltre, Alfonso Leo, Tanner Beighley, Salmane Benjelloun, Chris Bowmer, Johnny Walker, Chris Babcock, Chris Boyer, Samuel Hemphill, Michael Bitto, Troy Bozarth, Tony 'Amp' Brown aka Ghost, Apollo Busa, Eric 'Weeze' Cahill, Tony Card, Zac Marcano, Wayne 'Boogey' Martin, Shane Mcentegart, Adrian Mcfarland, Andy Mercer, Tony Mottley, Bryan Chubb, Chris Haskell, William Major, Ian Harris, Michael Hicks, Jason Itro, April Havens, Justin Johnson, Ernie Hernandez, Chase Kattell, Eric Jordan, Johnny Khalifa, Kyllan Purdon, Lucas Knight,

Matthew Knight, Ryan Koch, Tom Konier, Cameron Koss, Kurt Langel, Daniel Lero James Littleton, Shine CBR, Michael Cherry, Anthony Joe Mack, Ross Chrisman, Riko Martin Sr, Quintin Clark, Felix Colon, Luke Plasencia, Carlos Rivera-Silva, Mark 'Busa' Gomes, Elier Gonzalaz, Al Tobacco, Floyd Laycock, Buddy Reed, Sydney Pender, Xavier Alonso, Chasity Porrata, Devin Porrata, Chasity Rivera, Joshua Douglass, Mitchell Roberge, Darren Drysdale, Geoff Heil, Vance Ralph Eldridge Jr, Cassidy Manchester, Justin Carpenter, Kindred Carter, Eddy Castillo, Jessie Caudill, Lance Strickland, Joshua Custer, Anthony Avalos, Gage Sears, Sean Kunkle, Dustin Jay, David Mcintosh, James Beach, Keith Williamson, Robert Black Jr, Anthony Cook, Dallas Kirk, Eddie Lee Curry, Jason Prine, Aaron Daly, Matthew Deremer, Andrew Robinson, Erica Rodriguez, Francisco Gabriel Rodriguez, Anthony Jay Roe, Serrano Sebastian, Chase Shepperd, Nick Shontz, James Shortt, Austin Aiken, Zach Rogers, Brad Elder, Orlando 'Panda' Rodriguez Jr, Coty Ryhal, Sam Beede, Jose 'Jockey' Sanchez, Richard Schoeneck, Justin Stair, Chad Stephens, Corbin Stoltzfoos, Mason Storm, Philip Alan Theroux, Juwan 'A' Thomas, Fred Lanzo, Tyler Thompson, Kassidy Marie Titara, Terry Dillard Jr, Joshua Torny, Angel Correa, Zay Enrique Rodriguez, Hector Davila, Dakota Grimes, Jose Pena, Bradley Casler, Michael Henderson, Justin Mason, Justin Ennis, Lewis Joy, Phillip Ezell, Dylan Beauchamp, Anthony Farmer, Ryan 'Pig' Pignatelli, Cameron Farrer, Inkin Mike Pierce, Lex Fernandez, Armando Hernandez, Austin Grubb, Tyler John Pangrazio, James Figueroa, Roy Rainy, Melvin Cline Ford Jr, Kelvin Garay, Kenneth Gordils, Sarahjo Fuentes, Jarrett Gretebeck, Amanda Hacker, Casey Hahn, Tony Lee Hall Jr, Ryan Michael Bazell, Margarita Sagastizabal, Alphonso 'Poncho' Rodriguez, Dusty Duet, Jan Gabriel Melendez, Justin Mullins, Leilanie Ortiz, Josh Ortiz, Mark West, Christian Rozo, Robert Stafford, Sara Wheadon, Chris 'Chico' Watson, Wanderley Echemen, Sam Lougheed, Kevin Charles, Trevon Boose, Janell

McDougald, Alia Rogers, Donald Tyner, Aaron Barnhouse, Jario Hernandez, Dwight Harvey, Alexis Candelario Pacheco, James Redner-Gilmartin, Barrett 'Bodi' Phelps, Kyle Rush, Jimmy Butler, John Woodward Lauri Eastwood, Jason Shecter, John Sackett, Tony Perry, Eddie Jimenez, Jordan Renk, Tristan Velez Cody Snider, Gregory Johnson, Joseph 'Doughboy' Ryan Decubellis, Chris Mettao, Tony Cosdon Devante London, Ed 'Pops' Castleberry, Boston Mike, Dylan Press, Jerry Cedeno, James Littleton, Fred Pretorius, Suzette Pretorius, Thomas Slayter, Damon 'Da Kidd' Welle, Quwali Foster, Bryan Farrington, Lisa Bonwick, Bobby Fetty, KC Gilbow, Cody Delmar Beasly, Aaron Joseph Rathmann, Clifford J Flandreau III, Jeff Schlinger, Joe Zadina, Anton Potgieter, Derek Potgieter, Michael Hanson, Suavè Oog, Jason Itro, Supercat, Smoky, Chatterbox, Patches, Petrus Lukas van Mollendorf, John Solomon Lee, Jeremy Shane Denney, Gage Alizey Carroll, Wayne Patterson, Danny Kinkade, Richard Pilbeam, Billy Collins, Ed Sikich, Aaron Gardner

For all the BookTok girls,
Who want to know if the BikeTok guys fuck as hard as they ride.
They do.

TRIGGER WARNINGS

Abuse (Physical, Emotional, Verbal)
Murder
Non-Con
Vehicle Collision
Alcohol Use
Gaslighting
Manipulation
Bullying
Death
Choking
Spitting
Mentions SA

PROLOGUE
SAYSHEN

June 2020

Wait For You - Johnny Orlando

Bexley *fucking* Larson.

The girl every guy wants, and every girl wants to be. But that's not all she is. She's also the only chick to repeatedly shut down every attempt I make to get her on the back of my bike. Where other girls are beyond desperate to be seen backpacking with me, Bexley Larson is the first to tell me very bluntly just how she feels about my *fuckboy* tendencies.

She's not wrong, though. I may have a habit of hitting anything that comes within a five-mile radius, and never more than once. But hey, I'm an eighteen-year-old teenage dude with a shit ton of testosterone pumping through me. Can you really blame me? With her, though, I don't even have to hit it to know once would never be enough.

It's hot as hell today, and thankfully, school is officially out for the summer. For me, well, I'm never coming back to this shit hole. I don't need to. Racing is my life, and nothing these lazy underpaid fucks teach me is going to help me on the track, so I'm done wasting my time. Talon and Dad have been harassing me for months about dropping out, but I wouldn't. Being here is the only place I get to see her or be near her, and they knew that. It's why they would've loved to get me to drop out.

My obsession with Bexley is well known, though I doubt most people take it seriously. Everyone thinks it's a game, that I want her simply because she denies me. But it's so much more than that. Bexley is above the girls at Palms High. She's out of every dude's league, including mine. Not like that is ever going to stop me.

Bexley—well, she's got her senior year left, but this is it for me. Graduation was weeks ago, and I've run out of excuses to hang out at the school. While I have finished all my subjects, some seniors were still finishing off the last of their senior year. Allowing me the chance to go unnoticed a bit longer, and I have taken full advantage of it.

I watch as she leans against the metallic blue door to one of her friend's SUV. Her stack of books pressed tightly against her chest, pushing up her perky little tits. Just the sight of them has me adjusting myself in my gray sweats. Her thick dark hair blows about in the wind, carrying the scent of her familiar perfume right to my nose. I don't know what it is, but it's sweet, fresh. Like cactus and dragon fruit. *Fucking delicious.*

"Christ, when are you gonna give up on her man? There are much easier girls, just as hot as her, that will take one look at you and your bike and be begging for a shot." Cruz pipes in with a mockingly playful tone as he sits down next to me. Today is the final day for the remaining senior year, which means it's his last day too, but unlike me, he's more than happy to be done with this place.

"Yeah, yeah. You know you're starting to sound a lot like Talon," I snap back, keeping my eyes on Bexley.

"You've been trying since freshman year, dude. Bexley isn't

falling for your shit. Give it up already." I know he's right. Nothing I do ever works with her, but I don't have it in me to quit. Never did. It's not in my blood.

I'm a Shaw, and we always win.

"Have you seen me?" I smirk, nudging him in the ribs with my elbow. Us Shaw's were blessed with good looks, and we know it. Dark hair, tanned skin, and to top it all off, I tower over most of the senior class guys, and thanks to Dad and Talon always riding my ass about being fit for training, I'm a solid wall of muscle. What girl wouldn't want a piece of me?

Bexley Larson. That's who.

I bend my knees, pulling them into my chest as I lean forward and rest my arms across them. My gaze strays back in her direction. Bexley smiles, tucking her hair behind her ear as her friends giggle around her.

Fuck, she's gorgeous.

"She'll give in eventually. They always do," I add. It slips from my lips just as Bexley's hazel eyes meet mine.

The gold flecks in them glint in the sun, and for a brief moment, I feel like maybe she doesn't totally hate me. But it's short-lived. The moment I tilt my chin towards her, she scoffs and crinkles her cute nose with disgust. My smirk grows. She hates me, but hey, that means she feels something for me. Which means there's always a chance I can sway her, and *that* I can work with.

The race is just beginning, Bex.

The girls I hook up with don't mean shit. Not that I tell anyone that. They're just the laps around the track. A means to get off and warm up my tires before the final lap. Bexley.

To most of the girls I hook up with, that's all I am too. A really hot guy with a bike that can make them feel good for a night. It's an arrangement. But Bexley Larson, she's the fucking finish line. The goddamn checkered flag, and it might not happen today, but when the race is over, she will be in my hands for the winning lap.

Pushing off the SUV she locks arms with Cece, whom I've come to know as her best friend and bodyguard, and drags her off to the other side of the parking lot.

I watch, unwilling to tear my eyes from her tight little ass as she struts away toward where her white Lexus is parked and out of my line of sight. Only then do I let my head fall back, and my eyes find their way to the sunny Tampa sky.

Fuck, this is it.

Thankfully, the end of school signals the start of the race season. Something to at least help keep my mind off her. Hopefully.

"Baby Shaw, Van Doren, you coming or what fuckers? We got shit to do and places to be," Draygon shouts from where all our bikes are parked. Draygon is one of the older guys on the team. Knowing Talon, he sent him down here to meet us because he had a feeling we'd be in no rush to get to the track. "Coach is already at the track, and you know he ain't gonna like it if we show up late. By the way, Baby Shaw, your brother has been trying to get a hold of you since the third period."

"Yes, Mother, we're coming," Cruz croons with a childish tone as he stands up. "Let's go, Prince Charming, duty calls." He offers a hand to help me up. I take it, slapping my hand into his as I shake my head. Fucking guy thinks he's funny. Running my hand through my dark, thick hair, I lift my eyes back to Bexley's car just as she pulls out of the parking lot and takes off down the street. "Shaw!" Cruz shouts. "Snap out of it, she's just a chick, and it's summer. You know what that means!"

Cruz wraps his arm around my neck as we head toward Draygon and our bikes. "I do?" I reply, cocking a brow.

"It means by the end of the night, we'll have a revolving door of pussy, lining up at our door for you to choose from," he chuckles. "And seeing as I have my girl, you can have first dibs on whoever you want," he adds. He and his girl Lena have been together for a few years now, and though Cruz comes off like a joker, there's one thing I've learned about him. You never fuck with his girl. They're the Bonnie and Clyde type of couple. The ride or die type shit that most people dream of finding, and honestly the guys and I all get along great with her, so it's worked out. She's like one of the guys now.

Draygon revs his engine as we approach, and Cruz frees me from his hold as he climbs on his bike. Reaching mine, I grab my Shoei helmet from the seat and slide it on my head before lifting my leg over and climbing on. Turning the key, the engine purrs to life beneath me.

"You good, Baby Shaw?" Draygon shouts over the sound of the bikes.

"Yeah, man, I'm all good," I reply, nodding at him. I don't know who I'm trying to convince more, him or myself. He flicks his visor closed and revs his engine twice more before pulling out of the lot and onto the main strip towards the track. Cruz follows suit, shaking his head at me disapprovingly on his way by. I allow myself another glance around the lot, and the school I wasted four years of my life at, before lifting the kickstand and revving the engine again. Snapping my visor down, I head through the empty lot after my team.

It's weird seeing it so empty and quiet. Yet, no matter how different it is, every inch of it reminds me of nothing but her—Bexley.

CHAPTER 1

BEXLEY

Four Years Later

Friends - Chase Atlantic

The tiny bell hanging on the door of the cafe chimes every time someone comes and goes, sending a pulsating sharp pain through my head. I suspected last night I was suffering from yet another concussion, but the scent of food turning my stomach and the small cafe I'm standing in spinning around me confirms it. Nothing I haven't dealt with before. I'll be fine.

At least until Cece gets here.

My best friend has known me so long she can tell when I'm lying, and I have no doubt she'll call me out on my attempts to hide the newest collection of bruises across my skin.

She knows all about Christian, and what happens when he goes off. I can't even count the number of times she's threatened to put a bullet in his head and bury him six feet under for laying his hands on me. I know she's being protective, and I admire her for it, but sometimes I wish she wouldn't say anything. Walking on eggshells around him is hard enough. I don't need the added stress of wondering what will happen if he ever decides to snap on her the way he does me.

I have to admit though, it's rather funny, watching her chew him a new one. No one ever does. Only Cecilia. She's the only one who has the balls to give him a piece of her mind, but honestly, she's like that with everyone. Cece, despite being five foot nothing, never takes shit from anyone. Never has. There is no way in hell she'll miss the marks this time, and even if she does, she'll see right through my lies until she's forcing me to show them to her.

And as much as I hate that, if there is anyone I can't hide them from, I'm thankful it's her.

I pull the sleeves of my shirt down, fidgeting with the cotton fabric in my hands as I wait patiently in the lineup to place my order. Hopefully, now that race season is starting, Christian will be more focused on that than me.

Who am I kidding? If anything, it will only get worse.

Especially with the added pressure and stress of winning. It doesn't matter that I'm not one of his adrenaline-junkie opponents. I don't even involve myself in his race stuff other than show up to watch when I'm supposed to, and I definitely never touch his precious bike. Yet, every loss or every idiot he goes up against that does something to piss him off, is always somehow my fault.

It's me who always receives the brunt of his aggression and frustration.

His personal punching bag.

Cece always asks me why I stay. Why, no matter what he does to me, I find some reason, some excuse to stay. Sometimes, I even find myself defending him and what he does.

Idiot.

But no matter how many times she asks and how many times

I forgive him, I never know how to answer her. Because, if I'm honest, even I don't know the answer.

Fear, maybe? A sense of responsibility or hope that the man I met four years ago, who was funny, kind, and caring, is still in there. But even I know he isn't.

I don't think that man ever existed.

Not really.

Checking the time on my phone, I'm shocked to find I've been here for over fifteen minutes, and the line has barely moved. I roll my eyes and turn my attention outside. Summer is just beginning, and it's about time. The large cafe windows allow the bright rays of sun to pour in and illuminate the space. Outside, people are sitting at small bistro tables, where some are chatting away, and others are working. It's busy here, not that I'm surprised; Seaside Cafe makes the best coffee in Tampa, and with the return of the warm weather comes the tourists who all want a taste.

The familiar hum of sports bike engines meets my ears and draws my attention to the parking lot outside. A red BMW S1000 and matte black Yamaha R1 pull up and park. Bikes around here are a common sight. You rarely go anywhere without seeing them, especially with the warmer weather finally upon us. It's also opening weekend at the track, bringing bikes and teams from all over the country to this part of Tampa for the start of the race season.

One of the guys hangs back to make a phone call, and the other slides his helmet off and places it on his seat. I watch as he runs his tattooed hand through his hair, brushing it back from his face. The moment his face is in my view, my stomach catches in my throat.

Sayshen Shaw.

Biggest fuckboy from Palms High, the high school we both attended. The guy every girl fucked, and then bragged about for a week until she realized she was no different than any of the other chicks who were stupid enough to get under him before she did. His body count from senior year alone is more than most men fuck in their lifetime.

Girls always flocked to him, desperate for his attention and I never understood it. Don't get me wrong, he's hot, even I won't deny that. But I would never allow myself to be just another notch in his bedpost. Another girl he fucks for a night and forgets. While some girls want the guy all the girls want, it's a turn-off for me. Especially when they can actually get him. I don't want what anyone can get, and with Sayshen Shaw, if it walks, talks, and has a pussy, he'll fuck it.

I watch as the small bell above the door chimes with Sayshen's entrance into the cafe. At first, he takes his place at the back of the line. He's gotten taller since graduation and maybe a bit more buff. His arms, hands, and neck are covered in thick black traditional tattoos, and he has a small diamond stud earring through his nose. Other than that, he looks the same as he did then. The same dark hair, though now it's shaved around the sides and a bit longer on the top. His bangs hang down over his face, accentuating his dark whiskey-brown eyes as they roam the small space of the cafe. His skin is tanned and—

The lady in line behind me clears her throat, breaking my thought, "Are you going to move up? Or can I cut in front of you?" she asks with annoyance. Turning, I find the line has moved, but I was so focused on Sayshen I hadn't noticed.

Feeling slightly embarrassed, I apologize before moving up the line.

"Bexley Larson. Is that you?" Someone shouts from behind me.

Fuck.

I don't have to look back to know who it is. His tone, though deeper, is still familiar. Looking over my shoulder, I see him pushing through the line as he approaches me with his friend following behind him.

"Ha, I knew it was you," he adds as the lineup of people grunts and groans at them. Clearly pissed off at them for cutting through the line to reach me. Sayshen's friend pulls out a small pocketknife and uses it to pick his pearly white teeth as he eyes the lineup of impatient customers. I remember seeing this guy around a bit in high school. He was never a student, at least not that I remember, but he often sat out in the parking lot on his bike. Waiting for Sayshen and his friends, Cruz and Reign, to get out of school.

"Is there a problem?" The guy asks the crowd in a husky tone. It's a threat, for sure, but it works. Their complaints quickly disappear, and most turn their eyes away from Sayshen and his intimidating friend.

Returning my eyes forward, my lips pull into a small smile as I wrap my arms around myself, sleeves pulled tightly in my fists.

"Well, if it isn't Sayshen Shaw," I retort mockingly.

Finally reaching my side, he eyes me from head to toe before bringing himself to stand next to me in line. "Damn, girl. You haven't changed at all. Ass still tight as fuck and still just as gorgeous."

His friend hovers next to him, typing away on his phone. His jet-black hair is slicked back neatly on his head, and tattoos cover every inch of his exposed olive skin. He is taller than Sayshen and definitely older.

"Great, thanks. Don't think I could've survived my day without being eye fucked by the biggest fuckboy from my high school years," I spit cockily. "Great to know you've matured, Shaw,"

The line moves forward, and I move with it. Eager to get further away from Sayshen and the attention he's drawing. My eyes find their way to the ceiling as I release a breath. Cece can show up anytime now. This bitch is always late.

"Aw, come on, don't be like that, alright? I was trying to give you a compliment. Besides, I'm not the same guy I was back then," he explains.

"That's awesome, Sayshen, really. But to be honest, I don't care even if you are or not," I admit with annoyance.

"Why do you gotta be like that? Let me take you out sometime. We can catch up," he says, pressing his hand over his heart like my coldness inflicts pain. Sayshen Shaw might not be a bad guy, but he's not the right kind of guy for me. He never was. I rejected his every attempt all through high school, and when I say he tried, *he tried.* I was the only girl he spent all four years pinning for, the only one who didn't give into his looks and his charm. I'll admit, sometimes it wasn't easy. He was hot then, and he's even hotter now, but I'm with Christian.

"I can't, sorry. I'm taken, and I don't think my boyfriend would appreciate me hanging out with, well, a guy like you," I admit. The line moves up again, and it's finally my turn to order, yet there's still no sign of my best friend.

"A guy like me?" he laughs, following behind me as I approach the counter.

"Hi, welcome to Seaside Cafe. What can I get you?" The pretty blonde barista asks from her till. She looks exhausted. Her hair is a mess in her little visor cap, and her eyes are puffy as she puts on a fake smile for the line of customers.

"Hey, yeah, can I get a large strawberry matcha latte with oat milk and a large shaken espresso with vanilla cold foam—"

"Hey, do you think you could hurry those up for me, beautiful? We're in a bit of a hurry," Sayshen adds in a flirtatious tone, cutting me off mid-order as he leans on the counter next to me. The barista's eyes widen with excitement as she takes in his inked arms and chiseled jawline. One look at the protective chest plate, before her eyes flicker outside to where he and his friend's bikes are parked and she instantly caves.

"Right, of course. I can totally do that for you." She stammers nervously as Sayshen hands her a twenty. "I like your bike," she adds with a shy tone.

Sayshen grins, "Well thank you," he replies as his eyes lower to me, "she's pretty badass if I do say so myself."

Ignoring his comment, I cross my arms over my chest and lift my eyes to his. "What are you doing and why are you paying for my drinks?"

"I'm not," he replies, signaling the barista to keep the change. "I'm buying you *and* Cece drinks, because I can."

Thrown back by his response, I raise my brow. "How'd you know one was for Cece?" A genuine question I find myself wondering as we move over to the pickup area.

"I paid more attention in high school than you think I did. She was your best friend, the moment you ordered her nasty green drink I knew who it was for. Besides, you've always been a plain-Jane kind of coffee girl. Ain't no way that fancy shit was for you." I don't know what I find more surprising. The fact that there is a whole other side of Sayshen I apparently didn't know in high school, or the fact that years later, he somehow remembered not only my coffee order but my best friend's.

His friend's phone rings, and he quickly answers it in a foreign language, takes it and heads outside to talk, leaving Sayshen and me alone again as we wait for my drinks.

"Okay, well, thanks, I guess," I reply.

"So, are you going to tell me who the lucky guy is?" he asks, tucking his hands into the pockets of his jeans as he leans against the wall next to the pickup. I laugh, turning my eyes up to his. Even with him leaning against the wall, I feel short standing next to him. I'm guessing he's about 6"1", and god, don't get me started on how toned he is this close up.

"Nope," I reply, accentuating the P sound with my lips as I smile and turn my gaze back behind the counter where the barista is whipping up my order as quickly as she can. No doubt to impress fuckboy Sayshen over here.

"Why not?" he asks. Though he is out of my line of sight, I can feel his eyes on me. The weight of his gaze has my stomach in knots and my cheeks flushed.

I don't know why I like it. I shouldn't, especially because of Christian.

"Because it doesn't matter," I chuckle. The barista makes her way over and places my drinks on the counter, looking right past me and over to Sayshen.

"Here you go, enjoy. I hope to see you again," she adds excitedly.

Rolling my eyes, I unwrap my arms from myself and grab the drinks from the counter before turning to walk away. Catching me off guard, Sayshen's hand gently grabs my forearm, pulling me toward him.

"Bex, who did this to you?" he asks sternly as he examines the bruising along my exposed arm. Fuck. In grabbing the drinks, I hadn't thought about the marks on my arm I've been spending all morning keeping hidden. Lifting my eyes to his face, I find his attention fully focused on the bruising as he slowly pushes back the fabric of my sleeve to expose more of the purple and red marks.

"It's nothing," I whisper, pulling my arm from his grip.

"That isn't nothing. Don't give me that bullshit," he snaps, drawing the attention of the people in line next to us. "He put his hands on you? Who is he?" he asks with an aggressive tone. More people begin to notice the change in tension and set their sights on us. My cheeks flush with embarrassment just as Cece's voice hits my ears.

"Sorry, I'm late bitch, my car wouldn't start. I had to get my brother to–" Cece freezes, stopping mid-sentence when she notices Sayshen standing with me. But it's not the Sayshen that just paid for my drinks. The carefree, comical guy from just a few moments ago is gone. Though his eyes hold my stare, they have darkened, and his jaw clicks with anger. I find myself confused, puzzled as to why Sayshen would care at all about what's happened to me. Especially enough to have the reaction he's having now.

I am nothing to him. I never was. Just a girl he wanted and couldn't have, nothing more. Why does he care about the marks he found on my arm? What does it matter to him how they got there, or rather who put them there?

"Sayshen Shaw. Well, that's a face I never thought I'd see around here again," Cece admits as she locks her arm through mine. "You good, Bex?" Her long lavender hair cascades down her back in thick beachy waves with a few tiny braids randomly placed throughout. Paired with a cute crochet crop top that ties around the back of her neck and cute denim shorts, she's making quite the fashion statement.

Not that I'm surprised. I'm the one who told her what to wear when we were on video call this morning. If there's anything I know, it's fashion, and this year, crochet crops are definitely in, especially when you have a body like Cece's. Lucky bitch inherited the naturally tanned skin from her mother, who was born and raised in Mexico. Big brown doe eyes and lips the Kardashian's would literally pay for, it's a wonder why my bestie is single.

Actually, no it's not. She's more than a little spicy, and well, most men don't know how to handle heat.

"Yeah, I'm okay. We should, um, go now. We really don't want to be late," I stutter with a startled tone, trying my best not to sound like I'm internally freaking out.

"Yes, let's do that cause I don't know what's happening here," she gestures, pointing her finger from Sayshen to me, "but I don't like it, so let's go. See ya around, Shaw." And with that, Cece pulls me away until we're standing outside. The fresh sea salt air assaults my lungs as she drags me over to her small violet Honda Civic that she left parked in the lot. She heads to the driver's side while I climb inside the passenger seat. I exhale and let my head fall back on the headrest as my eyes flutter closed, and I try to get a grip on everything that just happened.

"What the fuck was that about?" Cece asks as she closes her door. Handing her drink over, I laugh.

"Nothing, it was nothing."

Lies.

"Puta, you are so full of shit, and what the fuck is this on your arm?" she snaps with a concerned tone as she takes her drink from me.

"It's fine. I'm fine," I reply, pulling down the fabric of my sleeve, suddenly feeling insecure in my own skin. "Why is everyone so fucking worried about marks on my arm. It could be from a million different things!" I snap.

"Oh, okay, so that's what was up Sayshen's ass, too, huh. Good," she adds as she takes a sip of her drink before placing it in her cup holder. "That boy was so obsessed with you all through high school I'm not even surprised he still wants a piece. Shit, maybe you should let him." She smirks coyly as she wiggles her eyebrows.

"Seriously?" I scoff, shoving her arm playfully.

"I was just kidding, kind of..." She laughs. "But in all seriousness, Bex, it could be from a million different things, but you and I, we both know damn well who and what those marks are from. When the fuck are you going to leave his stupid ass? Like, I'm trying to be patient, and kind but for the life of me I don't understand why you put yourself through this shit!" Her shouting sends sharp pains radiating through my temples, intensifying the lingering pain. Clenching my eyes closed, I bring my hand to my head.

"Stop, okay. I don't need this today. Especially not from you." I wince as the pain in my head throbs.

"I'll stop only because even I can tell you're in pain right now. But I fucking hate that piece of shit. You deserve so much better," she replies as she starts up the engine. "Fuck, I can't wait to give him a piece of my mind when I see him." As she backs out of her spot, I glance back to where Sayshen and his friend parked their bikes. Sayshen is sitting on his. His helmet is on, but his visor is open, and his eyes are fixated on me. The weight of his gaze has my stomach in knots.

He told me he isn't the same guy he was back then, and though I have my doubts about him, part of me feels like for once, Sayshen Shaw is telling me the truth. Something new and unexpected flickered in his whiskey eyes after he saw the marks Christian left on me—*rage*.

Since when did my pain matter to Sayshen Shaw?

CHAPTER 2

SAYSHEN

Cursed - WesGhost

It's mid-day, and the crowd at the track is growing by the hour. Trucks towing trailers of bikes and campers all heading in and crowding the long stretch of tarmac that makes up the pits. Everyone is prepping and setting up for the first race weekend of the season. Everyone but me, that is.

Talon, my older brother, is working on his bike under the tent next to our trailer a few feet in front of me. He doesn't fuck around. Every spare second he has is spent working on his damn bikes. Tweaking and fine-tuning everything he can to help him cross that finish line before any of the other teams. I should be doing the same, but I can't bring myself to give a shit about anything to do with my bike or the race weekend. Instead, I'm sitting here, flipping a water bottle up and down in the air.

My head is caught up on Bexley and the deep purple marks that painted her perfect fucking skin. The look in her hazel eyes when she realized I saw them reflected more than fear.

She was embarrassed.

Ashamed.

The Bexley I knew would never tolerate that shit, let alone from a guy, and the fact that he managed to break her, of all girls, has my blood boiling. I don't know what the fuck happened or who this dude is, but I plan on finding out. I'll show him what happens to scum like him. Men who prey on women and break them down. Because that is what he's done to her. To Bexley. He's broken her in every way he could, and now all that's left is the cold, empty shell of a beautiful girl that once housed the biggest and warmest of fires.

Because *that* is the Bexley Larson I remember.

"You gonna prep your shit or what? The R1 needs an oil change before tomorrow's heat," Talon explains as he lifts himself from the small stool next to his H2R. The heat race is the qualifier. Each competing team is made up of seven guys, and the heat race determines which three guys from each team will actually participate in the main race event on Sunday. He turns his attention to me, cocking a brow and nodding his chin at me as he pulls a rag from his back pocket and wipes his hands on it.

"Yeah, I know what my bike needs thanks, and I'll do it when I'm fucking ready," I reply with annoyance.

"When you're ready?" He laughs mockingly as he tosses the rag on the table of tools next to him. "Where the fuck is your head? We don't have time for this shit, Sayshen. Every other member of this team is prepping their shit. *They* are doing what they need to do to make sure they're ready for the heat race tomorrow morning. I don't give a shit that your head is off in la-la land. I'm not letting you fuck up this season for the team." His attitude strikes a nerve. He and Dad are always grinding my ass about training. Any second not spent riding my bike or working on it is a second wasted according to them, and lately, I'm just fucking tired of it.

Rising to my feet, I whip the water bottle where it smashes off the trailer. "Fuck off, Talon. I'm so fucking sick of this shit. You're acting like I don't give a shit about the team. Like, all I do is fuck up or waste my time. I work my ass off for the Demons, and you fucking know it. I train and hit the gym every fucking day. I barely have time to ride for fun anymore. So get off my back," I snap as I step up to my brother.

Barely two inches taller than me, I hold his stare. His short dark hair is damp with sweat that beads down his face, sticking to the newly grown stubble around his jaw. He, unlike me, inherited our mother's bright blue eyes, where I got stuck with our dad's deep brown eye color. It's something I've always been a little envious about. His long inked arms hang down at his sides and his fists are clenched tightly.

He's pissed.

Good, because so the fuck am I.

As if sensing the tension, Draygon pulls up on his red and black S1000—perfect timing. Talon, being himself, ignores my response and bumps his shoulder against mine as he makes his way toward Draygon. He doesn't care what I have to say—never does. Talon and Dad only hear what they want to hear, and to them, there is no excuse not to be one hundred percent focused on the team at any point in the season.

Draygon and Talon bump knuckles before he slides his helmet off his head. The dim lighting under the tent glints off his onyx hair as he pats it down with his hand and offers me a nod.

"You guys all good?" he asks as his gaze bounces from me to Talon.

Talon rolls his eyes and makes his way to the table, grabbing a wrench firmly in his hand before returning to the stool next to his bike. "Yeah, we're fine. Baby Shaw here just needed to be reminded about how important this season is to the Demons."

"The fuck I did," I seethe.

Confused, Draygon rests his elbows on his bike as he eyes us. At twenty-seven, Draygon is one of the oldest guys on the team, aside from my idiot brother, of course. But even he can agree that sometimes, *Talon* just doesn't know when to quit.

Talon shakes his head in disagreement, "I don't see anyone else just fucking sitting around with their head shoved up their ass, Sayshen. Do you?"

In an effort to calm shit down before it gets out of hand, Draygon turns his sights on me. "What's going on, kid? Is the R1 running okay?" he asks.

"The bike is fine," I snap as I return to my seat. "It just needs an oil change, and I don't feel like fucking doing it right now."

Confused, he furrows his brows before his eyes widen, and he laughs. "Ah! I know what's up!" he shouts, as he climbs off his bike and makes his way toward me. "It's that fucking chick. The one from the cafe. The one with the hot purple haired Latina friend, yeah? You've been in a mood since you saw her this morning. Fuck, what was her name…Becky?"

Leaning forward, I rest my elbows on my knees as I rub my face with my hands and release a breath. "Bexley," I admit.

"Bexley? Bexley Larson? From high school?" Talon laughs manically from the other side of his bike. "Don't tell me you saw her once, and you're all fucked up in the head all over again."

"Don't you fucking start, Talon," I reply, pointing my finger at him. "You don't know what you're talking about, so just fucking stop."

He doesn't stop.

Instead, he takes it like a challenge, and stands from his stool, making his way over to me. "You're really going to let a chick get in your head right now? Right when the Demons need you focused? Really, Sayshen? A fucking piece of ass. All because she wasn't willing to be one of the desperate bitches you brought home every night in high school?"

"Someone fucking put their hands on her, Talon. She was covered in bruises," I snap. Saying it out loud enrages me even more.

"So what? Not your problem."

I stand, bringing myself to stand mere inches from Talon. "The fuck do you mean it's not my problem? I'm not going to ignore that shit."

Talon digs his finger into my chest like a parent scolding their child. "Yes the fuck you will, because Bexley ain't shit to you. She's just a girl, and there are plenty of other chicks you can fuck for a night. Bexley is a goddamn distraction, and one we can't afford."

"Will you listen to yourself?" I laugh, a coping mechanism to stop me from slamming my fist into my brother's face. "You fucking know me, Talon. If she were just some girl, I'd have been over it when she turned me down junior year."

"You turned her denial into a fucking game, Sayshen. Everyone knows it. You wanted her because you couldn't have her. Well, guess what? You still can't. Not only does she clearly have a man in her life, but I'll be damned if you're going to end up back in the black hole that is Bexley fucking Larson."

"Listen, I think you both need to—"

"Fuck you," I spit, cutting Draygon's words off before shoving my brother's chest with my hands. I'm over this shit. It's a waste of my time and energy. The R1 can wait till the morning. Besides, ain't shit keeping me from winning tomorrow's heat, even if it's just to shut Talon up. I grab a beer from the cooler next to the chair and make my way back inside the trailer.

"Well shit, I didn't see—" Draygon starts, but his sentence is cut off by the sound of me slamming the trailer door. I'm not pissed at him. He didn't expect Talon to fly off on me like he did.

Just like I never expected to see Bexley Larson at the Seaside Cafe.

She's the last person I'd have thought to see there this morning, especially since it's a spot we frequent and I've never run into her before. I haven't seen much of her in person since high school, but that hasn't stopped me from stalking her socials.

Which unfortunately for me, are all set to private, limiting what I *can* see. I'll admit, I wasn't surprised to find out she had a boyfriend in her life, but it didn't make the sting of the information any less brutal. Bexley has been my dream girl since freshman year. The one girl I'll always want but probably never get.

It did make the chase more fun, though. She was different from the other girls, and I mean, maybe it's the competitive side in me, but the harder she made the game, the more I wanted to win.

As much as I'm pissed off at my brother, I have to admit, he is right about one thing. The moment I saw those marks on Bex, my whole world was flipped upside down. I can handle never having her and I was fine with her living her life and being happy without me being a part of it. But I'm not going to sit back and ignore what's happening to her. There is not a fucking chance that's happening.

After seeing her today, I don't care what it takes or what I have to sacrifice to help her get her fire back. Even if it means losing the race.

I can hear Talon and Draygon talking outside. Talon is still heated from our little disagreement, from the sounds of it. Draygon is trying to get him to calm down before people start asking questions, or Andre hears him. The last thing we need is our coach hearing him go off and worrying about cracks in the team.

The first round of heat races start at eight am sharp, and as much as I don't want to focus on racing, I know I can't miss them. I'm going to have to get up even earlier to prep the R1 and change its oil because there is no way in fucking hell I'm going back out there tonight to listen to my brother's bullshit.

Popping open my can of beer, I plop down on the small couch and pull my cell out of the pocket of my gray sweats. As I bring the beer to my lips, I open my search browser and type

Bexley's name into the search bar. A list of her socials pop up, with a few updated photos but nothing about a boyfriend. Her pictures show no evidence of anything going on behind the scenes. She looks happy and healthy. Like she's enjoying life. Not that I'm surprised. Her behavior today tells me she does her best to hide it from the world.

A new photo I haven't seen yet pops up in the feed. She's standing outside Tampa University, and she looks fucking stunning as always. Ripped mom jeans with a cute black crop top that shows off her petite figure. Her thick black hair slicked back into a long high ponytail at the back of her head. Simple, and yet Bexley could make any outfit look fucking fantastic.

Clicking it, I head to the comments, hoping to find some sign of the piece of shit who hit her. But there's nothing. Her friends have commented telling her the basic shit like how cute she looks or commenting about missing her. I do, however, end up learning that she's attending Tampa University as a Fashion Major in the fall. She wants to be a designer and create her own line of clothing and accessories. Good for her.

My lips pull into a smirk, and the weight of the argument with my brother seems to dissipate as I scroll through photos of Bexley, which I've seen at least a thousand times but never tire of because it's the closest I've ever been able to get to her. Tracing my thumb over the screen of my phone, I follow the curve of her perfect smile.

Don't worry, Bex. That guy who thought he could hurt you is about to realize his mistake. I'm coming for you, and this time, I'm not stopping until you're mine.

CHAPTER 3

BEXLEY

How Could You - Jessie Murph

Coffee with Cece was exactly what I needed after the night I had. After she chewed me out about Christian, she filled me in on the latest tea that's been happening in our small friend group—I say ours, but really, I mean hers. I don't get out much—not anymore, that is. After high school, my parents couldn't bring themself to understand my love for the fashion world. They refused to support me in my decision to make a career out of it, and cut me off entirely. Most of my friends from high school cut me off around the same time. With the loss of my parents' funding, I didn't have the money to hang out the way I did before, and so I was forgotten. By everyone except Cece that is. She's all that I have left. It's why these early morning coffee meets with my best friend mean so much to me.

However, I didn't expect this one to have me running into Sayshen Shaw, of all people. He looked good. Better than good if I'm honest with myself, and though his flirty personality used to drive me insane in high school, today I was thankful for it. Even if I didn't show it. It was nice, for once, to have someone just being playful and fun. His compliments weren't so bad either.

Christian used to be like that. But not anymore. Now, instead of compliments, I get criticism. It's always, "*you need to work out more,*" or "*that shirt makes your tits look too big, go change.*" It's no wonder I don't have the confidence I used to have. Today, with Sayshen, even though our encounter was brief. I was reminded of the girl I used to be. His presence reignited a spark that has been snuffed out by years spent with Christian. Whether or not it's a good thing has yet to be decided though.

Heading through the parking lot of our condo complex, I spot Christian's truck, with the trailer and bikes hitched on the end. Part of me was hoping he'd left without me, but obviously not. I have no doubt he has been waiting for me, and I'm sure the fact that coffee with Cece went a bit later than expected, means he's probably in a bitchy mood. I don't enjoy being forced to spend the summer weekends at the track. It's not that I don't enjoy the sport, I do. It's just that I wouldn't mind having the time alone and away from him.

To do something that maybe, I enjoy. However, any sign of me not supporting his racing, becomes a big problem. One I'll feel for weeks, and truthfully, it's just not worth it.

Making my way inside, I open the front door of our condo only to find the entranceway packed with all of Christian's track gear and suitcases. He rounds the corner just as I close the door softly behind me. His demeanor does little to hide his annoyance, and the moment his eyes meet mine, I know I'm in for it.

"Where have you been? For Christ's sake, I called you at least five times. We're going to be late. Where are your bags?" he asks sternly.

"They're upstairs. I didn't know I was going with you. I was kinda hoping to stay back. Cece said she—"

"Oh? You were hoping what? You could miss my race

weekend to party it up with Cece in *my* condo while I'm gone? I don't think so. You know I can't stand her and the bullshit she puts in your head about me," he shouts aggressively as he steps toward me. Christian isn't a fan of Cece and everyone close to him knows it. Cece refuses to put up with anyone's shit, especially his. But mostly, he hates her because he knows I tell her everything. It's hard to play the nice boyfriend role when the closest person to me knows the truth about all the shit that goes down between us.

As she often seems to say to me: *'He hates that I know everything, because when you forget the dumb shit he does, I won't'.*

She'll be there to always remind me.

To him, she's a threat.

"No, that's not what I was going to say," I add, my tone barely a whisper. "She said she'd come to hang out with me. We could get some schoolwork done and watch some movies. There's this big show coming up in New York, and well, I've been putting together a portfolio of my designs, and I'm almost done. I really think I have a shot of getting in if I apply," I explain as I back myself against the door. Christian's eyes widen with anger as he brings himself to stand directly in front of me.

"And what? You think you're going to get into this show in New York and just take off there?" he scoffs. "You don't belong out there, Bexley. You belong here. You're mine, remember? You have responsibilities to me. You can't just dip out to do your shit, not right in the middle of my race season."

"Well, it wouldn't be in the middle of your race season. It's in the fall," I try to explain, but I know it won't make any difference. To Christian, no time is ever going to be okay for me to go and pursue anything I want. If it's important to me, it's irrelevant. All that matters to him is his racing career, and he expects that to be the only thing that matters to me, too. "The show happens in your off-season. You could even come with me if I got in."

His jaw clicks as he looks down on me with darkened eyes. "Come with *you*? Why?"

"To support me? If I get into the show, that is."

"What makes you think I want to spend my off-season in New York at some stupid fashion show?" he scoffs.

"I don't know..." I whisper, "I just, I didn't think you'd need me during the off-season." The moment the last word slips from my lips, I realize my mistake. His fist flies past my face, slamming into the door behind me. My body begins to tremble uncontrollably, and my eyes follow my iced coffee as it slips from my hand and crashes to the white tile floor.

"Oh? That's what you thought, is it?" he spits with agitation.

He grips my chin firmly with his hand, forcing my eyes back to his. "Don't look away from me when we're talking, it's disrespectful." His thumb brushes over my swollen lip, wiping the concealer I used to hide it away before leaning into me. His hand glides down until it's wrapped around my throat. "Look at you, trying to hide the marks of your punishment," he whispers with heated breath against the shell of my ear. My heart races in my chest, and my head begins to throb as the hand around my throat tightens, cutting off my air supply. "I am not going to New York, Bexley, and neither are you. Is that clear?"

Desperate for air, my hands find their way to his in an effort to free me from his hold, which only makes him tighten his grip even more. I dig my nails into his forearm and pull on his arm, but it's no use. Christian is bigger and stronger. He laughs, mocking my attempt to free myself. "Is that clear?" he asks again, slapping my cheek with his other hand. The contact of his hand on my flesh stings. Unable to reply, I briskly nod my head in agreement. Hot tears begin to form on my waterline as he releases me and backs off. My body slides down the door as I slump to the tile floor, completely unbothered by the fact that I'm sitting in a puddle of ice-cold coffee that has surely ruined my outfit.

I gasp for air, filling my lungs with each panted breath as sobs slip from my lips. I lift my hands to my throat, running along the tender and burning skin. I can still feel him. Feel his hand like they're still holding me there.

"Stop your whining. I barely touched you. Clean up the mess you made before you pack your shit, and hurry the fuck up. You've had me waiting long enough," he snaps, kicking one of the small bags by the door. "And change your clothes. You're not getting in my truck looking like that," he adds before heading back out to the garage.

The door closes behind him, and with the click of the latch, the dam of tears break. They stream down my face as silent screams rip through me. A mix of fear, anger, and hatred. I hate myself for staying. For allowing him to treat me this way, but I know if I tried to leave, it would be even worse. I'll never escape Christian. Not alive anyway.

Pushing my trembling body from the floor, I head to the closet and grab a towel to clean up the coffee mess. When I'm done, I toss the cup in the trash and the towel into the laundry before heading upstairs to pack. The last thing I want to do, especially now, is spend the weekend at the track pretending everything is okay, but I know I don't have a choice.

Reaching my mirror, I lift my shirt over my head to reveal more of the deep purple bruises he left on me last night. They cover my rib cage and spread out around my back like stripes on a tiger. My neck, now sporting a bright crimson hand mark to match. Inspecting it, I can already tell it will also bruise, and neck bruises are among the hardest to hide. Especially in the Florida heat. The slap to the face only made my already busted lip swell and stand out even more, meaning I'm going to have to ice it on the way to the track.

Perfect.

Sliding out of my pants, I toss them in the hamper by the door before heading to my closet. I pull out black Lululemon leggings and a simple nude color Lululemon long-sleeved running shirt. The long sleeves will hide the marks on my arms and ribs, but not my neck. Shuffling through the hangers in the closet, I pull out an oversized black Balenciaga hoodie and pull it over me before heading back to the mirror. I free my thick, raven hair from the messy knot bun on the top of my head and brush it out quickly. Between my hair and the hood from the hoodie, I can hide most of the marks on my neck, thankfully.

I hate it when people notice them. I hate when their eyes fill with pity and concerns they won't mention for fear of upsetting me because usually, that's the looks I get. Sayshen's reaction today was new. It was different. His reaction reminded me more of Cece's. Where other people try to avoid asking about it but clearly struggle to take their eyes off the marks that paint my skin, Sayshen's eyes fill with anger. Rage. It was probably the most genuine expression I've ever seen from him. Like one small bruise on my skin and the fuckboy attitude was gone. Replaced by a boy, no, a *man*, who seemed to want to hurt whoever had touched me.

But why?

Sure, Sayshen always had a little thing for me in high school, but it was just a game. It was never serious enough for him to care what happens to me, especially so many years later.

Pulling my suitcase out from under my bed, I quickly pack enough clothes for the weekend, along with my toiletries and a couple of books to keep me entertained in the trailer. I grab my cosmetics bag and touch up my makeup, ensuring people won't be able to tell I am crying and hide the swollen and bruised lip as best as I can before tossing it into my oversized tote purse. I will most definitely need it to survive this weekend in public. I take one last look around the bedroom to make sure I haven't forgotten anything. This bedroom has never really felt like mine or like home.

Before Christian, I had a small walkup on the beach strip

with Cece. We'd spend our mornings on the cute little patio having coffee and bagels in the ocean breeze. It was beyond perfect. But then he insisted I move in here so we could have more time together since I'm always busy with school and he's busy with racing and training. It made sense at the time, but it wasn't long after that he changed, and his true colors began to show.

"Bexley!" Christian's voice echoes through the halls from downstairs, causing me to startle and jump. "Get a move on. I don't want to be stuck setting up and unloading the bikes in the fucking dark."

The track is about an hour drive from where we live, and I'm not looking forward to spending that time alone in a car with Christian. Grabbing my suitcase, I head down the hall to the stairs. The front door is wide open, and some of Christian's bags have been loaded into the truck. I leave my suitcase by the door, I head to the kitchen quickly to grab an ice pack. Pulling open one of the drawers, I wrap the ice pack in a small dish towel before grabbing a bottle of Fiji water from the fridge and making my way out to get in the truck.

Christian tosses the last bags in the back before locking up the house and climbing inside. Pressing the cool ice pack to my lip, I hiss at the contact, which causes Christian to look over at me.

He sighs. "I'm sorry, Bex, okay? You know I don't like being rough with you. I don't mean to be. I'm just under a lot of stress, and when you talk about leaving me, I just...I get upset, okay?" he adds as he places a soft hand on my thigh. "You don't need to worry about a career. I make enough money for both of us,"

His touch sends a chill down my spine, and I instantly feel sick to my stomach and the tiny spark Sayshen's encounter reignited, blows out. But I don't react. I turn my attention outside. To the beautiful sun as it begins to lower along the horizon. The way the wind blows through the tall palms that line the parking lot. He always apologizes. He never *means* to hurt me, and yet he always does. No matter how many times he says he's sorry, or swears he didn't mean it and that it won't happen again, we both know it will.

We both know in some sick and twisted way, he enjoys it. But what's worse is we both know I'm too afraid to do anything about it. I'll take it again and again because at this point, it's all I know.

Turning my eyes to his, I force a fake smile, "I know, it's okay. I'm okay," I reply with a shaky tone. "It's okay."

He smiles back, brushing his knuckles against my cheek before he starts up the engine.

"Let's go, baby. Time to kick some ass this weekend." With that, Christian pulls the truck out of the parking lot and onto the main street. I turn my eyes back outside as I curl up in my seat. Instinctively, my thoughts make their way back to Sayshen. To the look in his eyes today at the cafe. Part of me wonders what would've happened had I told him who they were from. How would he have reacted if I hadn't pulled away and he had seen just how bad they really are?

My eyes flutter closed, and my chest rises and falls with deep breaths. It doesn't matter. Even Sayshen Shaw can't help me. Not now.

CHAPTER 4
TALON

Like We Wrote - Lithe

One thing that never gets easier is fighting with my brother. Little fuck is so goddamn stubborn. He reminds me of our mom, and sometimes it stirs up memories. Some of them bring a smile to my face, but not all. We don't talk about her often, and Sayshen having been so young when she left, he has little to no memory of her.

Dad raised us as best as he could on his own, and as I got older, I tried to help out with Sayshen. Dad has always been more lenient with him. Leaving me, of course, to always be the bad guy as we got older. I mean, someone had to lay down the law and at least try to keep him in line and out of trouble. When it came to Sayshen, our dad didn't even try. I think he felt bad that Sayshen never got the chance to really know our mom. He still blames himself for her leaving, but we all know it was all on her. She was the one who chose to put her drinking before her responsibilities. Before her family, her kids. It was her choice to leave us instead of getting the help she needed.

Not Dad's.

It's getting late. The sun is setting, and after my little altercation with Sayshen, I needed a walk to clear my head, so I figured, why not cut through the pits on the way to the canteen for some food? At least that way, I can check out who has arrived and what the competition is running this season. It might not have been the best way to clear my head and find some quiet but it's definitely better than sitting at our trailer right now with how high the tension is between Sayshen and I.

The pits are packed, and as usual, the teams seem to have all parked together. I pass by rows of trailers with a line-up of red and black bikes, all belonging to the Naughty Nomads. They are one of the founding teams; but you wouldn't suspect it from their track record. Nomads have never made it past third place on the podium, and so far from the line-up, it's the same seven guys as last year. They're talented riders, but their bikes are not fast enough, and their coach isn't skilled enough in training for them to pose any real threat.

Next up is the Howling Heathens. Bikes sporting bright blue and orange bodywork are lined up outside their campers. I nod my head at a group of them as I walk by. Unlike the Nomads, the Heathens are one of the newer teams and though they're fast, they aren't skilled. Their team is constructed of the youngest guys in the league, besides Sayshen, Reign and Cruz, of course, and they are rowdy and impossible to control. Their coach struggles to keep them in line, which means a lot of the time, they're missing a member or two for misconduct.

The last row of bikes before ours, are sporting the black and gold colors of the Vicious Vipers. The only team in the league that poses a real threat to our chance at winning. As I make my way past their setup, their leader, Christian Cordova, pulls up in his silver F150, towing his BMWs behind it. Keeping his hands on the steering wheel, he waves two fingers at me and smirks as I stop, allowing him to pull into the parking spot next to me. He's a really cocky piece of shit, but unlike the rest of the assholes walking around the pits, he has the talent and training to back it up.

The moment he shuts down the engine, the passenger door facing me pops open, and a petite brunette in an oversized hoodie hops out. She's fumbling with arms full of empty water bottles while trying to close the truck door, which causes her to drop something wrapped in a dish towel to the ground. Noticing her struggle, I step forward and pick it up. It's cold in my hand, and I realize it's an ice pack.

"Uh, thanks," she mutters quickly as she takes the ice pack from my hand. The moment she does, her large hood pulled up over her head blows back with the wind, revealing her face.

Bexley *fucking* Larson.

If we weren't fucked before, we sure are now. In high school, Sayshen was obsessed with her. Sickly obsessed. She was his drug of choice, and it has taken years of rehab away from high school and her to get him sober, and focused back on racing. Thankfully, after years of staying on his ass and pushing him to train and take the team along with racing seriously, it seems like Coach, Dad and I have gotten through to him. For a while, Bexley was a distant memory. Forgotten.

But that's all gone to shit now.

Seeing her this morning at the cafe in town already has him all fucked up and now she's at the track. The one place the Demons and I really need him to remain focused on the race, and winning.

She clears her throat, and I realize I never replied to her.

"Yeah, no problem," I say. She doesn't recognize me, and she shouldn't. We've never actually met. But thanks to my little brother's obsession, the entire team knows what Bexley looks like. I bet there are still pictures of her hung up in the garage back home.

I rake my eyes across her from head to toe. Up close, I can better understand my brother's obsession. She is fucking gorgeous. Big hazel doe eyes with thick lashes, a light dusting of freckles across her high cheekbones, and plump pouty lips. Even in the oversized hoodie, I can tell her frame is small and tight. But it's the fresh purple marks covering her throat that draw my attention. For the first time in a while, I find myself rendered completely speechless. Her eyes lock with mine briefly before her cheeks flush a pretty rose color, and she turns away, clearly ashamed of the marks on her skin.

Something in me doesn't like them.

My eyes snap to Christian, who's on the other side of the truck talking to his teammates, completely unbothered that his girl is walking around with marks on her. Marks that *he* put there. I spit to the ground as an unfamiliar taste coats my tongue. Turning my eyes back to Bex, I find her quickly heading inside the trailer they parked next to.

Shaking my head, I force myself to turn around and continue back down the pits to where the Demons are set up with my fists clenched tightly at my sides. I can't afford to be worried about her. Why the fuck do I care how Christian chooses to treat his chick? I shouldn't. My focus, like Sayshen's, needs to be on the races. On winning. We don't have time to worry about anything else, let alone a girl. Especially one who chooses to stay with a piece of shit who puts hands on her.

Sayshen won't see it that way though. He only mentioned marks on her arms, not the ones on her *neck*, and by the deep purple color of them I'm going to bet they're new. Which means Sayshen is going to be nearly uncontrollable. Knowing how stubborn he is, I'm going to have to push him hard to stay focused. After his reaction earlier today, that won't be fucking easy. He's going to fight me, and it's going to cause a lot of tension, which also isn't good for the team, but there's nothing I can do about that now. It's only a matter of time before Sayshen finds out about Bexley being here with Christian, and when he does, I need it to come from me.

When I get back to the trailer, I find Sayshen, Cruz, Reign, and Lena all in the small living room area playing on the Xbox. Sayshen and Reign are battling it out on Mortal Kombat from the couch, while Cruz sits in the lazy boy recliner with Lena, his girlfriend, on his lap. They're both watching reels on Lena's phone and laughing together while she runs her hand through his short blonde hair. Reign and Cruz are Sayshen's best friends. Cruz and Sayshen went to high school together and Reign moved here from Greece in the summer of their senior year, after Andre signed him to the Demons roster.

Even though they're all a few years younger than myself or the rest of the guys, all of us Demons are pretty tight. We're always together, even in the off-season, but being the youngest three on the team, they tend to gravitate together.

"Oh, come on. That's bullshit! How do you always get your special bro?" Reign shouts as he jumps up from the couch. He turns, whipping the controller at the couch with frustration while Sayshen breaks out in laughter.

"Aw, come on, bro. Don't be such a whiny little bitch," Sayshen shrugs. "I'm just better than you."

Reign grabs the controller and sits back down. "Yeah, right. Keep dreaming, Baby Shaw. Let's go again. I'm going to fucking ruin you this round, watch."

"Hold up," I cut in, pulling their attention before they can load into another game. "Sayshen, we need to talk,"

"Oh, for fuck's sake, Talon. I know I have to get the R1 ready, okay? I'll do it in the morning before the heat. Lay off me."

"Can I fucking talk before you jump down my throat? This isn't even about the fucking R1," I add. Sensing the seriousness in my voice, everyone's attention falls on me. Sayshen lays his controller on the table and leans back on the couch. He wipes the sweat from his palm on his sweatpants before pulling out his phone as he waits for me to continue. "Christian just pulled up. He's camped over with the Vipers."

"Okay, and? Why is that so fucking important? It's not like we didn't all expect him to be here," Cruz chimes in with a confused tone. "He's the best fucking rider on their team."

"Yeah, we did. But he brought someone with him this year who could become a problem. A girl."

The guys break out in laughter. "What do we care if he brought some chick with him? Shit, maybe she'll suck him off so good his head will explode," Reign adds jokingly, as he punches Sayshen in the shoulder. "Then the podium will be as good as ours."

"Nah, if we beat that mother fucker, it's going to be a fair fucking race," Cruz cuts in. "Ain't no way I'm taking any less. Not with fucking Cordova."

Lifting my hand to my head, I rub my temples in slow circular motions. I know the next thing to leave my mouth is going to ignite unwanted chaos. But it's chaos I can't avoid.

"It's Bexley."

The laughter and joking around stops the moment her name slips from my lips, and Sayshen's eyes snap to mine as the vibe of the room changes.

"What do you mean it's Bexley?" he asks, rising from the couch, clearly distraught with the news. "My Bexley?"

"Give me a break, she's not *your* Bexley. I was walking back from the canteen and ended up seeing Christian when he pulled up. She hopped out of his truck." Sayshen's hands fall to his sides in clenched fists and his eyes fall to the floor as he slowly begins to pace the small space.

"No way." Reign's expression changes to one of disbelief as he raises his fist to his mouth. "Are you sure it was her?"

"Who's Bexley?" Lena asks Cruz with a quiet tone.

"Bexley Larson. She's the girl Baby Shaw had the hots for through high school, but she would never give him a chance."

"Ohhh. The pretty brunette from the yearbook pics in the garage?" she asks.

"Yep. That's the one," Cruz answers, clearly doing his best to not fuel the fire we all know is burning inside my little brother right now.

The tension in the room is thick. No one really knows what to expect from Sayshen's silence. It could be either a good thing or a bad thing, but something tells me he's not going to take this news the way I hope he will. He's not going to listen to me when I warn him to stay away from her, nor will he care what Christian will have to say about it. Sayshen has always been one to go for what he wants, full throttle. And he wants Bexley.

"Cruz, get over here. Let's play a match and let the Shaw brothers figure their shit out," Reign mutters in an attempt to break the silence as he starts up the menu for the game.

"Alright, but you're about to get your ass handed to you again," Cruz adds as he scoops Lena up in his arms and carries her over to the couch, where they both plop down. Cruz, Lena, and Reign talk among themselves about the game, allowing Sayshen and me the time to figure this shit out.

Flooded with uncertainty on how my brother is going to react, my eyes remain on him as he stands there for a few minutes, completely unresponsive. He's thinking. Just knowing Bexley is here is already having an effect on him, and he hasn't even seen the newest marks on her yet. Marks he now knows, Christian, our biggest competitor, put there. He grabs his hoodie from the hook by the door and pulls it over his head before sitting on one of the dining room chairs and grabbing his shoes.

"Where the fuck are you going?" I snap.

Confused, my brother eyes me. "Where do you think I'm going? This is good. It means I can convince her to get away from that piece of shit."

"Are you listening to yourself?" I shout loudly. Everyone falls silent, and Sayshen freezes in place before slowly spinning to turn his attention to me. "What the hell are you going to do for that girl besides cause her more problems? Not to mention, the

Demons need your head in the races this weekend, not wrapped up in Bexley Larson, and the life she chooses to live."

Sayshen storms toward me, and presses his chest against mine aggressively. His eyes widening with rage. He knows to some extent, I'm right. Bexley clearly allows Christian to do what he does to her. She could leave; stop it. But she doesn't. Why? Fuck if I know, but Sayshen isn't going to be the thing that makes her change her mind.

"You saw her, yeah?" he huffs with a tightly clenched jaw. "So you saw the marks on her arms. The bruises that fucking Cordova put—"

"Yeah, I saw them. I saw the fresh ones on her neck, too, and you know what I thought? If she's so unbothered by it, why the fuck is my brother so bent out of shape over it. Shit, maybe she fucking likes it, Sayshen. Did you ever think of that?" I spit, instantly regretting the words as they slip from my mouth. I don't have to know Bexley to know being smacked around definitely isn't her kink. Her eyes told me exactly how she felt, even without her speaking words. She was scared. Terrified.

Sayshen's fist slams into my jaw, and my head whips to the side.

Cruz drops his controller to the carpeted floor. My jaw clicks with rage, and I'm forced to slow my breathing and calm myself before I react. I know I'm pushing him. I'm walking a thin line with my brother right now, but that's nothing new. The rage I felt before is nothing compared to what's flowing through my veins with the impact of my brother's fist. I will admit, I'm surprised he did it. Clearly, he has more balls than I gave him credit for. I wipe the blood from my lip with my thumb and suck it into my mouth. Sayshen and I butting heads is basically a daily occurrence. It getting physical, however, isn't. We don't lay hands on each other and never have. Not even as kids.

Shaking my head, I turn my eyes back to my little brother. His chest rising and falling with panted heavy breaths. Cruz and

Reign cautiously make their way toward us, ready to step in if things get out of hand.

But they won't. As angered as I am right now that he's letting a girl have this much of an effect on him, I won't allow my temper to get the better of me. I won't allow myself to snap, even if the little fuck deserves a wake-up call.

"Okay," I add, slowly nodding my head as I turn back to my brother. "You wanna throw your season away for a piece of ass, go for it. But when you get thrown off the team and lose the support of the Demons, don't come crying to me, little brother." With that, I storm off toward the back of the trailer, bumping shoulders with Reign as I pass him on my way to my bedroom and slam the door closed behind me.

CHAPTER 5
SAYSHEN

Anything For Her - Bryce Savage

My knuckles are still swollen and aching from punching Talon last night. He deserved it. At least that's what I've been telling myself all morning. It helps with the guilt rotting inside me. I've hit plenty of guys before, but never my brother. Considering how hard he rides my ass about training and my life choices, it's probably a fucking miracle I have managed to control my temper with him as long as I have. When it comes to him bitching about racing or training, I can handle it. The same can't be said about him pushing me about Bexley. Something about her is just different for me, and him shit-talking my feelings for her, is just unacceptable.

Everyone always thought my fixation with her was a game, and I don't blame them. I know I've created the fuckboy image of myself to people around me and the team, and I've allowed them to think of me that way for so long that I shouldn't expect anything else. But Talon is my fucking brother. He should know *me* better, and the fact that he is either too oblivious to see what

Bex means to me or he doesn't give a shit, pisses me off more than anything.

Leaning against the counter at the canteen, I wait for the lady on the other side to prepare the coffee and bagels I ordered for the team. I spent the morning changing the oil and filter on the R1, and now it's all ready for the heat race. Since I didn't work on it yesterday, I was stuck getting up before dawn today to ensure she was all set to go and would pass the early morning inspection without issue. Not that getting sleep was really an option for me last night after what went down between Talon and me.

My head falls back against the thin glass of the canteen window, and I slide my hands into the pockets of my gray sweatpants as I scan the area around the small building with my eyes. As usual on race weekends, though it's barely eight am, the pits and track are getting busier by the minute. Guys are lined up with their bikes at inspection, waiting to get the all clear before they head out. The first round of heat racers are out on the track, the hum of their 600s filling the quiet morning air as they get their laps in.

A familiar laugh draws my attention to the long lineup for the canteen. A glimpse of thick raven hair in the sea of people. *Bexley.*

Without hesitation, I push myself off the wall completely disregarding the team's breakfast and coffee order as I rush toward where she's standing in line. Her eyes are on the gravel ground as she pushes the tiny rocks around nervously with the toe of her checkered Vans sneaker and chats with someone on her phone.

"You know I can't do that," she giggles as I reach her side. I grab her upper arm tightly and pull her out of the line. "Ow, what the fuck!" she shouts, drawing the attention of the people around us.

"It's all good, everyone. We just need to have a chat," I

explain calmly as I drag her to the back of the canteen building and away from watching eyes.

Clearly confused and annoyed, she fights me. Tugging to try to free it from my hold. "Sayshen, what the hell are you doing? Where are you taking me?" she asks. "No, it's fine, Cece. I'll call you later, okay? Yeah, I'm sure. I can handle this fucking psycho," she adds sarcastically before ending her call.

Only when we're away from the crowds do I release my hold on her arm.

"What do you think you're doing?" she snaps as she steps toward me defensively. The gold flecks in her hazel eyes glimmer in the rays of morning sun as it rises above the treetops in the horizon. They flicker from one to the next as she searches my face for an explanation. The thick locks of her hair cascade down her back and around her shoulders, framing her gorgeous face. But even with the collared sweater she chose to wear today, I can make out new purple bruising along her neck in the morning light. Purple bruising that wasn't there when I saw her at Seaside Cafe.

I slowly lift my hand to her hair, tucking it back behind her ear before gently tilting her chin as I take in the severity of her new marks.

My jaw clicks. Every fiber of my being is enraged by what my eyes find. Marks that no woman should bear, let alone have them placed there by a man they trusted to care for them. Deep purple and crimson bruising circle around her thin neck, no doubt left there by a hand.

A hand I'd like to fucking break.

She pushes against me, shoving my hand away from her. She tries to turn away from me, but before she can. I grab her chin firmly, and force her eyes back to mine. At first glimpse, they fill with sadness, but it doesn't take long for her to put on her mask. A mask I already know she must have to wear daily to fool the world around her and keep them from finding out about the shit that is happening behind closed doors.

But it doesn't work for me.

I see right through her facade.

Bexley pulls away from my touch again, her eyes narrowing as she straightens her back. Gripping her phone tightly in her hand, she slowly steps backward to get away from me.

"Why are you with him?" I growl. "Why do you let him do this? Touch you like this," I spit with disgust. The fact that any man could do this to a woman makes me sick to my stomach. Knowing it's Christian, the Demons biggest rival, doing it to Bexley—my fucking Bexley—has me ready to commit murder. Lifting my hand, I gesture to the bruises along her delicate neck. "I'll fucking kill him, Bexley." I'd happily spend the rest of my days rotting in a max security prison if it meant Christian was six feet under. Rotting in the dry Tampa earth, while the worms feast on his woman beating flesh. Then, Bexley could start new, and live the life she fucking deserves.

I'd kill to see her get her fire back.

Rolling her eyes, she tucks her phone into her pocket before crossing her arms in front of her chest. "I don't know what you're talking about. No one touched me," she snaps with a sharp tone.

"Don't give me that bullshit, Bex. I see right through your lies. What happened to you, huh? Where's that feisty girl from high school? The one who wouldn't take crap from a guy. You deserve so much better than this, and you know it."

"Who are you to say what I do or don't deserve? You don't fucking know me, Sayshen. Wow, you had a little crush on me a million years ago when we were fucking kids, for Christ's sake. You have no right to dictate my life and tell me how to live it," she snaps.

There she is.

It's not the roaring blaze I remember, but there's a spark that I saw at the cafe.

There is hope.

I don't like that this is happening to her, but now, knowing who's doing it, it's even worse. I have to race against this guy. See him daily on and off the track and somehow not beat his fucking face in. All while knowing somewhere in the crowd is Bexley. She's not the Bexley I remember, though. No. This girl, she's but a fraction of the girl I remember. The empty look in her eyes shows me how broken she is. No amount of makeup or oversized clothing can hide the marks he leaves on her. Not from me. Because I know her well enough to know that they run deeper than her skin.

"You're wasting your breath trying to lie to me," I snicker. I take one of her loose curls in my hand. Threading the raven colored softness between my fingers as I take a step closer to her. She gasps and steps back again, pressing herself up against the brick wall of the small canteen building. Realizing she's trapped, she drops her eyes to the ground, unwilling to show her vulnerable side. Gripping her chin softly, I force her to look at me. The fact that eye contact is so hard for her is no doubt a result of her treatment.

Her abuse.

My other hand slams down on the brick wall behind her, supporting me as I box her in.

"Your eyes give you away. That and the way your body trembles when I bring it up. Bring *him* up. You're not angry, Bexley. You're scared. You've given up, and I don't blame you for having no fight left in you. Fuck only knows how long you've been silently battling behind the closed doors. But lucky for you, I'm here now. I see you, I see your pain, and I haven't given up on you. Hell, I never did," I confess as I softly brush my knuckles along her blushing cheek. Tears brim along her lashes, as she holds my stare. Her lip trembles, "It's okay, Bex. You're allowed to be sad. I'm angry enough for the both of us, and I promise, Christian is going to get his."

She holds my stare for a few more seconds, absorbing everything I've just told her. In high school, it was no secret how I felt about Bex, but I think, like everyone else, she believed it to be a game. That she was just another girl to me. Back then, I was okay with her thinking that, but not anymore. Not if thinking she doesn't have any other options, is what keeps her with Christian. Because she does.

She has me.

Her calm expression quickly fades, replaced with one of anger and annoyance as she shoves my hand from her face and ducks under my arm to get past me.

"Leave me alone, Sayshen. You don't know anything." *Oh fuck, here we go.* "You don't know me or what I'm feeling, so fuck off before—" she snaps from behind me.

"Before what?" I laugh, turning around to face her. She's flustered. "Before you tell Christian how bad I'm going to beat his face in for fucking touching you? For hurting you?"

"He didn't hurt me!" she shouts.

"Stop the bullshit! Anyone with eyes can see those fucking marks on your neck, Bex. It's not just me!" Looking around, she quickly pulls the collar up in an attempt to hide the marks.

"So what? Maybe I like it rough? Did you ever think of that? Hmm?" she spits, stepping towards me with purpose. "Did you ever think of the possibility that I like it when he's rough with me? That I fucking enjoy being made into his little slut. Maybe shit got wild in the bedroom. What if he was hitting it so good we both got caught up in the moment, and he gripped a little tighter? Then what Sayshen?"

"Bexley," I growl. My body tenses. It doesn't matter that I know her claim is bullshit. The very thought of him touching her in any way gets my blood pumping. Especially *that* way. The way she'd never let me touch her.

"Or what? Because you, the famous Sayshen Shaw, couldn't hit it, there's no way Christian can, right? You've always been a cocky asshole. Well, news flash, but he gets it. He gets all the wild hot horny sex he could want, and it gets damn rough and rowdy. I fucking love it. He'll bite me, choke me... the rougher he is, the wetter I get. That's how I have marks on my body. If you want, I can show you these—" She snaps as she starts to pull her sweatpants down.

I stop her, smacking her hands away from her waistband as my chest rises and falls with heavy, panted breaths. I know none of what she's telling me is true, but it doesn't make it hurt any less. That's what she wants, though. To hurt me. Scare me away because I'm calling her out on all the shit she's been hiding for god knows how long. I'm seeing *her*, and to her, that's dangerous.

Holding her hands to her sides, I slow my breathing and soften my tone. Her eyes meet mine again. Searching. Silently pleading for me to stop. To give up.

"Why are you doing this? Why are you protecting him? You can't fucking lie to me, Bex. I know you better than you think I do, and I can tell when you're full of shit. I can read you like a fucking book. So stop trying to hide shit, cause it's wasting both of our time."

"I'm not hiding anything," she snaps, pulling her hands from my hold as she backs away. "Stay the fuck away from me, Sayshen. You think you know me, know my relationship, but you don't."

"Fuck that. I can't just turn a blind eye, and I won't," I admit, and I mean it. There's no way I'm going back to acting like Bexley doesn't exist. Like she isn't right here, within arm's reach.

"You will, or I'll have you thrown out of the races. All it takes is one complaint. One paper file claiming you touched me, harassed me, and you're out. Stay the fuck away from me," she adds as she heads back around to the front of the canteen.

"Do it then. You think I would put racing before *you*? Fucking go for it," I bark back at her. "I don't give a fuck about racing, Bex, not if it means sitting here and watching you let that piece of shit do this to you."

"I mean it, fuck off." With that, she turns her back to me. She holds her hand up over her head and she flips her middle finger up to me as she rounds the corner of the building and leaves my sight.

I groan with annoyance. My jaw clicking as I begin to pace the small space behind the canteen. I kick up the gravel, and my already bruised fist slams into the brick wall of the canteen building, causing me to cry out. The pain radiates through my hand and up my arm as my knuckles begin to bleed.

"What the fuck d'you do that for, bruv?" Thorne's voice shouts. Lifting my head, I cup my injured hand with the other and make my way over to where he and Cruz are rolling by with their bikes.

Thorne Rosewood is one of the more chill guys on the team. He's one of the newer guys, having moved here from Peckham, London after Andre signed him to the Speed Demons. Despite being a fulltime racer, he's one talented fucker with a pen and paper. Guy can draw just as good as he can ride a bike, and while graphic novels and comics have never really been my thing, any that have his work in them, I buy and put away. Standing six foot five, with a buzz cut, he loves to remind us all he's the tallest guy on the team and though most of the time he's a big goofball who never takes anything seriously, he's been known to try and play the role of peacekeeper within the team. Which is what I'm sure he's doing right now.

"Don't worry about it. How was it out there?" I ask, squinting my eyes as I nod my head in the direction of the track.

"It's fuckin brass monkeys out there…" Thorne replies.

I cock a brow in confusion "Brass what?"

"Brass monkeys, cold enough to freeze the balls off one..." Thorne explains.

"How would the balls even—"

Cruz flips his visor open. "Never mind, Sayshen. Just make sure you have your warmers on or you'll be sliding all over the place. They called your line out next. Are you sure your hand is good to ride?"

"Who's on my line?" I ask.

"You and Wolfe for us. Uh, the Ackerman twins from the Heathens, Josh Slatter and Thomas Raker from Nomads—"

"Cordova, too," Cruz adds. My eyes snap to his, and Thorne shoves him. "What? It's the only fucking name he wants to hear, and we both know it." He's right. I might not be able to handle Cordova the way I want to without pissing off a lot of people and benched for the season, but I sure as fuck can teach him a lesson on the track.

Thorne shakes his head with disapproval. "Why you gotta muddy the water? You heard what Tal—"

"What did my brother say this time?" I ask, cutting him off. My knuckles throb. Truthfully, my riding today is a risk. The swelling in my hand after hitting not only Talon but the fucking wall is going to make holding the throttle dangerous and risky, but what's a little fun without some danger. And the heat race this morning is definitely going to be fun.

"Damn," Thorne laughs. "For once, you weren't takin' the piss, Cruz."

"What the fuck are you on about?" I snap, spitting to the ground as I turn my sights on the growing crowd of people making their way to the bleachers.

"Cruz was talking to the team all morning about you landing a blow on Talon last night. Reign swore up and down that he saw it, too, but I don't think any of the other guys believed them. I sure as fuck didn't."

"And?"

"Look at you, fam. Your hand is smashed up too, and you're obviously fuming about something. I doubt they've lied to us but this can't just be over something, can it?" Thorne adds as he kisses his teeth.

"Don't," I warn. Snapping my eyes back to him.

"Woo," Cruz laughs. "I told you, fucking idiot." He smacks Thorne in the arm, nearly knocking him off his bike. Thorne lifts his hands in submission as the loudspeaker cracks and the announcer gives the crowds the ten-minute warning before the next heat.

"You better get a move on if you wanna get out there, Baby Shaw," he adds.

"Yeah, knowing Cordova, he'll be one of the first guys out there. Are you sure you're good to ride?" Cruz asks, eyeing my hand.

Rubbing my injured knuckles with my other hand, I hiss at the sting of the contact "Fucking right, I am. A little blood isn't stopping me from getting out there," I reply. Accepting my response, the guys close their visors and head off toward the pits.

My hand could be broken, and I'd still be planning to head out. Nothing would stop me from getting out there, not even Bex warning me to stop meddling in her shit. If she doesn't want to face Christian, then I sure as fuck will.

On and off the track.

CHAPTER 6

BEXLEY

Battlefield - SkyDxddy

My heart races as I make my way back to our trailer. Part of me wanted to confess it all to him. Confess everything that Sayshen so clearly sees already, but I can't. All it would do is make things worse. He can't help me even though I can tell he wants to. No one can. I can feel how deeply he seems to care, even if I don't understand why. The way he looked at me. Touched me so cautiously, like I was a China doll he was afraid to break. It made me feel things. Things I shouldn't be feeling for another guy. Not when I'm with Christian.

I do find myself believing that all those things he claimed to feel for me in high school were genuine. I mean, it didn't seem like it at the time, but now, I've seen a new side of him. A side I wish I'd known back then, maybe then things would be different. Back then, he just let me and everyone else think it was all a game. Something is different about him now. He's bolder.

But now that gorgeous, flirty smile he's always thrown my way has been replaced with a concerning frown. Now when he looks at me his eyes reveal his heartbreak and rage. It's like he sees something broken inside of me, and he wants to fix it. Especially when he confronts me about the marks Christian leaves behind. Marks I clearly need to do a better job at hiding.

How sad is that?

Instead of admitting to myself that I need to leave. To end my relationship and walk away because even I know Christian is never going to stop, I'm thinking of new ways to hide the marks he leaves across my skin. I don't know when it happened, but I've come to realize at some point I just started accepting it. Accepting that this is my life now, and the only way I'll ever get out is if one day I set him off so bad that he takes it too far. So far that it will be my face on the missing posters hanging downtown. Stapled to the poles and taped up in the shop windows.

What would Sayshen do then?

Making my way through the pits, I pass the next round of guys headed out for the morning heat. I know Christian is in this round, too, and though I don't normally make it to the stands this early to watch, today I need to—especially if word of mine and Sayshen's little altercation makes its way to his ears. That won't be good for either of us. Christian won't take lightly to Sayshen sticking his nose into what goes on between us or hearing about me being behind the canteen with another guy. Not only do I know it would be the cause of yet another beating, I know it would be a bad one. One where the marks he leaves behind are impossible to hide, and I find myself in the emergency room, spinning some wild tale about how they got there. Another mugging perhaps? Or maybe this time, I got hit by a bus.

Wouldn't that be lovely. I mean, on one hand, it's a way out.

When I approach the trailer, I find Christian still on his bike under the large black and gold tent set up outside. Which is odd, normally he's one of the first guys out. His coach, Julian, is beside him, giving him directions and strategizing for the heat.

Knowing Christian, he won't listen—never does. He thinks that because he's the fastest guy on the team, he knows everything and usually tends to do whatever he wants. I'll admit, more often than not, the choices he makes out on the track end up paying off for him and the Vipers.

Christian's visor is open, and his cold eyes trail me as I make my way to the trailer door. Feeling the weight of his condescending glare I tuck my hair behind my ear and avert my gaze. I don't even have to meet his eyes to know he's pissed. There's no way he's heard about Sayshen and I getting into it yet, which means he's pissed about something else. My guess is the fact that I wasn't here earlier to help him get ready to head out. Julian pats Christian on the shoulder and heads to the front of the bike. He checks the temperature gauge before removing the Velcro tire warmers off both the front and back and hanging them over the top bars of the tent.

The tire warmers. Fuck.

One of my many duties for Christian when at the track is to ensure his warmers are always on. Heated tires are needed on the track for proper traction. If the tires aren't hot enough on the cool tarmac, the tires will spin and slide around, making going fast or taking turns too dangerous. This morning, in my rush to get coffee, and then being delayed by Sayshen, I realize, I never turned them on.

Christian snaps his visor closed, and Julian pulls the bike stand off the back wheels, freeing the bike. Christian twists the throttle, revving the engine loudly three times before he turns his head in my direction and pulls out down the laneway of the pits, headed toward the track.

Well, at least I know his anger isn't about Sayshen.

The announcer's voice cracks through the loudspeakers around the pits, announcing the start of the next round. Quickly heading inside, I grab a water bottle from the fridge and head back out toward the bleachers. It's not the coffee I was hoping for, but it's better than nothing. Reaching the top row of the bleachers, I find a seat next to an older couple and turn my sights on the starting line. It doesn't take long for me to spot Christian. But it's when the black and neon green bike with the Speed Demons logo pulls up next to him my stomach ends up in my throat.

Number twelve. Sayshen Shaw.

Frozen in my seat, I watch as he pulls right up to Christian with his visor still open. He snaps his head in Christian's direction, who in return opens his visor. Even from here, I can see words being exchanged between them, and by their body language and the way Christian grips the throttle it doesn't look like a friendly conversation.

Shit.

My heart thumps violently in my chest. No. This can't be happening. Maybe it's nothing. I could be overreacting and making normal competition about me when it's not. But the moment Christian briefly lifts his eyes to where I'm seated in the crowd, I know Sayshen most definitely mentioned me, and Christian is pissed.

Sayshen turns his sights back on the track just as the horn blows, signaling the start of the race. The bikes take off. Speeding around the track for the first lap of three. I stand, trying to keep my eyes on Sayshen and Christian as they fall to the back of the swarm.

The morning wind whips around me, blowing my hair around my face, and I quickly brush it away to keep my eyes focused on the race. It's clear early on that neither Christian nor Sayshen will be placing very highly in this round, but that doesn't stop them. By the second lap, they're still in the last two places, battling it out in their own race. I don't know who I want to see win. Part of me hopes Christian winning might lessen the blow I know he'll inflict tonight. But fuck what a rush it would be to see Sayshen show him up.

As the others begin their third lap, the people around me in the bleachers start to make their way down the narrow stairs and back to the pits.

Unable to tear my eyes from them, my head spins. Playing out all the different scenarios and ways the rest of my day could go, depending on how the race ends. How will Christian react to losing not only to Sayshen, but everyone else on the track? It's only a heat race, but to Christian there is no race that doesn't matter. I already know being in the last two spots most likely has him internally raging. Losing to Sayshen now, would only fuel that fire.

He'd be setting out for him moving forward with the season. I shouldn't be concerned for Sayshen. But I am. When it comes to Christian, I've come to recognize the telltale signs over the years that he's about to explode. The way his body moved and shifted when they were lined up before the race told me everything I needed to know about the effect Sayshen has on him. The sheer signs go unnoticed by some, but not by me. Not when each and every one of them has been followed up with fists and pain.

You'd think since I'll most likely be the one on the receiving end of Christian's wrath, I'd be afraid for myself. But I'm not. It's Sayshen I find myself worried for. That flirty boy from high school with the gorgeous smile. The blunt and bold man from this morning, with the gentle touch. A touch that sent shockwaves through my body. It's him I'm worried about. But I don't know why. It's not like he's ever been anything to me besides a pain in the ass.

A really hot pain in the ass.

Christian and Sayshen are the last two bikes to cross the finish line and of course, Sayshen crosses it first. Christian slams his gloved hand down on his handlebars, and gestures aggressively to Sayshen before they make their way back to the pits in parallel. Shit. Rushing down the stairs I quickly push through the crowds of people and bikes, and head toward mine and Christian's trailer.

Christian, however, beats me there. Julian is already behind him with the bike stand as he backs the bike into its spot under the tent. Turning off the engine, he opens up his visor before climbing off. Julian goes right to work, getting the warmers wrapped around the back tire. I fluff up the collar of my sweater before heading under and taking the cords for the front warmer in my hands. I pull it down from the bars, and start wrapping the heated fabric around the tire. Christian grabs me by the forearm roughly and pulls me away from the bike.

"Let Julian do it, that way at least I know it fucking gets done," he snaps as he looks down on me. I gulp. Julian pays no mind to Christian's aggression toward me. Not surprising, I've met his wife and though we're not close, people in our situations tend to recognize each other.

A bike pulls ups, drawing Christian's attention. He releases me, shoving me away before pulling his helmet over his head and slamming it down on the table next to the trailer. I rub my arm where he grabbed me. A pathetic attempt to ease the aching pain his tight hold left on my muscles.

My eyes follow Christian as he makes his way toward the bike. My heart stops when I spot the neon green number twelve on the front fender.

Sayshen.

He brings his bike right up to the gold and black tent as he violently revs the engine at Christian before opening the visor of his helmet. Looking at me, he trails his eyes down my body to where my hand is rubbing my arm through the thick sweater before they snap back to Christian.

"So, you like putting your hands on women I see, Cordova," Sayshen spits aggressively. "You're a fucking dead man." Christian laughs, finding humor in Sayshen's threat. He's always thought himself to be untouchable. He brings himself to stand a few inches from Sayshen, whose hand grips the throttle of his bike tightly.

"Better watch your tone, Shaw. Don't let your little early morning win go to your head. We both know who the better rider is."

"Yeah, me. That's why you're so hard pressed you came back to your trailer and put hands on your woman, right?" Sayshen replies with sarcasm. "You know, it takes a real piece of shit to lay hands on a woman," he adds, nodding toward me. "You think people don't see it? We do. We all see you for the weak fucker you are, and your days are numbered."

"Tough talk for a kid with no proof. She's got some bruises, so what? Maybe she's clumsy," he laughs as he looks over at me. "Shit maybe she's a freak in the sheets. Did you consider that before accusing me of beating my woman? Maybe that tight cunt of hers feels so fucking good wrapped around me that shit gets out of hand and she likes it. I mean why would she stay with me if I was beating her, right? Regardless, I'll handle my woman however I see fit, cause she's *my* woman," Christian replies.

Tension between them rises. Clearly sensing it, Julian heads toward them, and stands between them to prevent it going any further. "Ain't it cute, babe?" Christian asks, directing the question to me.

"W—What?" I stammer with a cracked voice.

"This little crush Baby Shaw seems to have developed for you." Christian makes his way toward me, and pulls me into his arms tightly as he holds Sayshen's stare. "Look at him thinking he's your white knight, saving you from the evil villain so he can take you away with him. But you don't want to go anywhere, do you baby?" he asks.

"No," I whisper. Lowering my eyes to the ground. Christian pulls me tighter against him, digging his nose into my hair as he inhales my scent.

"Louder baby, I don't think he can hear you over there."

"No!" I shout. "I—I don't want to leave you, Christian." Bile rises in my throat as the words slip from my lips. Lies. It's all lies. I should've told Sayshen the truth. I should've told him everything, but all I can do now is hope he sees through these lies as easily as he did all the others I told him.

Slowly, I lift my eyes from the ground to meet Sayshen's. If I thought his eyes were full of rage earlier, then I was wrong. Pure and utter carnal anger flashes back at me for a few brief seconds before he snaps his visor closed and takes off on his bike. Christian pushes me away, nearly causing me to trip over one of the small chairs against the trailer. He makes his way back over to where Julian is standing next to his bike and they laugh about the altercation.

I inhale slow and deep. Filling my lungs. A single tear cascades down my heated cheek, but I quickly wipe it away as I watch him take off. Leaving me behind. Leaving me with my abuser. There is no one to blame but myself. Because I allowed this to happen. Sayshen spoke up for me. Defended me and made me feel safe for the first time in years. He fought for me, gave me multiple outs, and like a fool, I turned them all down.

I'm a coward.

I deserve what comes next.

CHAPTER 7

BEXLEY

Don't Talk About It (Sad Version) - SkyDxddy

Christian kicks my chair, pulling me back to reality.

"So, are you going to tell me who the fuck Sayshen Shaw is to you?" Christian snaps. After he and Sayshen went at it, I needed to decompress; the only way to do that is to draw. Drawing up new designs and fabrics is how I cope. It's my outlet. So, while Julian and Christian chatted about the heat and how to move forward with the race weekend, I sat in my chair—allowing myself to be completely consumed with sketching until nothing else seemed to matter. That is, until their little convo finished up, and Julian left. Now that there is no one around to keep him occupied, Christian can let loose and show me just how fucking angry he really is about Sayshen not only showing up here, but saying whatever he did before the heat race today.

"What are you talking about?"

"Don't play dumb with me, Bexley. Who the fuck is he to you? How do you two even know each other?" He questions with a condescending tone.

"I don't even know him that well. We went to the same high school, that's it," I answer quietly.

"Bullshit. It's more than that. Has to be. Everyone knows Sayshen is a fuckboy. Kid never has the same chick with him, and he sure as fuck never behaves the way he did today. Not over a piece of ass. So I'll ask you one more fucking time. Who is he to you?"

"Okay, well, I don't know anything about any of that, Christian. I swear to you I don't even know him that well. I don't know why he's acting the way he is. I haven't done anything wrong."

"Right, just like you didn't purposely forget to turn my warmers on this morning," he snaps. "You wanted him to beat me, didn't you? You ungrateful bitch. You left them off on purpose, so your little boyfriend would be able to win. God only knows that's the only way he could ever stand a chance of beating me,"

"Do you hear yourself?" I shout back. I instantly regret the words and the tone I used to speak them. I've only made the mistake of speaking up to Christian once, and then I never let it happen again. The beating he inflicted when I stood my ground was by far the worst. I spent nearly a week in the hospital. I had to lie and say I was mugged just to be able to explain the marks littered across my body. I had a severe concussion. Multiple broken ribs, a hairline fracture in my right arm and internal bleeding, all because I didn't put enough sauce on his pasta and when he asked me for more, I told him he could help himself.

"Yes, I forgot to turn on the warmers this morning. I'm sorry, but it wasn't intentional, I promise. I am human, and I make mistakes. I just forgot, okay?" I reply, quicky taking a seat in the chair behind me.

"Mistake?" He laughs as his hand finds its way to the top of my head. He threads his thick fingers through my hair before gripping tightly at the root and pulling me up. The burning pain radiates across my scalp, and I drop my sketchbook and pencil as my hands cover his in desperation. A sob escapes me, and the intense pull on my hair guides me to stand. "Your little mistake cost me the race. I was sliding all over that fucking track, completely unable to keep up with the rest of them. But that's what you wanted, wasn't it!" he shouts inches from my face. I can feel his heated breath on my face, and my stomach lurches.

He slams my back against the steel exterior of the trailer when I don't answer him quickly enough. Pain vibrates up my spine from the impact.

"Wasn't it!" he shouts again.

"No. Christian—" I whimper. "I didn't want that, I swear. I'm sorry—"

"Sorry, you cost me the race? Or sorry that now I know about your little boyfriend? Hmm? I never took you for a whore, Bexley, but shit I guess there's a lot about you I don't know."

"No, it's not like that," his grip on my hair tightens as he holds me firmly against the side of the trailer. I'm scared. But I also knew this was coming. I knew Sayshen showing up here had sealed my fate tonight, and honestly, I was okay with that. I've taken Christian's beatings before, and I can do it again.

As long as he leaves Sayshen alone.

What I didn't expect was his hand to slide under the waistband of my sweatpants, cupping my pussy. I cringe at the contact of his rough hands on my sensitive flesh.

"No? So, it's not this whore pussy he's after then? Tell me, Bexley, how many times have you let him have it?" he whispers with husky breath as he shoves two fingers inside me. I cry out at the burning pain as he forces them through my opening. He leans against me, pressing his hardened cock against my thigh.

Him being turned on by the pain he inflicts on me is nothing new. Most often than not his beatings end with me being fucked raw and senseless, and not in the enjoyable way. I can't even remember the last time I actually wanted to be touched. Even on the good days, my thoughts trail back to the bad ones and sex becomes more of a chore than something I genuinely want or crave.

"Please, Christian. Stop," I plead as I try to squirm away from him. It's useless. His hold on me is too tight.

"Stop?" he seethes through tightly clenched teeth. He pulls his hand from my pants and slaps my face with the back of it. My head whips to the side as the stinging pain of the impact radiates across my cheek. "You didn't stop him though, did you? Fucking whore."

"He never even touched me, Christian. Aren't you listening? I told you it's not like that!"

"Oh, I know he did. To have the balls he did today, I know he fucked you at least once. But you know what, Bex," he spits, forcefully grabbing my chin in his hand. "That," he adds, gesturing to my crotch, "is my fucking pussy," he whispers against my face. He tugs on my sweatpants, pulling them down my body. "And I'll claim it whenever and wherever the fuck I want. You want to act like a whore? I'll ruin your pretty little cunt so that boy toy of yours never wants to touch you again."

No. Please no.

My stomach twists at the very thought of what's to come. Even though it wouldn't be the first time Christian has taken me against my will and it most likely won't be the last either. I should fight him. But I don't. I can't. Instead, I stand there. Pinned against the exterior of the trailer, silently praying and begging for someone, anyone, to stop it—to stop him.

But who am I kidding? I had my chance, but I didn't take it.

This is my fate.

TALON

"Talon, it's not the same with Bexley for him. You *have* to see that dude. I know you fucking do," Reign explains. "I know you guys have this weird ass brother shit, and you feel like you have to be the hard-ass all the time because your dad isn't, and shit I'll even admit that sometimes, Sayshen fucking needs it. But when it comes to her, you're fighting a losing battle man." After the guys told me what happened during the heat, I knew I had to find Sayshen and stop him from making anything worse.

"I don't care, Reign. He needs to forget about her and get his shit together before he fucks the whole team over for some chick. This is our fucking season. The Demons' season. No piece of ass is worth being so distracted over, that you let your team down."

"Why can't you just fucking accept that Bexley isn't just some chick or 'piece of ass' to him? Would it be such a bad thing if he found a girl he was actually down for? Shit, maybe he'd settle down and actually focus more on the shit that's important, like racing," he snaps back with annoyance. "You keep acting like Bexley is the problem, but did it ever occur to you that maybe she's the fucking solution here?"

I stop, turning my eyes to Reign. Wearing a black sweater, with the hood pulled up over his head, he tucks his hands into the front pocket, and straightens his back. His green eyes hold my stare as he waits for my response. A response I don't have yet, because though I don't want to admit it, in a way, he's got a point.

I shouldn't be surprised Reign seems to rush to defend Bexley. While he doesn't know her from high school like Cruz and Sayshen, he's always naturally been protective of women. I guess being raised by a single mother does that to you. His dad left before he was ever even born, leaving him to be the man of the house. He spent a few years in a juvenile detention center for shoplifting around age twelve when his mom was let go of her job and money was tight. Fucking kid just wanted to put food on the table to help his mom out, and was locked up for it. Thankfully, shortly after, his mom met a decent dude through some friends, and things seemed to get better for them.

I never considered that Bexley could be the one to actually settle Sayshen down. Shit, I don't think I ever considered any girl could be the one that gets my little brother to settle down and get his head right. I struggle to picture anyone being that for him, let alone some girl he wanted in high school. I mean, they were just kids. They didn't know fuck all about love or what it meant to commit to someone. I was a teenager once too, and the only thing we cared about, was getting drunk, busting some heads and fucking chicks. I guess I never considered that maybe, it was different for my brother. That maybe despite me wanting to see it, the little shit is more mature than I give him credit for.

"You go check the canteen, and I'll finish having a walk down the pits to see if I can find him. I'll meet you back at ours," I add. Reign nods and heads off through the crowd in a light jog toward the canteen building while I continue down the pits in search of my little brother. When Wolfe told me about Sayshen paying Christian a visit after the heat, I knew shit was about to pop off. Especially when he didn't come back to the trailer afterward. Sayshen has a temper. I don't know what his plan was going back there, but it clearly didn't go his way.

He's pressed, and that's not a good thing for any of us. Andre has been looking for him since the heat ended, and the longer it takes me to find him, the worse off shit will be.

I continue down the pits, nearing Christian's trailer when the sound of a commotion hits my ears. Curious, I duck my head under the black tent set up over the Viper's bikes and find Christian with Bexley pinned against the side of his trailer by her hair.

This mother fucker.

I know before I act that my next move is fucking stupid. It's everything I've been bitching at Sayshen about, and yet I know I can't walk away and leave her like that. I don't even have to know her the way Sayshen does, to know there is no fucking way I'm turning my back, and walking away. I need to stop him. Her head slowly turns to the side. Her eyes lifting to mine as her plump bottom lip trembles with fear. A silent plea for help floods her wide tear-filled eyes.

Without another thought, I rush over in a fit of rage. Swinging my arm back before slamming my fist into the side of Christian's head. The impact catches him off guard, causing him to release his hold on her hair as he's thrown back. Bexley falls to the ground.

I grab her and help her to her feet before placing myself between her and Christian.

She's trembling and clearly terrified, and for some reason, it only angers me more to see it myself. Something inside me is infuriated by the fear in her eyes. I see now what Sayshen was trying to explain. Bexley is a broken shell of a once beautiful and lively girl. She has no fight left in her. There is no doubt in my mind that without someone to fight for her, she'd eventually die by Christian's hands. My heart pumps rapidly, pushing my blood through my veins. My head cocks to the side as I look down on Christian. He rises from the ground, his eyes zoning in on me as he wipes the blood from his lip.

"Well, if it isn't Big Shaw now. What is it with you and that bitch brother of yours? Both of you have an obsession with my girl, I see," he spits, sending crimson blood to the tarmac. He steps toward me, and I mimic his movement, keeping Bexley safely tucked behind me.

"The only bitch I see here is you, Cordova. After all, one has to be one in order to hit a woman," I reply cockily. There's no way I'm backing down. I'm not going anywhere without Bexley, even if that means going blow for blow with Christian.

"Right, okay, well, why don't you mind your own fucking business. Bexley and I can figure our own shit out. No one asked for you to get involved. We were just having a little argument, weren't we, babe?" he asks, tipping his chin toward Bexley, who is cowering behind me.

"Don't answer him. Go get your shit."

"What—?" She stammers with confusion.

"You heard me. Go pack your shit. You're coming with me."

"Going with you?" Christian laughs. "Do you think you can walk up here and take my girl? And what? I'm supposed to just let you walk away with her."

"I don't really give a fuck what you do, Cordova," I reply. People around the pits begin to crowd around us. Christian's shouting is drawing more attention than either of us wants. He eyes the passers as they whisper and gossip on their way by. "Bexley, go and get your stuff."

Without another word, she cautiously makes her way to the entrance of the trailer behind us, softly closing the door behind her. She's in there less than five minutes before she returns with a backpack. She picks up a large spiral-bound sketch pad and pencil from the ground before returning to the safety behind me.

"Fine, take her. She's a fucking whore anyways, but I'm sure you know all about that, don't you. I have no use for her anymore," Christian laughs, but we both know he's putting up a front for the people watching. However, with so many people watching, his hands are tied. He can't do or say anything about it without someone seeing it, and he knows it.

"You ready?" I ask over my shoulder.

"I—I think so," she whispers. I offer her my hand behind my back, and she takes it.

"Stay the fuck away from her from here on out, Cordova."

"Aww, so protective of your baby bro's little whore. And here he thought he was her white knight. Wait till he finds out it was his big brother," he laughs as he takes a seat in one of the chairs propped up against the trailer.

Turning my back on him, I make my way back down the pits, dragging Bexley along with me.

Fuck. What the fuck did I just do.

Her hand trembles in my grasp, and though I know I'm most likely going to regret everything that just happened, I clench my hand around hers tighter, running my thumb across the soft flesh of the top of her hand as I pull her in under my arm. Keeping her petite frame close to mine.

My heart hurts for her in a way I've never experienced before. Though I still have my concerns about Sayshen's mindset with her around, I have to admit that even I feel this need to protect her.

Like I expected, shit is about to get really tough for the team. What I didn't see coming was me being the reason for it. However, from the look in Cordova's eyes tonight, he took this like an act of war. Like Bexley is Helena of Troy, and I'm the Trojan prince who just stole her away.

Christian is the least of my worries right now. There is something more important for me to focus on, and that's my brother when he finds out what I just did. I have no idea how this is going to play out with Sayshen and I after how hard I've pushed him away from doing the very thing I just did.

What I do know is that Bexley is safe, and Christian will eat a fucking bullet before he ever touches her again.

CHAPTER 8

SAYSHEN

Miss You - Bryce Savage

There's a deep pain in my chest. Driving away from Bexley today was the hardest thing I've ever had to do. But even I know I can't force her to leave him. It has to be her choice. All I can do is hope that in time, she'll make the right one. When I get back to the trailer, Cruz, Wolfe, and Thorne are posted outside. Wolfe and Thorne are filming some shit on their phones for TikTok while Cruz and Lena are busy grilling us all up some burgers for dinner. The racing for us is done for the day, meaning we all get to chill out for the rest of the night.

"Here, it looks like you could use it," Lena adds, handing me a cold beer from the cooler. "She'll come around, just give her time."

Confused, I look up at Lena, who tilts her head toward Cruz. "He tells me everything, you should know that by now," she laughs.

"Of course he does," I smirk, popping the cap off my beer. I bring the bottle to my lips, guzzling down the cool liquid.

Lena's a pretty girl. Thick long blonde hair and big blue eyes that could cut you like knives. She's sweet, most of the time, but I can't say I'd ever want to be on her bad side. Girl can fucking land a punch, and her tongue smacks so hard sometimes you'd think she was actually spitting venom. Her and Cruz have been together so long now that she's practically one of us. She even rides, though she enjoys the stunt side of riding rather than the speed. She's always just fit in, so perfectly with the team.

After I left Christian's, I took the bike out to the back of the track to get away from everyone. No one goes back there since it's all swamp and forest, but it was just what I needed to cool off. It's quiet, secluded, and there was no way I was processing the shit that went down today surrounded by crowds of people.

Especially when my brother is one of those people.

Once the guys told me Reign and Talon were out looking for me, I sent a quick text letting them know I was fine and that I was back at the trailer. Reign is already on his way back, but Talon never replied, which is unlike him. But I have no doubt he's ready to lay into me. I already know he's heard about me and Christian, and if I know my brother, he's ready to chew me out about how my blowing up on Christian is probably fucking shit up for the team. Typical.

Pulling one of the small stools closer to me, I prop my feet up on it as I lean back in my chair and take another swig of my beer. It's early evening and still scorching hot outside, especially under the black tarp tent next to our trailer. Don't even get me started on the humidity. I'm sweating buckets just sitting here.

"Sayshen," my brother's stern voice booms over the noise of the radio.

Here we fucking go.

I take another sip, preparing myself for the lecture I know I'm about to get, before placing my bottle on the ground next to my chair. Turning my attention towards my brother, I freeze when I see he's not alone. Bexley is with him, and they are hand in hand as he pulls her under the tent.

What the fuck.

"Bexley?" I shout, jumping up from my chair and I rushing toward her. She instantly lets go of my brother's hand and rushes to me. Wrapping my arms around her, I can feel her small and fragile body trembling. Looking over her head, I lock eyes with Talon as I pull her in close to me.

"What the fuck is going on?" I ask. Lena and the guys all crowd around us, equally eager to know what the hell is happening.

"Where's Draygon and Reign?" Talon asks with panted breaths. He itches his nose with his hand allowing me a clear view of the fresh cuts and swollen knuckles.

He had to have hit Christian.

Which means it was fucking bad. Talon looks around the area before resting his hands on his waists.

"Reign is on his way back from looking for Sayshen, and Draygon is back at his trailer with some chick he met, but if it's important, I can go get him—" Wolfe explains with a calm tone.

"No, it's fine. You can fill him in after." Talon adds.

"Fill him in on what exactly? What the fuck is happening?" I ask with annoyance. Whatever it is, I know it isn't good. By the way that Bexley is shaking in my arms, I have no doubt some serious shit went down, and it's taking every ounce of my self-control not to go off right now.

"I was walking through the pits, looking for you. I heard about you, and Christian—"

I scoff aggressively, "Yeah, well, that fucker had it coming."

"Don't fucking cut me off," Talon shouts, pointing his finger at me. "This isn't a fucking game. Shit is about to get real, little brother. So I hope you're fucking ready for it."

"We're all ready for it," Cruz cuts in. "This isn't just Sayshen's problem, and whatever is coming, we handle it together. We're a fucking team. A family. No one is facing shit alone," he adds, and the rest of the guys step forward in agreement. Bex turns her head slightly to the side so she can see what's happening.

Talon takes a deep breath to calm himself before continuing. "I was looking for you. I heard about what went down, and when you didn't come back, I knew you had to be fuming. I didn't want you to make any more stupid decisions," he explains, eyeing me. "Anyway, I was walking past Cordova's trailer when I heard some shit. I went to investigate cause I was worried it was you and him brawling it out, but instead I found him with Bexley. He had her pressed up against the trailer." His eyes moved from me to Bex before locking with mine again. "It wasn't fucking good."

She sobs, and I pull her closer. Wrapping my arms around her tighter as I rest my chin on the top of her head, "You're okay, Bex. I have you now," I whisper softly, hoping it will calm her.

"So what's the plan? When do we get to give this piece a shit what he deserves?" Wolfe asks, clearly as eager as me to lay into Christian.

"We don't, not yet. For now, we need to get Bexley out of here," Talon replies. "Go pack a bag, get Bexley out of here for a few days. Cordova isn't going to just let this go, and I don't want either of you around when shit pops off."

"What about tomorrow's race?" Bexley whispers in a cracked voice. "Doesn't Sayshen race tomorrow?"

"We'll cover that, love. Don't you worry about that?" Thorne adds with a gentle tone.

"Yeah, you just worry about yourself, okay, Bexley. Let the rest of us worry about the races while Sayshen gets you away from that piece of shit," Wolfe chimes in from where he's standing. Lifting my eyes to his, I can see a mirror of my rage flowing through him.

Cruz wraps his arm around Lena, pulling her into his chest

before looking toward Bexley "You're one of us now, Bex. Might as well get used to it."

"Here," Lena says as she leaves Cruz and makes her way toward Bex, who's still in my arms. "Take this with you," she adds, handing her Demons hoodie over to Bexley. Slowly, I free her from my arms, allowing her to take the hoodie from Lena and wrap it around her shoulders like a blanket.

That's when I got a really good look at her. She's a mess. I don't know all that went down today, but I do know it had to be bad if Talon stepped in to stop it and fuck if that doesn't both break my heart and fuel my hatred for that piece of shit.

"Oh, thanks," Bex replies. "I didn't realize how cold I felt until now." Unable to hide the pity she feels for Bex, Lena pulls Bexley in for a supportive hug, whispering reassuring things in her ear.

"Well, you just went through some traumatic shit, girl. Your body is probably in shock after all that, I'd say it's normal," Wolfe adds, reaching our side.

Bex smiles. It's small, but genuine.

"Thanks for that super helpful lesson, Dude," I add, smacking my hand down on his back. "Fucking smart ass. Here, Bex, sit down." I guide her to the chair I had been sitting in earlier and kneel down in front of her. "I'm going to go grab my shit real quick, and then I'll get you out of here, okay?" I explain with a soft tone. I tuck a loose strand of her hair behind her ear as we lock eyes. Her eyes are red and puffy from crying. Her plump lips are cut open and speckled with dried blood.

"Okay." She nods, pulling the hoodie around her tighter. Seeing her like this is destroying me inside. Not that I will show it. Showing it will only hurt her, and she's suffered enough. But one thing is certain… Christian Cordova is a fucking dead man.

Bexley

"Wolfe, go fill Draygon in. I don't want to take any chances. We don't know how Christian is going to handle this, but I know it won't end here. We all need to pay close attention to him and watch his every move. He can't be trusted," Talon explains as he makes his way over to me.

"Got it," Wolfe adds before taking off down the pits in a light jog. I never really realized how close these guys all are. I mean, Christian and his team aren't close like this. They don't consider themselves a family, and they sure as fuck wouldn't go to bat for each other. Not like these guys. They don't even know me, but are ready to fight for me, defend me, all because one of their own has deemed me important to him.

I didn't even know Sayshen had a brother, let alone one that is as good-looking as Talon is. He has to be 6'2, and based on the fact that he's Sayshen's older brother, I'd say he's about twenty-seven if I had to guess. If Cece were here, she'd be squirming in her chair over his tatted-up body alone, and don't even get me started on those broad shoulders and chiseled jawline. The way he just ran up and hit Christian stirred something in me. Something about these Shaw men has my jaw on the floor and my thighs clenched. The way they take no shit and give no fucks. Are just ready to defend those who matter to them is something I've never experienced before, not from a guy at least.

I could feel his anger. His rage for Christian when he saw what was being done to me. What is even more confusing was that he is a total stranger to me, yet I feel so incredibly safe with him.

Sayshen exits the trailer with a bag on his back and his helmet in his hand. Talon grabs a helmet off the seat of an H2R which I assume is his, and slowly steps toward me. He offers me his hand and I take it as he helps me to my feet. The wind blows by, softly carrying his scent to my nose. Oak, Sandalwood, and something else, cedar maybe. It's woodsy and warm. Cautiously, he brushes my hair away from my face, before sliding the helmet over my head.

"It's going to be a bit big on you, but it's better than nothing," he explains, guiding my chin up and buckling the helmet. I lift my eyes to his face, taking in his features as he messes with the helmet straps. Where Sayshen has brown eyes, Talon's are a piercing deep blue color—like the deepest parts of the ocean. I find myself drowning in them, unable to look away. His features, though similar to Sayshen's, are more mature. Full lips and a jaw that could cut glass.

"Bex, take what you need out of that bag and stuff it in mine. We can only take one bag with us," Sayshen explains, tossing his bag at my feet. The weight of the bag hitting my legs startles me, and I jump, but Talon's hands grip my shoulders, holding me still.

"It's okay. You're safe now," he whispers. His eyes soften as he looks down on me, but he clears his throat, and backs away.

I turn toward Sayshen and find him sliding his helmet on his head. Kneeling down next to his bag, I move whatever clothes I need from mine to his, some leggings, a change of underwear and socks, a few t-shirts, and my favorite neon green bikini. I grab my small bag of toiletries, a hairbrush along with my pencils and sketchbook, laying them across the top before zipping the bag closed. Rising to my feet, I slide my arms into the Demons hoodie from Lena and zip it up before sliding Sayshen's bag onto my back.

The guys are all talking amongst themselves quietly. I watch them, reading their body language. It tells me they're all on guard. Ready to act on a moment's notice. Lena is cuddled up to Cruz, and I find myself wondering if it's always like this for them. It must be different to have people around you who always want to protect you and have your back. Christian was never that for me. Looking back, I don't even know what I ever saw in him. I mean sure, he was sweet in the start, and I may have fallen for the fake act he put on, but I'll never understand why I didn't leave the first time he showed me the man he really is.

The first time he hurt me.

Maybe I was just lonely. Leaving home and losing the love and support of my parents left me with no one but Cece, and while she's always going to be my favorite person in the world, part of me just needed more.

Craved more.

I never should've settled for Christian. I never should've let the shit that happened happen. I watch them, fascinated by this group of strangers for whom I find myself so thankful. Because without them, without Sayshen, Talon...I would have never been brave enough to leave Christian on my own.

Sayshen climbs onto his R1 and starts it up. Talon approaches my side and cautiously guides me to the bike, and I climb behind Sayshen.

"Do you have somewhere you can go?" Talon asks with a concerned tone.

"I—I can go to Cece's," I answer.

"Does he know where Cece lives? Has he been there before?" Sayshen asks over his shoulder. I nod in response.

"Take her back to the beach house for a few days, that way shit can settle down before you take her to Cece's. If he's going to go there looking for her, it will be in the next couple of days. He's not going to wait. Assuming that's okay with you, Bexley," Talon questions.

I nod in agreement, unable to find words for all the thoughts flowing through my head. Would Christian go to Cece's looking for me? I mean it's clear he never cared about me, so why would he waste his time going through all the trouble of finding me?

"If anything happens in the meantime—" Sayshen adds, meeting eyes with his brother.

"Nothing is going to happen, Baby Shaw," Draygon adds as he joins the group with Wolfe at his side. "We'll handle shit here, and you just get Bex the fuck out of here. The Demons ain't afraid of a little Viper venom, are we boys?" he laughs, wrapping his arms around Thorne and Talon's necks.

Sayshen revs the engine, and my nostrils fill with the scent of exhaust. He looks over his shoulder as he takes my shaky hands.

"I'm assuming you've ridden as a backpack before, yes?" he asks. I nod in response as he wraps my hands around his waist. "Okay, hold on, Bex." I do as he tells me, gripping the thin fabric of his T-shirt in my hands as they wrap around his toned stomach. He flicks his visor closed and starts to back out as the guys move out of the way. Before I know it, we're speeding down the pits aisle and heading onto the highway.

I don't know where this beach house is he's taking me to, but I do know anywhere is better than where I was.

CHAPTER 9

SAYSHEN

Molly - Chase Atlantic

Nothing has ever felt as good as finally having Bexley's arms wrapped around my waist. The sun is beginning to set now. We've been riding for a little over an hour, and I can still feel her body trembling as she's pressed up against my back. Internally, I'm fucking fuming. I hate that it had to get this bad for her to allow someone to help her finally get away. Part of me is pissed it was Talon who found her and convinced her to leave, especially since I had been trying to convince her to leave him just a few hours before. To let me help her get out.

But in the end, I'm just thankful she finally got out. She's finally safe, and I will never fucking let this happen to her again. She's going to be okay.

I take a left, heading off the highway toward the secluded road that goes along the coast. It's less busy than the highway and will give Bex a prettier view for the last stretch of the ride to the beach house.

Talon and I bought a small beach house together a few years ago. It's nothing fancy, but it's enough for us. We spend most of our time either at the track training or at the warehouse working on the bikes anyway. But when we do get time there, it's nice. There's something about the beach that relaxes me. Maybe it's the salty air or the cool breeze as it comes in off of the ocean. Either way, I know it's the safest place for Bexley right now.

There is one thing I still haven't been able to figure out. Why, after all the bullshit Talon has put me through over Bexley, did he step in and stop shit? I don't know what he saw go down, and part of me doesn't want to know, but it had to be bad for Talon to go against everything he's said and bring her to me. One thing was clear when my brother and I exchanged looks — he cares for her more than he's letting on. Having your own brother care for the same girl as you would probably bother most guys, but not me. I'm not even ashamed to admit Talon and I have shared girls before. Bexley would be the first one to actually mean something to me, at least.

At some point, I'm going to have to talk to my brother and figure out where his head is when it comes to all this. To her. Though knowing my brother, he's not going to want to admit shit. Not after how hard he's been on my ass about Bexley fucking shit up. The thing is, my brother has never been a soft guy. Not even with girls, yet today, he was with Bexley. So he can't hide shit from me.

Gently, I pull her hand from my waist and hold it. I softly rub my gloved thumb over the top of her hand, and slowly, her trembling seems to fade.

Thank fuck.

BEXLEY

Sayshen's hand over mine is a comfort I didn't know I needed. Slowly, I intertwine my fingers with his and rest my head on his back as I turn my eyes to the ocean. Pressed up against him, I'm intoxicated by his scent. It's woodsy, with notes of leafy citrus greens and violets.

Part of me still can't believe this is really happening. After everything. After all the years of abuse and fear— I'm finally free. I'm happy. Relieved, and yet, I can't tell if those are emotions I should be feeling given the circumstances. One thing I do know is that I believe the guys when they say I'm safe, and for that, I'm thankful.

The ocean view fades as we reach a row of beach houses lined up along the white sandy shore. Sayshen slows down and pulls into a large driveway. Lifting my head, I watch as he pulls right up, stopping under a section covered by a large overhanging deck, and turns the bike off. He climbs off the bike before helping me off. My legs are numb and shaky, so I'm forced to use the bike to keep my balance until the blood flow returns. Popping his visor open, he eyes me through the slot before taking the straps for mine in his hands. He unbuckles it before slowly lifting it off my head.

Patting my hair back down, I hold his stare as he removes his next.

"You okay?" he asks, once free of his helmet.

"Mhmm," I mumble. He takes the helmets and puts them on the bike seat before offering me his hand. "Alright, let's go."

"This is your house?" I ask, taking his hand.

"Mine and Talon's, yeah. It's nothing fancy, but it beats living with our dad," he explains.

Flashbacks of the look in Talon's ocean eyes when he found me pinned against the trailer invade my thoughts. The way he rushed in and, without a thought, slammed his fist into Christian. How safe he made me feel, even without knowing him. I find myself hoping he's wrong about Christian. That nothing becomes of what happened tonight and that Christian doesn't do anything to Talon or the team. They don't deserve it.

Not for me.

I'm not worth it.

Sayshen guides me up a narrow white staircase that leads from the driveway to the overhanging deck. When we reach the top, my jaw drops at the sheer beauty captured in the view from their deck. He slowly releases my hand as he unlocks the door. I take a few steps away, I rest my arms across the distressed wood railing as I look out at the ocean. The moon's glow casts a silver sheen over the rolling waves, and the night sky is littered with thousands of glittering stars.

"I don't know. I think this view alone is pretty great," I whisper.

He laughs softly from behind me, "Yeah, it is." When I turn, his eyes are glued to me, and he has a familiar flirty smirk on his face. "Come on, let's get you inside," he adds as he opens the door.

Taking his hand, I let him guide me into the dark house, before he wanders off to find the lights. When the lights flick on around, I close the door behind me, and lock it before sliding the bag off my back and dropping it to the floor.

The light reveals a small, simple living space. It's an open floor area with a large kitchen and living room. An oversized black leather sectional couch sits in the sunken living room, complete with a huge flatscreen TV mounted on the wall. Cool gray tones paint the walls around the whole space. The kitchen is open, with white granite counters and black cupboards. It's cleaner than I expected for two guys living here.

Too clean.

"We don't stay here much," Sayshen adds as if hearing my thoughts. He opens the large stainless-steel fridge. "There's not much to eat, but I can head to the shops in the morning, and stock up."

"It's fine," I reply. "You've already done plenty for me, Sayshen. Really. I'm okay."

He sighs and closes the fridge door. "No, you're not, Bex. But

I don't expect you to be after everything you've been through," he adds softly. Turning his attention to me, he steps toward me. His tall frame standing before me makes me feel so small. The veins in his inked neck pulse. He's angry, but he's doing a good job hiding it.

"Just know you don't have to put up that front. Not anymore, okay? I'm here for it all, whatever you need from me." Feeling the weight of his words, I turn my eyes from him, but he quickly cups my face in his hands and forces my eyes back to him. "No. That's the only thing I won't let you do. You can't hide from me, Bex. Not anymore. You wanna cry? Scream? Then do it. I'll hold you through it all. Shit, if you want me to scream and cry with you, I will, but we do it together. Just tell me what you need."

My body stiffens. Suddenly, any doubt I had of Sayshen, having changed from the guy I knew in high school has completely faded. The way his eyes flicker back and forth between mine—searching, silently begging me to trust him—lets me know just how genuine he and his words are.

"A shower. Please," I mumble, holding his stare. His thumb brushes slowly across the cut on my swollen lip, sending a stinging pain across it. Tears form along my lash line. A natural reaction to the realization of just how real all of this is. I'll never hurt again. Christian can never hurt me again.

"Okay," he whispers. Pulling his hands from my face, he takes my hand in his and guides me through the house, flicking lights on along the way. I can't explain why, but I'm comforted by having my hand in his. After what just happened, you'd think I'd want to be alone, but that's the last thing I want. It's easier to cope with Sayshen here. To forget about my pain when someone else is near me. Reminding me that I'm okay. That I'm safe now.

Doing all the things that Christian never did.

Because Sayshen isn't Christian.

We pass through a long hallway with a huge Speed Demons

logo painted across the wall like a mural. From what I've seen, it's the only color in the entire house.

When we reach the stairs, he leads me up them and stops at a small closet at the top. Opening the door, he pulls out some folded towels before closing it. He flicks on the bathroom lights and releases my hand as he starts up the shower. Hot steam quickly fills the room. The bathroom color matches the rest of the house, but it has more of a beachy feel to it. Framed art prints of starfish and corals hang along the walls, and the shower curtain is a powder blue color, with tiny white fish scattered around it.

"I'll be right downstairs if you need anything, okay?" he whispers as he starts to exit the room.

"No!" I snap. He stops and turns to face me with a concerned expression. "Stay. Please. I—I don't want to be alone, Sayshen," I admit. Saying it out loud makes it all seem so much more real. My heart hurts, and though I know I'm better off without Christian, I still feel like part of me inside is breaking. Tears begin to trail down my cheeks, and my body once again begins to tremble.

Sayshen nods and turns his back to me so I can undress. Unzipping the Demons hoodie Lena gave me, I hang it on the hook on the wall before undressing. Once done, I step into the shower stall. The steam billows around me, but it's a relief on my cool clammy skin. I can hear Sayshen on the other side of the curtain, and though I find comfort in that, I find myself wanting more. I slide my hand out through the curtain in search of his. A silent plea for the comfort he provides me.

Within seconds, his warm hand covers mine. Our fingers intertwining as he softly squeezes, and that's all I need. I step under the cascading water. Welcoming it as it washes away any trace left of Christian on my body and my life. Taking it right down the drain.

CHAPTER 10

TALON

I Need - Lithe

To my surprise, it's been quiet around the pits since my brother and Bexley left. I don't expect it to stay that way. Guys like Christian hate not getting their way. They don't take well to being put in their place, and like the narcissist that I know he is, I know it's only a matter of time until he's bored without the drama and has to do something to stir shit up.

Lena, Reign, and Draygon are all cooking up breakfast for the team. Reign, Thorne, and Wolfe all crashed here last night, not that any of us really slept. One thing I love about track weekends is that we all always eat together. Wolfe said something last night that's stuck with me. He said we're a family, and I guess we really are, though I never viewed it that way. There isn't a member on this team I wouldn't go to bat for, and I know it's the same for them.

And that's how a family should be.

It doesn't matter that we all come from different walks of life. All that matters is that when push comes to shove, there is no one we're more loyal to.

We'll die for each other, and on days like today, I'm thankful for that loyalty.

I lean back in my chair and pop my shades on over my eyes. The sun is bright and blinding this morning, and there isn't a cloud to be seen in the blue sky. Which is good. The races kick off in just a few hours, and this weather is the best weather to race in.

"Talon, grab your plate," Lena shouts from the kitchen inside the trailer. "Your bacon is done," she adds.

"Is it charcoal?" Wolfe shouts from his chair on the other side of the tent. "Cause this fucker only eats it if it literally crumbles when you touch that shit," he laughs, running his hand through his shaggy dirty blonde hair. Wolfe is the newest Demons member. He moved here from Alberta when Andre signed him and it didn't take long for him to fit in with the team. Raised on a big ranch up there, he is a lover of anything that involves being out in the wild with nature. So naturally, moving to Tampa was a huge culture shock to him at first, but he's gotten used to it.

Lowering my eyes at him, my shades slide down my nose. "Just cause you like your meat raw doesn't mean I have to," I spit jokingly before pushing myself up from my chair. It's no secret Wolfe likes to dabble with both women and men. It's why Thorne calls him greedy.

"I'd be careful riding bareback so often, that causes dick rot," Thorne snickers.

Wolfe laughs. "Aw, you jealous?"

"In your fucking dreams, bruv," Thorne laughs.

Wolfe puckers his lips toward Thorne. "Exactly,"

"Oh so that's why you've been so tired out on the track," I add with a cocky grin.

"Ya' know what, go fuck yourselves," Thorne replies as he playfully whips a dishtowel at Wolfe.

I make my way to the door still laughing when Andre, our Coach, pulls up on his small pit bike. He is dressed in the usual team colors. Wearing a black tee with the team logo on the front and the roster list complete with team numbers down the back like an old school rock band tour shirt. His buzz-cut hair cut glints in the sun as he rolls his bike up to the tent to park, and shuts off the engine. He is no doubt here to tell us the lineup plans based on the team's qualifier times. Draygon and Reign head out of the trailer upon his arrival, and we all head over to him.

"Demons," he nods, greeting us.

"What's up, Coach," Reign replies, tipping his chin up at Andre. "Did you come to tell the guys how bad I beat their asses out there yesterday?" he adds cockily. Wolfe elbows him, causing Reign to wrap his arm around his neck, putting him in a playful headlock.

"Ha, funny guy you are this morning, Matthews." Andre laughs.

Thorne snickers. "Ah, shit. You get the last name treatment, bruv."

"Where's your brother?" Andre asks, turning his attention on me as the guys continue to fuck around.

"He wasn't feeling so hot, so I sent him into the city to get checked out."

He crosses his arms in front of himself and rests them on the front of his bike. "Why? We have medical here. They could've checked him out," he asks, clearly not buying into my bullshit.

"Yeah, but his fever was pretty high last night, and it was after medical closed. I figured it was best to get him checked out and not wait until morning."

"Right. Okay, well, I guess that means he's not racing today then?" he asks. I shake my head in agreement. "Is your dad here yet?" Dad never misses a race. So I have no doubt he'll be here today as usual. But the last few years he's been absent from the pits. He's busy with work and his new girlfriend. Which honestly, Sayshen and I prefer. The last thing we need is to spend days with him pressuring us before a race. "Does he know Sayshen is missing the race yet?" He questions again.

Fuck.

"Nah, I didn't think it was that big of a deal. He'll be here today as usual and he'll find out then. It's nothing to worry about. I mean, we have the guys to cover Sayshen, and it's just one race," I lie. Sure, any of the guys can step in and race my little brother's laps, but even I don't believe this will be the only race he misses because of Bexley.

"Right, well, I'll call him when I get back to the office and fill him in. Maybe he should head over and check on him," Andre adds. Fuck, that's the last thing we want.

"Ha. It's unlikely he'd miss the race to go and check on Sayshen," Reign cuts in. "We all know Mr Shaw isn't missing the races to drive into Tampa. Besides, Baby Shaw is a grown-ass man. I'd hope he can handle a stomach bug on his own."

Our coach eyes him questionably but nods. "You know, you're right," He laughs. "Not that I blame Mr Shaw. I hate missing the races, too."

The guys and I all exchange looks, hoping we've convinced him not to call my dad. Dad wouldn't care about Sayshen missing the race for being sick. Don't get me wrong, he pushes us hard and always has, but he'll never push us when he knows physically we can't do it. He's not that much of a hard-ass, at least when it comes to Sayshen. However, missing the race to take another racer's girlfriend back to our house...Dad will definitely have something to say about that.

"Right, well, without Baby Shaw, it looks like—" He opens up the time sheets on his cellphone. "Talon, Wolfe, and Reign are headed out for today. So make sure your bikes are prepped. It's a hot one out there today, so stay hydrated and kick some fucking ass. Reign, I hope this year you have learned to tone down that cockiness on the track, yeah? I don't want a repeat of last year."

"You got it, Coach," Reign nods with a smirk.

"Don't fuck this up. I want to see Demons all over that podium this year," Andre adds before starting up his pit bike. He takes off back down the pits to where the main office building overlooks the track.

"Just one race," Reign laughs as he plops back down in one of the chairs under the tent. Draygon heads back inside to help Lena with the food.

"What's so funny, Matthews?" I mock as I sit down next to him.

"What's funny is after all that shit talking, you brought Bex right to your brother and then sent them off into the sunset, and you think, he's just going to what? Spend the weekend with her and then drop her and come back to racing?" Reign explains.

I understand why my intervening with Christian and Bexley is confusing to the team. Fuck, it's confusing to me too. But regardless of how concerned I am for my brother and the team, I couldn't just walk away from what I saw happening to Bexley. I couldn't just leave her.

"I mean, I'm not saying he won't be back. Cause I know, despite what you think, he does take the team and racing seriously. But you'll never get him to leave Bex now. He'll never let another guy touch her, let alone Christian."

"Fuck that guy," Thorne spits as he shoves a spoonful of eggs into his mouth.

"Talon!" Lena shouts through the trailer's window. "Your bacon is officially cold charcoal now," she adds.

The guys burst out laughing as I push myself from the chair and head to the trailer. Draygon pops the screen door open and hands me my plate. Peeking my head inside, I nod at Lena, "Thanks, Lena, sorry."

"All good, I get it," she adds with a smile.

The guys talk amongst themselves as I take my food back to my chair and sit down. I don't want to admit it, but I know Reign is right. I knew what I was doing, and yet I still handed my little brother the only girl he ever truly wanted, right to him. The image of her pinned against that trailer haunted me all night. I barely slept because every time I closed my eyes, all I saw was her face.

Those gorgeous hazel eyes she hides behind thick dark lashes. So full of sadness, defeat and fear.

The freckles that dance across her nose. I could see her pouty and bruised lips as they trembled. I kept trying to picture her smile and what it would feel like to be the one to put it on her face after so much pain and heartbreak.

Part of me wishes I had been the one to take her away from here. Not that I'll ever admit that to Sayshen or the guys. But I haven't been able to stop myself from wondering how she's doing and how she's feeling being away from Christian. Is she afraid? Does she still jump at every sound and look over her shoulder, fearing that he'll be behind her? Because he never will.

I'll never let that prick near her again.

Something in me feels for her. I care about her more than I probably should, especially considering what she means to my brother.

But I can't help how I feel.

All I can do is do my best to try to hide it from everyone.

CHAPTER 11

BEXLEY

Cold - Jessie Murph

Four days. That's how long it's been since Talon stepped in when I needed him and Sayshen whisked me away to their quiet little beach house.

To safety.

The bruises left behind by Christian have begun to fade. Each day, they grow fainter when I look in the mirror. I can't yet say the same about the other marks. The ones you can't see. The ones that still seem to plague my thoughts. Nightmares are a daily occurrence. Every night, my head is still plagued by thoughts and visions of Christian. They always wake me up in the dead of night, when I'm drenched in sweat and terrified. Sayshen, however, is always close by, always rushing to my side whenever I need him.

He's been nothing but kind to me. Respectful even.

A far cry from the cocky and immature fuckboy I knew so long ago. I'm thankful for everything he and his brother have done for me. But mostly, I'm thankful that when he looks at me, it's not pity that reflects in his eyes. It's pain. Rage. I've grown quite attached to him the last few days. Having him here has been a much-needed comfort. We've spent the last few days filling each other in on what happened between high school and now—watching movies where we place bets on how it's going to end. The loser has to wash the dishes. But mostly, just relaxing with each other.

Decompressing.

This morning, Sayshen is in the kitchen preparing breakfast for both of us while I sit on a barstool at the oversized island, watching and praying he doesn't burn down the house. I may also be secretly checking out his tight ass in those goddamn gray sweatpants as he bends down to grab pans from the cupboard too.

I swear those pants were made by the devil himself. To tease and torture women. The way they hug his hips and reveal just the right amount of his goods to drive a woman insane, is completely unfair.

But it's so much more than just physical attraction, especially after how he's treated me over the last couple of days. It's like this pull to him has been building up since that day at the cafe. He has been so kind and good to me. Sayshen was always sweet to me back in high school. He had always said I was never going to be just another number, one of the many girls he took home and spent a night with. I just never took any of what he said seriously.

Now, I do.

Now, when he talks, I find myself staring at his full lips, wondering how they'd feel against mine. I crave to run my fingers along the lines of the tattoos across his chest, arms, and stomach, dipping and swerving down the ridges of his toned abs.

"Pancakes today, then?" Sayshen asks, pulling me back to reality.

I tightly clench my thighs and clear my throat.

"Ye—yeah," I stutter.

Cocking a brow, he looks at me with confusion. "You good?"

"Yeah," I laugh, doing my best to hide the fact that I've spent the entire morning checking him out and silently drooling over him. Part of me wonders if I should feel guilty about it. I mean, after everything I just went through—not just the breakup with Christian, but everything that's been done to me—is it even normal for my body to want or crave the touch of another man so soon?

"Blueberry or banana?" he asks, seeming to believe my lie.

"Umm, blueberry. Please," I reply with a sweet smile.

"Mind grabbing them from the fridge for me?"

"Sure," I add, hopping down from my barstool. The short summer dress I chose to wear today brushes against my legs as I make my way around the island toward the fridge. It's a simple dress that Sayshen and I grabbed when we went into town for supplies: light denim, cute spaghetti straps, and a little fringe around the bottom. One of my favorite local designers made it as a piece in her summer line a few years ago, and though it's technically *out of style,* it will always be one of my go-to's for summer.

Nearing the fridge, my foot lands on something wet on the floor, and my foot slides across the floor. I fall backward, gasping until strong hands wrap around my back, stopping me before I hit the tile floor.

Sayshen.

He holds me tightly against him, the spatula still tightly grasped in his other hand as he smiles at me with that flirtatious grin that makes me weak in the knees.

"Thought you said you were good?" he smirks coyly as he looks down at me.

"I am! It's not my fault you got pancake batter on the floor!" I retort sassily.

He looks over his shoulder to where I slipped. "I did, well… I didn't mean to. Sorry, Bex," He adds as she slowly helps me upright. Standing inches from me, his hooded eyes lock with mine as he brushes some of my hair off my face. This close to him, I can feel the warmth of his body. A warmth I want to feel more of. I search his eyes for any sign of him feeling the same way I do. As I inhale his woodsy fresh scent, my body tingles, and I silently find myself hoping he'll kiss me.

Everything around us seems to freeze. The pancakes in the pan continue to sizzle and crack on the stove behind him, and yet neither of us flinches. His eyes make their way to my lips. Darkening as his tongue darts out to glide across his bottom lip.

Fuck it.

Without thinking, I give in to temptation and place my palms flat on his hard chest to steady myself. His eyes snap back to mine. I can feel his heartbeat increasing under my touch. His dark bangs hang down around his whiskey eyes. Holding his hunger-filled stare, I push myself up on my toes and press my lips against his.

He instantly kisses me back. His hand shifting to the small of my back as he pulls me in closer against him, deepening the kiss. Wrapping my arms around the back of his neck, I part my lips for his tongue. Soft moans slip from his lips, bringing a small smile to my face as he gently pushes me back against the counter of the island.

My body craves more of him. A tingling sensation courses through me, and I beg for more of his sweet kisses and gentle touch. Sayshen breaks the kiss, and we briefly share panted breaths before he rests his forehead against mine.

"Fuck, Bex. You have no idea how long I've been waiting to do that," he whispers from swollen lips. I giggle because though he doesn't think I do, I do. "Shit," he shouts, quickly leaving me to return to the stove where, if the scent is anything to go off of, the pancakes are completely burnt.

I wrap my arms around myself. My cheeks flush, and my lips pull into the biggest smile as I gently bite my lip.

I'm falling for fucking *Sayshen Shaw.*

Walking over to him, I look over his arm at the pan to find one side of my pancakes completely burnt. Taking the spatula from him, I push myself in front of him to assess the damage. "Well, at least it's only one side," I laugh.

From behind me, Sayshen pushes my hair over one side of my shoulder before wrapping his arms around my waist. He presses his hardened cock against my ass. The gesture causes my eyes to snap forward to the subway tile backsplash behind the stove. "I'll make you new ones. It's no big deal," he whispers, pressing soft kisses down my shoulder.

Elbowing him playfully, I smile. "Don't. These will be fine. Really."

"You sure? I don't mind."

"I'm sure," I laugh as I plate the burnt pancakes. Behind me, Sayshen grows quiet, and he pulls his arms from around me. Looking over, I find him using one of the dish towels to clean up the batter off the floor before opening the fridge door and pulling out a carton of orange juice.

With my plate in my hand, I return to my place on the island, where I left my sketchbooks and pencils.

"You should stay here," Sayshen says, as he places a glass of juice in front of me.

Confused by his statement, I reply, "Stay here?"

"Yeah. I mean, you obviously aren't going back to *his* place." His voice darkens with the mere mention of Christian. "You'll need somewhere to stay, so why not here?"

"That's a sweet offer, but I don't want to impose. Besides, I told you and Talon the other night, I can stay with Cece, it's not a big deal."

"No," he adds with a stern voice.

"Christian knows where Cece lives," he explains as he reaches my side. I watch him as I bring the glass of orange juice to my lips. It's sour and pulping but delicious and just what I needed to quench my thirst. "Just because it's been a couple of days, doesn't mean Christian will just drop it. We really don't know when going to Cece's will be considered safe for you. I mean what's to stop him from showing up a week or two from now?"

"I mean, you're right about Christian being able to find me there anytime, I guess. I don't know, though. Are you sure that Talon will be okay with me staying here?" I ask. Talon may have saved me from Christian, but that doesn't mean he'll be okay with me totally invading their lives. The last thing I want to do is cause any more problems than I already have.

"He'll be fine with it, Bex. Besides, it is my house too ya' know, and if I want my girl here, he can't really say much about it," he adds with a cocky smirk before taking a forkful of my burnt pancakes and shoving them in his mouth. "That is fucking disgusting," he mummers with a mouth full of food.

I smile, tucking my hair behind my ear. "Your girl, huh?"

"Yep!" he replies, accentuating the p sound.

"You do realize I haven't even been single for a week, and you're already laying claim to me."

"And? Why does it matter how long it's been since you and the douchebag broke up? I've wanted you longer. Everyone knows it. Besides, he didn't deserve you," he adds.

Taking a bite of my pancakes, I let his confession float around in my thoughts before replying. "Well, don't you think it's a little soon? I mean, considering everything that went down. People will talk."

"Let them. Bex, listen to me. I don't care what anyone says. I want you, and I know you want me, too. But I also know you've been through a lot of shit. I know in many ways you're still broken inside, and that's okay. I want to be the one that is here for you, to help you heal all the pieces of yourself that he broke. So when your fire returns, I'll know I helped get it going again," He adds, pressing a soft kiss to my head. "If you'll let me."

Tears build on the brim of my lashes and begin to glide down my cheeks. Cupping my face in his hands, he wipes them away with his thumbs and forces my eyes to his as his expression softens.

"Let me be that for you, please," he begs.

"Okay," I stammer, placing my hands over his.

He pulls me in for a hug and rests his chin on the top of my head as he holds me for a long moment. With my face pressed against his bare chest, I slow my breathing and allow his scent and warmth to calm me.

Releasing me, he takes my hands in his and looks down at me. "I'm going to take a quick shower, and then maybe we can go down to the beach for a swim. How does that sound?"

"That actually sounds really good," I reply.

"Alright, cool. I'll be right out," he adds before lowering his face and softly pressing his lips to mine. I watch as he walks down the hall toward the stairs. Checking out his tight ass the entire way as a smile grows on my face and my cheeks flush.

God, why did I wait so long to give Sayshen a chance?

I quickly finish my pancakes, which Sayshen was right—they are disgusting. I tidy up the mess in the kitchen and wash the breakfast dishes before heading out to the large deck at the back of the house. The cool ocean air whisks by me the moment I step outside, blowing my hair around my face. The left side of the deck is set up with a large black wicker patio set, complete with dark gray cushions with a palm tree pattern. In the middle, sits a large round fire pit table that looks like it's never been used. A massive grill and barbeque station sits under a small gazebo in the back corner making it the ideal deck for entertaining. Especially, for a group the size of the guy's team. Tropical potted plants and palms are placed around the deck, offering some privacy from the neighbors and beach visitors. Reaching the distressed white railing, I rest my arms across it and inhale a deep breath and look out at the ocean.

Living with Sayshen temporarily might not be so bad. After all, the house is gorgeous—this view is literally to die for. Having him around so much also isn't something I think I'll complain about, especially after that kiss. Somehow, even after what I've been through, the simplest touch from Sayshen makes me feel things. Things I haven't felt in a very long fucking time.

It's clear my feelings and needs matter more to him than what anyone else thinks and when we kissed, I could feel how badly he wanted it. Wanted me, and yet, he didn't push me any further.

He makes me want and crave things I truly never saw myself wanting again, not after Christian. With him, it was always about him and his needs. Never me. I never mattered. Most importantly, though, I feel safe here—safer than I've felt in a long time.

Sure, the nightmares are still there, but having Sayshen next to me when I wake up helps. My thoughts find their way to my best friend and all the things I need to fill her in on. Sliding my cell out from the small hidden pocket of my sundress, I dial Cece's number.

She's going to lose it when I tell her everything she's missed.

CHAPTER 12

SAYSHEN

Always Been You - Chris Grey

As I turn off the cool shower water, I can still feel Bexley's soft lips against mine. My cock is hard and throbbing for more of her intoxicating touch. I've waited so long to be with her like that, and in that moment, when she finally kissed me, it took every ounce of my strength to control myself. To stop it all before it went further than she or I wanted. Don't get me wrong, I want Bexley. I want her in every fucking way I can have her, but not until she's ready. Not until she can look me in the eyes and tell me she wants me to touch her.

A smile forms on my face at the thought of just how much she must trust me to be this open and vulnerable with me so soon after what Christian has put her through. The way she looked at me today, is how I spent every day of high school hoping she would, and now that she finally has, I feel like a horny teenager all over again. Patiently waiting for the chance to claim her as mine.

She wanted me to kiss her. I could see it in her hazel eyes.

Feel it in the way the energy of the room changed. But, if there's one girl I never want to fuck shit up with, it's Bexley. I don't want to rush a single thing when it comes to her. So no matter how badly I wanted to kiss her. I didn't. But never did I expect her to take things into her own hands.

And fuck, if that wasn't the hottest thing ever.

The problem is, now that I *know* for sure she craves the same thing I do, it's going to be that much harder to resist the urge to fucking take her. The last few days have honestly been a struggle. Not only because every waking minute spent with her has my body and soul craving hers, but because I'm forced to sit here and watch her go through a pain I can't take from her. All I can do is get up through the night any time I hear her crying and hold her tightly in my arms while she sheds years' worth of pent-up tears and pain. It not only angers me but fucking hurts me. No girl deserves to ever feel that kind of pain–least of all her.

I want to touch every inch of her perfect fucking body that still holds even the tiniest inkling of his memory. When she's ready, I'll replace every memory, every touch, with my own. He will no longer exist in Bexley's world, nor her memories.

I grab my towel from the hook on the wall and quickly run it across my body. The soft cotton fabric soaks up the last beads of water dripping down from my wet hair. I'm excited to take her down to the beach today. I think it might be just what she needs to de-stress a bit. There's something about the salty ocean water that just seems to help with pain. Both physical and emotional. After Mom left, though my memories of her are very vague, I do know the ocean became one of my favorite places to visit.

Talon and Dad would bring me every Sunday after track practice. They may have been hard on my ass about staying focused and training every other day of the week, but Sundays were for family.

After drying my hair with the towel, I toss it in the laundry bin by the door, step into my black swim trunks, and head back out to the living room. Rounding the corner, I spot Bex outside on the deck through the large floor-to-ceiling windows. She's chatting to someone on the phone while she looks out at the ocean. Bent over the old wooden railing with her arms resting across it, the wind whips around her, blowing about her raven-colored hair. Hair, I find myself wanting to thread my fingers through. Especially while she's bent over with her ass out just like she is right now.

I smirk as I head out to the deck. Bex ends the call just as I close the door behind me. The clicking sound draws her beautiful eyes in my direction.

"It was just Cece, don't worry." She smiles, before her eyes find their way back to the ocean.

Confused, I come up behind her, wrapping my arms around her petite waist as I inhale her sweet scent. To this day, she still smells the same as she did in high school. My nose fills with the familiar sweet and fresh scent of dragonfruit and citrus. It's nostalgic and soothing, and even when I went years without seeing her, any time that scent hit my nose, I always found myself looking around, scanning the crowds of people around me in search of the only person I truly wanted to see.

Bexley.

"Why would I worry?" I ask before pressing a gentle kiss to her ear.

"Well honestly, I don't know," she laughs. "I guess I'm just not used to having so much freedom," she adds.

"Well, get used to it. I never want to control you, Bex," I admit softly. Bexley turns in my arms to face me and lifts her arms to wrap around my neck.

"Good. I don't think I could go through that again."

"You'll never have to. Not while I'm around," I whisper, before lowering my lips to ghost over hers. "You smell so fucking good."

"I do?" she laughs. Even the small laugh coming from her is goddamn addictive.

"You do," I reply, before pressing my lips against hers. She pulls me into her, and we stumble until her back presses into the railing behind her. The impact causes a moan to slip from her lips, and I growl.

Fuck. I'm going to need another cool shower after this.

My hands find their way to her face, cupping it as I part her lips with my tongue. She tastes like summer rain—sweet and minty. My cock hardens, and without thinking, I can feel myself pulling her closer against me. Shit, I need to stop.

I break the kiss and gently release her as I move to step back, but she grabs my hand to stop me. Her lust-filled eyes lift to mine.

"Don't," she mutters from swollen lips. "Don't stop."

I wipe my mouth with my thumb as my lips pull into a smile, "I have to stop. It's taking everything in me not to bend you over that railing and fuck you right here on this deck for all my neighbors to watch, Bex."

"Then do it," she challenges. Her reply catches me off guard, and I freeze, staring at her in disbelief.

There's no way she's ready for that. Is there?

She pulls again on my arm, trying to bring me back to her.

"Bex. I'm not messing around. Just give me a minute to get myself under control."

Slowly, she steps toward me. "No," she whispers. "I want this. I need this, and I need it to be with you. I trust you." She ghosts her lips over mine, holding my stare.

"Are you sure?" I ask with panted breath. Fuck, this girl knows how to drive me crazy, and she isn't even trying. She pauses before licking her lips and nodding before she replies.

"Sayshen, I want you to touch me in every way he never could," she mutters. Her hungry eyes flicker back and forth with mine, before she swiftly slams her lips against mine.

Yep, I'm fucked.

Taking her ass in my hands, I wrap her legs around my waist and lift her into the air as I carry her back into the house and up to my bedroom. Closing the door behind us, I gently lay her down on the black silk sheets of the bed. Breaking the kiss, I hold myself up above her, and allow myself a moment to take in the sight of her flushed skin as she lays beneath me.

"You are so goddamn beautiful, Bex," I whisper before placing soft kisses along the soft skin of her neck and collar bone. I hold her gaze, looking up at her as I trail my kisses down her body, slowly pulling the short denim dress along down with me. When I reach her legs, I pull it the rest of the way down, and toss it to the floor before standing up.

If I thought Bex was gorgeous before, it was nothing compared to seeing her like this. Wearing nothing more than a pair of white cotton panties in the middle of my bed. She has small silver barbell piercings through her nipples that draw my attention as her perky tits rise and fall with each ragged breath. The bruises that covered her body have almost completely healed, revealing small patches of freckles and beauty marks scattered around her soft skin.

Standing at the edge of the bed, I follow every curve of her exposed body with my eyes while she watches. Fuck, I could bust just from the view of her like this. I don't know what the hell I did to deserve this fucking moment, but goddamn am I thankful.

Under the weight of my stare, Bex giggles, and pushes herself up on her elbows to look at me. Scooting herself to the edge of the bed, she holds our stare as she hooks her fingers into the waistband of my swim trunks and pulls them down.

"Bex—" I warn through a clenched jaw as she takes my cock in her hand. She holds it firmly, and slowly pumps it. Once. Twice. Her tongue slips through her teeth, and flattens it as it runs up the length of my shaft.

"Oh Fuck," I hiss as I suck in a breath.

My head falls back and my eyes roll back as I lift my hands to her head. Threading them gently through her thick hair as she teases me. Swirling her warm tongue up and over my cock's swollen tip. Fuck. Bex knows what she's doing.

"Sayshen," she moans. Looking down at her, I find her with her panties pulled to the side, using her free hand to play with herself as she pumps my cock with the other. My grip on her hair tightens as just the right amount of her teeth scrapes across the tip sending a shudder through me. She moans again and the hand around my cock picks up speed.

That's it.

Pulling my cock from her beautifully swollen lips, I bend down and pick her up to lift her back up onto the bed. Her arms instantly wrap around my neck and we kiss as I lay her back down, keeping myself above her. Positioning myself between her thighs. She grinds against me, lifting her pelvis as I hold her panties to the side with my thumb and line myself up at her opening.

"Are you sure you want this?" I ask huskily, breaking the kiss. I want this. Shit, I've wanted this since the moment I first saw her in junior year. But I also know there will be no going back. Not from this. Bexley Larson will be mine, and there's no way I'll ever let her go. I'll spend every day of my life protecting her. Loving her. Nothing will ever come before her. Not even racing.

Locking eyes with me, she nods her head in acceptance, and I slowly thrust myself inside her. Her tight walls clench and spasm around me. Her back arching off the bed as my sheer size stretches and fills every inch of her.

"Oh my god," she cries out. Her nails dig into my back as I hold myself still inside her, allowing her time to adjust. Slowly, I lower my lips to hers, and begin to pull back, before slamming back into her. Again, and again, slowly, gently. I swallow her moans as she lifts her hips to meet my thrusts.

"Fuck, Bex. You feel so fucking good," I whisper against her lips. "Too fucking good. You're mine now. When I'm done with you, it will only be my touch you remember. It will be my touch that you think about at night, that you crave," I whisper as I pump in and out of her. The wet sounds of our bodies coming together echoes around my bedroom; mixed with the soft whimpers that slip from her lips. Her hands glide down my body to grip my hips as she pulls me in against her. Deeper. Harder.

"Sayshen. Please," she moans. Her teeth sink into my bottom lip, breaking the skin. Her legs wrap around me as she grinds her pelvis vigorously in search of the friction she needs to find her release. Pushing myself up, I grab her hip with one hand, and slowly slide the thumb of my other hand into her mouth.

"Suck on it," I command. "Lick it like you did my cock, Bex." She does. Firmly gripping my wrist in her hand, she licks and laps at my thumb with her warm silky tongue. "That's it, fuck, such a good girl." Pulling my thumb from her mouth, I lower my hand to her clit. Circling it with my thumb as I continue to thrust up inside her. Taking her deeper and harder each time. Her hooded eyes begin to roll into the back of her head. Her hips bucking about as my thumb continues to massage her swollen nub.

"Fuck. Sayshen—" she cries out. Fuck she is so goddamn close. Releasing her hip, I place my flattened hand on her pelvis, holding her down with the perfect amount of pressure as I fuck her, knowing each thrust is bringing us both closer to the edge.

"Eyes up here, baby. You're going to fucking look at me while you come on my cock, Bex," I whisper. "I want you to watch me make you come. I want you to remember what my touch feels like and just how much your body fucking loves it."

"Oh god. Oh fuck," she mewls, gripping the sheets of the bed as her body begins to convulse and her orgasm hits her.

Removing my hand from her clit, I grip her hips tightly. Slightly lifting her off the bed as I pound into her. Her pussy clamps down on me. Vibrating and squeezing along my shaft, guiding me to my own release as I thrust into her one last time.

Lowering myself. I rest my head in the crook of her neck while we share heated breaths. Pushing myself to the side of her, I wrap my arms around her body and pull her into me.

"Are you okay?" I question, pressing my lips to her soft hair.

"You know, I'm actually perfect," she purrs, nuzzling herself against me. I don't expect her to be perfect. I know she has a long road to recovering, and an even longer one before she'll ever probably fully trust someone again. But I'm okay with all of that. As long as I get to be by her side through it. To help her, and to protect her, that's all that matters. "Oh, I'm on the pill by the way," she laughs.

"Huh? Oh," I reply. "Honestly wasn't even thinking about that."

"Well, regardless. Now you know. So, are we still going to the beach? I was really looking forward to that swim," she adds as she traces her fingers around the tattoos on my chest as her chin tilts up toward me.

"If that's what my girl wants," I reply with a smirk as I look down at her. "But first, I need to find my swim shorts, cause someone...ripped them off me."

She cocks a brow at me before replying. "Oh I would hardly call that 'ripping them off'," she laughs as she climbs out of the bed. "But I mean, if you weren't a fan, I can make sure I never do it again."

Panicked, I jump up from the bed, "No. No, I didn't mean it in a bad way. I loved every second of it, I promise."

"Mhmm, I bet you did," she winks. "I'm going to go grab my swimsuit from my bag, meet you on the deck?"

"Sure thing, babe. I'll be out in a few," I reply, pressing a soft kiss to her lips. With that she heads downstairs. Grabbing my swim shorts from the floor, I slide them back on before collapsing on my bed. My lips pull into a smile, and a small uncontainable laugh escapes me.

Bexley fucking Larson.

Goddamn.

CHAPTER 13

TALON

AirplaneMode - BONES

When the guys and I pull up to the house, I find Sayshen's bike parked in the driveway with both helmets resting neatly on the seat. The team all file in behind me, shutting down their bikes and stepping off to stretch. The ride from the track to the beach house isn't long, but after we lost the race Sunday, Coach forced us all to stay at the track for a few extra days to practice, leaving our bodies pretty much done. Which is awesome considering we have to be back there tonight to prepare for this weekend's races.

Dad didn't buy the story I gave Andre. He might not have made the drive down here himself to check on Sayshen, but he knows something is up. Sayshen and I have never missed a race, and we've been sick for plenty of them. The team has just always come first. Exactly like he wanted. It's how he raised us. So having Sayshen sit out this past weekend, and not even be at the track to spectate and cheer for the guys definitely raised some concerns with Dad.

I have no doubt that is exactly why, even though the race

ended Sunday, Dad is still hanging around the pits and planning to stay until this weekend's races are over. He made special arrangements with work just to be able to stay here. He even had his girlfriend drive him up a bag of clothing and their little pop-up camper so he had somewhere to stay. Which means I need to get Sayshen back to the track as soon as possible.

We have barely spoken since he left with Bexley on the back of his bike, and though the track was relatively quiet with no more altercations with Christian, I still have this gut feeling it's not the end of it. Can't even say I'd blame him for starting shit. I'd be pissed too if I lost a girl like Bexley.

"Damn, I'm pumped to hit the beach," Reign adds as he pulls his helmet off his head before placing it on the seat of his bike. "You think it's cold?"

"Shit, I don't even care. Ain't no way I'm not hitting the beach before we head back, bruv," Thorne adds, nudging Reign with his shoulder. Wolfe and Reign take off up the stairs, pushing and shoving each other excitedly along the way.

"Baby Shaw, Daddy's home! Where you at, man," Cruz coos, as he heads up the narrow staircase to the upper deck dragging Lena along behind him. Shaking my head with amusement, I climb off my bike and rest my helmet on the back before following them up.

"I'll be up in a minute. Need to make a few calls for Ma about some issues at the restaurant," Draygon explains before strolling down the long palm tree lined driveway with his phone pressed to his ear. His parents moved here from Korea when his mom was pregnant. They opened up a small Korean restaurant in downtown Tampa using all his mom's old family recipes and surprisingly, though downtown Tampa is a difficult place to start out for restaurants due to competition, it took off. Now, it's one of the busiest restaurants in the city. Since they don't speak much English, Draygon is left to handle most of the business side of things. He bitches about it, but secretly, we all know he actually loves it. That guy fucking loves his food.

The salty ocean breeze blows past me as I make my way up the narrow staircase to the deck, and when I take that last step I'm thrown back by what my eyes find. Laying on her stomach in one of the long black wicker lounges, is fucking Bexley Larson.

She's wearing what has to be the tiniest neon green bikini I think anyone has ever worn. The way it hugs her curves should be fucking illegal. Her thick dark hair is pulled up into a messy bun on the top of her head with a white scrunchie. A pair of aviator glasses cover her deadly hazel eyes as she lies sprawled out in the sun with the same sketchbook she dropped at the track. Drawing away like she doesn't have a care in the world. My eyes trail along her, taking in each inch of her perfect body. The deep purple bruising left by Christian is barely visible in the sunlight.

Fucking hell, she is gorgeous. So much so that I have to turn my eyes away from her and toward the ocean to keep myself calm. But what is she doing here? I thought I told my brother to bring her here just until shit settled down, and then he could take her to her friend Cece's? I don't know why I am even surprised he didn't listen to me. I should've expected this with how badly he has wanted her, and I handed her right to him. I should've known he'd never let her go.

Maybe I did. Maybe that's why I did it. After all, though I don't want to admit it, part of me is happy to find her here. Because since the night I found her, I haven't been able to shake her from my thoughts. Shit, maybe in some twisted fairytale in my head, I sent her with Sayshen that night because I knew this is exactly what would happen.

Exactly what I wanted to happen.

But why would I want that? After all, the more she's around, the less Sayshen or I will be able to focus on racing, and we can't afford to *not* be focused. Especially with Dad at the pits waiting for us and now having to watch our back for retaliation from Christian. Which means she has to go, and she has to go as soon as possible.

"What are you doing here?" I spit, trying to sound annoyed by her presence. The rest of the guys have all taken seats around the deck. Some joined Bexley on the wicker patio set, others leaning over the railing while they look out at the beach.

She lifts her eyes to mine, clearly thrown off by my question. Looking down on her, I can't help but notice how good her ass looks in the thin thong bottom of her bikini. The neon green color is almost a perfect match to the Demons team logo color, and the perfect complement to her sun kissed skin.

Averting my eyes, I clear my throat. "I said, what are you still doing here?" I ask again.

"Talon, chill man. Leave the girl alone," Cruz chimes in from one of the chairs across the deck. Lena eyes me from Cruz's lap as she swirls the golden hair at the nape of his neck between her fingers.

I know my issues with Bexley are not something the team shares. They all think she's good for Sayshen, and maybe in some ways she is. But she's not good for his racing career. She's not good for the team, and she sure as fuck isn't good for me. Especially when she's lying about in barely any goddamn clothes.

Sitting up, she places her notebook down on the chair beside her and pushes her glasses up to rest on her head, "I thought you knew I was here? I mean, you sent me away with your brother after—"

"Yeah, well, I didn't know that meant you'd be residing with us. I thought he'd keep you for a night and be done with it."

She scoffs. "So you thought you'd get me away from my abusive ex, hand me to your little brother, and he would what? Just bring me back to this adorable beach house, woo me for a few hours, and I'd spend the night riding his dick before he dropped me off in the morning. Is that it?" she adds with an accusatory tone.

I don't answer her. Because, for once, I find myself unsure of how to respond. She's not necessarily wrong. Part of me has always thought that most likely that's exactly what Sayshen would do, though he has always denied it. I think I always just assumed that yeah, maybe he thought she was different, but the moment he finally got a taste of her, he'd realize I was right all along and drop her. It would be like she never existed.

Clearly, what he's been telling us all these years, is the truth.

Which means I shouldn't want her.

Yet, I can't stop thinking about her.

Sayshen and I have shared girls before. But never a girl that ever meant anything. None of them ever mattered. The more I push Sayshen away from Bex, the more I'm starting to see that she does genuinely mean something to him. And though she is a distraction to both of us, I can't honestly say that I don't feel the same way. There is just something about her I can't shake, and I don't know if I want to.

"What's going on?" Sayshen asks as he makes his way out onto the deck in only a pair of swim trunks. He runs his hand through his hair as he brings himself to stand next to me.

"What the hell is she still doing here? Is she why you haven't been back to the track for practices this week? You know we lost, right?" I ask, stepping close to my brother.

"Yeah, I know we lost. Reign filled me in. It's not a big deal. It was the first race of the season. Now we at least have a better idea of who to watch out for on the track," Sayshen replies.

I laugh, crossing my arms over my chest. "Do we? Because you haven't been there to watch, to study anyone's movement or lines. You've been too busy playing house, apparently."

"Talon," he hisses, clearly pissed off. "Can I talk to you inside? Alone." Sayshen opens the door to the house, gesturing for me to follow him inside. Everyone's eyes seem to have fallen on me, and they don't look pleased. They're looking at me like I'm the asshole, and maybe I am, but I find myself confused about how one girl made an entire team forget about their goal.

Winning.

BEXLEY

Reign sits on the lounger next to me and picks up my sketchbook as Talon and Sayshen head inside. His hood is pulled up over his head to shade his buzz cut from the radiating sun. He pulls off his thick black Oakley glasses and hangs them on the collar of the oversized tee he has on underneath as he flips through the pages.

"Damn, Larson. You got some serious talent," he explains in an effort to break the awkward silence that seems to have taken over the deck.

"Thanks. They're nothing special," I reply, appreciating that he's trying to make me feel more comfortable.

"So what, are you like a designer then?" he asks as he continues flipping through the pages.

"Well, not yet," I laugh. "But I hope to be, one day."

"Is that what you take in school?" Cruz shouts from the chair where he and Lena are sitting. "Baby Shaw mentioned you were in college, but never said what for."

"Yep," I nod. "This will be my second year."

"That's sick though. Good for you, girl." Reign adds with encouragement. I'm thankful for his genuine support. Thankfully, despite everything, the team and Lena have been nothing but kind to me. Well, that is except for Talon. His hot and cold behavior confuses the fuck out of me.

Sayshen did tell me Talon isn't my biggest fan. He's even told me why, but I'm not sure why he seems to think I'd ever allow myself to be a distraction for Sayshen. After spending the last few days with him, and catching up, I know how important racing is to him. To his team and to his family. I'd never want to be the thing that changes that. What's confusing is I've never done anything to him or his brother for him to think that would be my goal, so I'm not sure where his hatred for me stems. I mean if he hates me so much, why did he step in that night? Why bring me right to Sayshen afterward?

Something in me feels like his hatred is an act. A front to hide feelings he doesn't want to admit. Maybe it's because of how Sayshen feels about me, which I could understand. I definitely don't want to be the cause of tension between them. Especially right at the start of the race season. All I know is that night, when Christian had me pinned against the trailer, and my eyes locked with Talon's, I felt something.

And I thought he did too.

"No, really. I mean it. You got skills, girl," Reign laughs, pulling me back from my thoughts. "It's clear you have an eye for it. I wouldn't be surprised to see your designs on the runway next to that dude's," he adds, trying to play it off like he knows the name of any designers, as he hands me the sketchbook and rises to his feet.

Thorne laughs loudly as he pushes off the railing and sits next to Wolfe on one of the couches. "Bruv, you wouldn't know fashion if it sat on your face. Stop chattin' shit and leave the girl alone, ay."

"I wanna see!" Lena shouts excitedly. Her long, beachy blonde hair swaying behind her as she makes her way over. The cute jean shorts and white bikini top she chose to wear today reveal the ink that paints her tanned skin. Lena has a certain aura about her. She's confident, kind but also super badass, and to be honest I kind of envy her. To be so sure of yourself, so comfortable in your own skin, is a true blessing.

Sitting beside me, she takes the book from my hand and flips through the pages. "Oh, I love this one," she explains as she points to a small short and blazer set I designed for one of my student projects last year. "Reign is right! Your designs are all so cute." Her bright blue eyes lift to mine, and I can tell her responses are genuine. "If you ever need a model, or anything, I'd love to help. I mean I don't know much about fashion either, but I'm willing to learn. That is if you ever want to guide me and give me some pointers," she laughs.

"Yeah, I'd love that," I add feeling hopeful. Having Lena be so kind toward me is something I'm thankful for. Especially with her being the only other girl in the group. They've all been so welcoming to me, just like Sayshen said they would. Well, all except Talon.

"Yo, let's hit the beach. I'm fucking melting out here," Reign shouts.

Cruz laughs, "Maybe cause you're the only idiot wearing a fucking hoodie today, dick weed."

"Well, I'm ready to hit the beach," Wolfe adds in. "I saw some top-notch babes heading down that way when we first got up here, and let me tell you…so fucking hot."

"Well, if Wolfey boy here has a shot at some pussy, how can we say no?" Cruz replies as he grabs Lena and tosses her over his shoulder. She screams playfully and pats his back, cheering him on as he hops from foot to foot. "You coming, Bex?"

"Hey, all I said was babes, I didn't say fuck all about them having pussies," he replies with a wink. I didn't know Wolfe was bisexual, but I can't say I'm surprised. After all I have seen him checking out Thorne once or twice, though I seem to be the only one who notices it.

"I think I'll just hang around here for now, I want to finish this design while it's fresh in my mind," It's a lie. I don't want to head down to the beach, not without knowing how things are going with Sayshen and Talon inside. I know their fight is about me, so taking off to swim at the beach just doesn't feel right.

"Suit yourself. But don't let their little quarrel keep you from enjoying yourself today, okay? They'll figure it out. They always do," Cruz adds. "To the beach!" he shouts, throwing his fist up to the air before he takes off down the stairs with Lena still draped over his shoulder.

They all take off down the stairs to the driveway and toward the beach. Rising from the large wicker lounger, I make my way to the railing and watch as they all run off toward the ocean. All accept Sayshen and Talon of course. Guilt-ridden, I turn, focusing my attention inside to where I know they're arguing. Because of me.

Clearly, though I've been welcomed into the circle by most of the team and into the house by Sayshen, Talon still has something against me and that is only causing problems for them. Right now, the best thing for me to do, for everyone, is to pack my bags and go stay with Cece.

It won't be easy, and it could very well be a dangerous move if Christian ever decides to pop in there looking for me. But it's better than causing problems for the team, or for Talon and Sayshen. It doesn't matter that I've grown to feel safe here, or that honestly, this is the only place I want to be right now.

Heading inside, their voices echo through the empty beach house, but I do my best to ignore them as I quietly walk across the open living space and up the stairs to Sayshen's room. The door clicks closed behind me, and I grab the bag and start to pack my things.

Well, it was fun while it lasted.

CHAPTER 14
SAYSHEN

Way Out - Colorblind

“What is your fucking problem? And don’t even start with me on racing. I fucking know we have to be up at the track tonight. Andre called me, and I was planning on heading back up there with Bex, I just wanted her to have the day to chill before I brought it up,” I snap, leaning my back against the island in the kitchen. After the morning Bex and I had, the last thing I’m in the mood for is Talon’s bullshit. This fucking game bitching and complaining about how Bexley is a distraction, a problem, is frustrating as fuck. When in the end, it’s clear to everyone else, even he doesn’t believe that shit.

“Why is she still here? And what do you mean you and Bex were heading back up there? You’re bringing her right back to the track? To him? What is the game plan here, huh, little brother?” Talon replies defensively.

“Where else would she be, Talon? Think about it. She has nowhere else to go where he won’t find her. I told her to stay, because I want her here. This is where she is the safest. So get the fuck over it," I reply, stepping toward him. "You know this bullshit about Bex being a distraction is getting really fucking old. You don't even know her. You shit talk her left and right, but then you turn around and beat the shit out of her ex and steal her away? It doesn't add up."

"Are you really that fucking oblivious to it all? She has her nails so deep in you that she consumes your every thought. When was the last time you trained? Sayshen, she's been back what, like a week, and already you've missed a race and a week's worth of training. And for what? To spend your days fucking the one chick from Palms High that wouldn't let you hit it? But I mean, now her options are pretty limited, right? So, of course, you're finally getting your chance. Finally getting your shot between her legs, huh, Baby Brother?"

Before I know it, I'm standing inches from his face. My chest rising and falling with heavy, panted breaths as I try to remain calm. "You think you have us all fooled, Big Brother? You think we don't all see the way you look at her. That I don't see you watching her every move when you're around her," I retort through a clenched jaw.

"The difference between me and you, *Brother*, is that I can protect her, and not stick my dick in her," Talon snaps back. "After what she went through, I feel obligated to protect her, and I will. But one thing I won't do is let it affect my racing, or my training. I will not put pussy before the Demons."

Rolling my eyes, I run my hands through my hair, "Oh stop with your fucking bullshit. Everyone fucking sees right through you. Even she fucking sees it. Feels it. Whatever the fuck this hatred you have for her is...it has nothing to do with racing or the fucking team. This is because you feel something for her, and you don't want to admit it. So go on. Tell me how she's just like every other fucking girl I've stuck my dick in because even you know she's not even close." I bump shoulders with him as I walk by, making my way back out to the deck having noticed everyone took off down to the beach.

"Oh? So you haven't fucked her then," he adds from behind me as he joins me on the deck.

"I didn't say that. I said even you fucking know she isn't just pussy. If she were, then her being here, being around me, it wouldn't bother you. That's what this is really about, right? The fact that my feelings for Bex are fucking real. That you know I'd give it all up for her in a goddamn heartbeat." I'm so fucking tired of arguing with my brother. So tired of having the same fucking arguments. It's time he accepts that Bex is staying. That my feelings for her are genuine. That they are real.

He paces back and forth on the deck.

"I'm fucking tired, Talon. I'm tired of having this argument over and over. Everyone else has accepted her, why the fuck can't you. Would it be so fucking terrible to just admit that she makes you feel something? That you were wrong about my intentions with her? Because I can't keep fucking doing this. Not with you."

He sighs. His head falls back as his eyes find their way to the clear blue sky.

"Promise me you'll get back to training. Regain your focus. The Demons need you. I need you," he admits with a calm tone.

"I promise, like I said, I planned to return to the track tonight, and I'm bringing her with me," I explain.

He laughs. "And how were you expecting Christian to react to that?"

"Like I give a fuck what he thinks about it. I'm not letting him near her," I add.

"That makes two of us," he replies as we bump knuckles. "How is she doing, anyway?" he asks, seemingly more calm now.

Cocking a brow, my lips pull into a sly grin as I eye him. "I fucking knew it," Talon punches me in the shoulder playfully, and he clicks his tongue as he smiles.

"Yeah, yeah. Don't let it go to your head. I don't even know what the fuck I'm feeling. She is something else, though, I'll give you that."

"Fucking right she is," I snicker. "And that body—"

"Do not even go there," he cuts me off, pointing his finger at me. "You should go pack your shit if you're planning on heading to the track tonight. It's supposed to rain tonight, so we'll probably head out once they've had their fun."

"You guys coming or what?" Cruz shouts from the edges of the property, where it meets the sandy beach. "Get Bex and get your asses down here, man, the water's great."

Get Bex?

"Is Bex not down there with you guys?" Talon replies, clearly sharing the same concern as me.

"Nah, she didn't come down with us. She said she had to finish her design," Cruz explains.

Looking over, I find Bexley's sketchpad and pencil on the chair where she left them. Fuck.

Feeling concerned, I head inside to find her, but Talon stops me. "I'll go find her. You head down to the beach with the team, and we'll meet you there."

"Are you sure?" I ask. I knew something was going on between them, even if neither had accepted it yet. It's obvious. There's a tension between them, one most guys in my position should be jealous of. But not me. Nah, I'm happy to share Bex with my brother. There isn't another guy on the planet I'd let near her other than him. Mostly because I trust him with her. I know he'd never hurt her.

But also because deep down, even I can see that they need each other.

And I need both of them.

TALON

The floorboards creak under my weight as I quickly head upstairs searching for Bexley. My heart is racing, and the conversation that Sayshen and I just had is still spinning around in my head. Inside, I feel a sense of pride for my little brother for standing his ground and calling me out the way he did. He's never been one to do that before, probably because if it had been about anything other than Bexley, my reaction might not have been so chill.

Reaching the landing, I head down the hall to Sayshen's room, where I know Bexley has been staying with him. She is standing at the edge of the bed, folding clothing before shoving it into her black backpack. I lean against the door frame and cross my arms over my chest while I watch her with confusion.

"What are you doing?" Bexley startles at the sound of my voice. Her cute little ass jiggling in her thong bikini bottoms as she jumps slightly.

She sighs. "What does it look like I'm doing?" Her reply is cold, but I can't say I don't deserve it. "You've made it perfectly clear numerous times that you don't want me around, Talon. I thought you'd be the one person happy to see me packing."

Pushing myself off the door frame, I cross the room's small space, pausing when I'm a few inches behind her. "So that's it. Now you're just going to give up? Just going to run to your little friend's house because you know I don't want you here?" She freezes, before whipping the clothes she was folding into the bag and turning around to face me.

"No. I'm going because I care too much about your brother to stay!" she snaps. "I'm tired of being around arguing, Talon. I don't like the negative energy or feeling guilty or like I'm constantly walking on eggshells. I just went through all that with Christian, I can't do it anymore," she adds as she releases a breath.

What could she possibly feel guilty for?

Then it hits me— my coldness, my refusal to see how sincere Sayshen's feelings for her really are, have affected more than just him. The more I push him about her, the more we fight, and Bexley blames herself for it all. When in reality, it's because of me.

Fuck.

I step closer to her—so close that she tilts her head up to look at me. Holding her stare, I soften my tone because not only do I not want to upset her, but I want her to know how genuine the next words from my lips are.

"The fighting between Sayshen and me is my fault. All of it. Not yours."

She rolls her goddamn eyes, and my cock twitches. It takes everything in me not to grab her by the throat and fuck the attitude right out of her. Even if I know I deserve every bit of it.

"How can you say that when it's always *me* you two seem to be fighting about? You know what kills me? I don't even know why you hate me so much," she replies.

"I don't hate you."

"Well you could have fucking fooled me," she retorts with a snarky tone.

"Because I didn't know you!" I snap and inhale deeply, calming myself before continuing, "I didn't know you, Bex. At first, I thought you were just another girl—one of the many my brother would bring home for the night and forget about. Then I realized that all of the years he told me you weren't, that you actually meant something to him. It meant that you were more dangerous to him and the team than I originally thought."

"Do you even hear yourself? How can I be dangerous to him? I'd never hurt Sayshen," she sighs and backs away from me. Without thinking, my hand grips her wrist, forcing her back to me.

"You think I don't know that? I know you wouldn't hurt him.

It's never been about you, it's what he's willing to sacrifice for you. Don't you see that? When it comes to you, there is nothing my brother won't do. He will literally die for you."

"Do you think I'm blind to that? I can see how much he cares for me. But I hate the tension between the two of you. I hate that you're both hurting and arguing over me. Why do you think I'm packing my things?" she snaps, pulling her arm free of my hold. "I don't want to be the thing that causes a rift in the team. I won't be."

"You're not listening. You were never the reason. I was. Hell, I still am. I've been unwilling to consider the possibility that maybe you could be good for him. That maybe you being here would motivate him, not distract him," I add. I know it doesn't make up for my behavior, but I'm hoping it will at least convince her to stay. Gently taking her hand in mine, I pull her back to me and brush her hair off her shoulder. "You bring out a different side of him. Out of both of us, and to me, there is nothing more terrifying. Nothing more dangerous. Our whole lives have been dedicated to racing, and it's all I know. I don't know how to make room for anything else, but I want to try. I— I need you to be patient with me." The confession slips softly from my lips as I look down at her.

With it, a weight seems to lift off my shoulders. Lifting my free hand, I trail my fingers down the exposed flesh of her arm, causing little goosebumps to prickle along her skin. Fuck she is so soft. So warm.

"Okay," she mutters, with a short breath, as her fingers intertwine with mine. Sayshen was right. I just told her how I feel, and yet there isn't a sign of surprise on her face. Instead, it's like she feels as relieved as I do. She lifts her eyes to mine and slowly steps closer toward me. So close her warm body is pressed up against my chest. Her hooded eyes search mine, and her lips begin to part, silently begging for me to press mine against them. Taking her chin in my hand, I tilt her face up before lowering my lips while my other hand presses against the small of her back. Inching her closer. I teasingly ghost my lips over hers, feeling her warm breath across my mine.

Behind us, Sayshen clears his throat. Snapping my head to the side, I find him leaning against the doorframe with a shit-eating grin across his face.

Little fucker.

"What's going on in here huh?" he adds cockily as he crosses his arms over his chest. Bexley, panicked, backs away from me almost instantly and pretends to be digging through her bag in search of something.

"Oh, I was just looking for my lotion," she answers.

"Is that right? Well, when you find it, make sure you put it back in that bag, we're heading back to the track tonight." Sayshen explains as he enters the room. He stands next to me, as we both wait to see how she'll react to the news. We both know going back and being forced to see Christian again will be hard for her.

"Back to the track?" she whispers, her eyes bouncing from his to mine.

"Bex, you don't have to worry. Nothing will happen to you. One of the Demons will be with you at all times. We'll ensure you're never alone, and that Christian is kept far away from you," I explain with a reassuring tone. I mean every word of it. There is no way in hell Christian or anyone else will ever touch Bexley again.

"Okay, if you're sure. But can we still hit the beach first?" she adds. It's clear from her expression she's skeptical but doing her best to give us the benefit of the doubt. I don't even blame her.

"Fuck yeah, we can. The team is already down there, and Lena has been waiting for you. I think she likes having another girl around, to be honest."

"Lena is pretty great. So is this all good now, then?" she adds, gesturing between Sayshen and me. "No more fighting?"

"We're all good, babe. Don't stress," Sayshen replies as he steps toward her. He presses a soft kiss to her forehead. "Let's go have some fun, I think we all deserve it."

With that, we all head out to join the team on the beach. To enjoy a bit of the sun before we drive back into the shit storm awaiting us at the track. I told Bexley nothing would happen to her, and I meant every word. There is no way in hell Christian or anyone else will ever touch Bexley again.

Now, Bexley Larson, is ours.

CHAPTER 15
SAYSHEN

Staying Up - PLVTINUM Ft. Riley

Driving through the pits with Bex riding as a backpack on my bike felt better than I expected. To be a dick, I drove right past Christian's trailer and just at the right time. He and his team were outside, and there was no way they missed us as we passed by. It felt fucking good. But not as good as having Bexley's arms wrapped around me. Nothing competes with having her finally be mine.

Ours.

After seeing the moment Talon and Bexley shared today, I have no doubt there is something between them. My brother seems to be accepting of it, which is a relief, finally. I don't think anyone could've handled any more of our fighting. The team doesn't need the added tension, especially with us all waiting to see how Christian is going to react to not only Bexley being back here but also being with me.

It's early evening, and things around the track are all settling down for the night. On the way here we stopped by Corsa Moto Works and grabbed the supplies we'll need for the bikes over the weekend, so thankfully we can all just chill for the rest of the night. Talon is laid out on the couch watching TV while Bex is unpacking. She wanted to lay low, and truthfully, I don't blame her. Talon and I know her being back here is uncomfortable for her, but hopefully in time, she'll come to realize that as long as she's with us, it doesn't matter how close Christian is. She is safe.

Heading over to Cruz's trailer, which is one over from ours, Lena is in her usual chair under the tent wearing one of Cruz's Demons hoodies and a pair of leggings, while Reign and Cruz mess around with his bike. Tomorrow's heat is important, especially now, with everyone wanting to give Christian a little slap to the face both on and off the track.

"Yo, Baby Shaw. Shouldn't you be working on the R1?" Cruz shouts as I approach.

"Probably, but you know me. I thrive when I leave shit to the last minute," I reply with a smirk. Reign reaches down into a small blue cooler beside them and pulls out two beers. Handing me one before twisting the cap off his.

Cruz stands, wiping his grease covered hands on a rag, "Well, excuse me for thinking now that your woman is here, you might want to spend the time prepping your bike so you don't look like a—"

"My god, Van Doren. Do you ever listen to yourself talk? You think now that his woman is here, that he's magically going to want to spend more time on his bike? When he could be spending it with her? Doing all the dirty things he's been dreaming about doing since junior year. Come on now, even I know how fucking dumb you sound," Reign adds with a laugh as he pats Cruz on the back.

"I don't blame you, Sayshen." Lena joins in from her chair. "I like Bex. She seems sweet. I can see why you've liked her for so long."

"Thank you, Lena. At least someone gets it," I reply, twisting the cap off my beer and tossing it at Reign playfully.

"You think you're slick, don't you!" Christian yells as he and a couple of his teammates approach us. "Acting like the big shot coming in here with her on your bike. Like you won or some shit." Cruz stands and nods his head toward Lena to get her to head inside the trailer.

My lips pull into a menacing smile as Reign and Cruz step up behind me, ready to have my back if needed. I'll admit, I was hoping this would happen. I knew exactly what I was doing, pulling up past his team with Bex on the back of my bike. I wanted it to bother him. Immature, maybe, but I knew it would get this reaction out of him and I want to see what he does when it's someone his own size that he has a problem with.

When he can't silence me with his fists like he did Bex, what's he got left?

Nothing.

Christian isn't shit.

"Ah, so you saw that did you. Sorry, I couldn't help myself. I just had to show her off. I mean, look at her," I reply cockily. Itching my jaw, my grin grows when I can practically see smoke billowing from Christian's big ears.

"You didn't win shit. You think cause you fucked her that she's yours? Ha, she'll come back to me. When she realizes only a man's touch can make her feel as good as I did," He laughs.

Reign cuts in from behind me. "As good as you did? Well fuck me, if beating a girl senseless is what it takes to feel good, then shit, I'm failing all the ladies I get with."

"She'll never come back to you, that I can promise," I add, stepping forward. "I have seen close up the marks your so-called *touch* leaves behind, and if it weren't for Bexley, I'd be leaving the same marks on you, except you wouldn't live to see them."

Christian steps toward me, leaving mere inches between us. My fists are clenched tightly at my sides. Every fiber of me wants to beat his face in. To make him feel all the fucking pain I know he put her through. The only thing stopping me is that I know

Bexley enough to know it wouldn't help. If anything, it would only hurt her more.

And that is the last thing that I want.

He laughs. "You think you're so big, don't you? Go on then, try it. You'll be dead before you land your first shot."

"You best watch who you're spitting death threats to, Cordova. After all, everyone here knows you're only tough when you're hitting women," Cruz chimes in. Pushing me out of the way, he presses his chest against Christian's. "A threat to one of us is a threat to all of us, and us Demons, we don't play nice when threatened," he adds.

"Cruz, it's all good. Just let it go. Christian ain't going to do shit," I add, placing my hand on Cruz's shoulder in an attempt to pull him back. He shrugs my hand off his arm.

"I will piss on your grave before you touch anyone in my family," Cruz spits aggressively. Cruz has always been a hothead. Guy has been through more than most people could even comprehend. He never takes shit from anyone, and he will protect those who matter to him to death. Literally. The trauma he went through in the system as a kid fucked with him. He's known nothing but loss, until Lena and the Demons of course, which is why he takes threats to us so seriously.

"Enough!" Andre shouts. His voice booms over the area, and everyone expects Christian and Cruz's attention to snap to Andre as he approaches. "Van Doren, back the fuck off right now otherwise I'll bench you tomorrow."

Lena, knowing she's the only one who will actually be able to pull Cruz back, slowly emerges from the trailer. She calmly approaches him and takes his hand in hers, pulling slightly to get him to back away. Sensing it's her, he holds Christian's stare while he lets her guide him back to the chair she was seated in before.

"Cordova, why the fuck are you in my team's section of the pits?" Andre steps up to Christian, crossing his arms over his chest in a condescending manner as he eyes him. “You and the Vipers, get back to your posts, and if I catch you over here starting shit with my team again, I’ll have you thrown out.”

Christian laughs, as do the two guys he brought with him. His eyes shift to mine, and he grins. “This ain’t over, Baby Shaw, and you better get a rein on your little pitbull over there before he finds himself on the other end of my fist.”

“I won’t tell you again, Cordova. Get the fuck out of here. Now!” Andre shouts. Christian smiles at him cockily before he and his teammates back off and head back down the pits to where their team is set up.

“That piece of shit needs to be put down. Respectfully,” Cruz says, pulling Lena into his lap as he laughs.

“Yeah, well, whatever the fuck is going on between you guys, handle it on the track. Not off,” Andre commands. “You’re lucky I came over here when I did.”

“For real,” Reign chimes in. “Cruz, I legit thought you were about to lose it for a second there.”

“I almost did. Fucking guy deserves it, though. Especially after what he’s done to Bexley.”

“I can’t believe he thinks she’d ever go back to that,” Lena adds in a soft tone. “I mean, I might not know her that well yet, but even I can see the damage he’s done, and I don’t just mean the marks we’ve all seen on her skin.”

Andre clears his throat. “Does someone want to fill me in on what that was all about?”

“It’s fine, Coach, we have it handled,” I reply, patting my hand on his back.

“Right, well, Shaw, glad to see you’re back and feeling better. Next time, give me a heads up before you decided to fuck off into to the city, sick or not. And do the team a favor, leave your personal shit at home,” he adds, with a commanding tone. “Van Doren, you, Reign, and Wolfe are out for the first heat tomorrow. Cordova is on your line. I don’t know what the fuck is going on but handle it there. Show him what happens when you mess with Demons. Keep your hands free of any blood."

"You got it, Coach," Cruz adds, lifting his beer to his lips as he pulls Lena in higher against him.

The gesture makes me miss Bex. Miss the feeling of her warm body pressed up against mine.

"Shaw, you're out second round with Draygon, and your brother. Make sure you're ready to go and don't fuck it up. I expect your dad will be there watching. Seeing as he's remained here through the week, I'm guessing that has something to do with your absence last weekend," he adds as his eyes move to me.

"Yeah, I'm sure he'll be up everyone's asses bright and early," I laugh, trying to make light of the fact that I know Dad is going to be watching my every move. He knows something is up, and the last thing I need right now is a lecture on him about putting a girl before racing.

"Well, I'm glad you're feeling better. Now, everyone get some rest, and don't drink too many of those, Matthews," he adds, pointing to Reign's beer.

"You got it, Coach," he replies, lifting his bottle in cheers to Andre as he heads back down the pits.

"Your dad doesn't buy the whole you being sick shit, just so you know," Cruz explains. "He's been questioning everyone about you not being here."

"Yeah well, I'll worry about him and his bullshit tomorrow," I reply, lifting the beer to my lips. "Tonight, there's someone else I'd rather handle."

Reign laughs, "Aw, shit."

"Well, what are you standing here for, Baby Shaw? Go find your girl," Cruz smirks.

"I think I just might." Tossing back the last of my beer, Lena sticks her hand out to take the empty from me. "Thanks, Lena. Night dipshits, don't do anything I wouldn't do."

"Oh I'm going to do everything you're going to do, and then some. Just to my own girl," Cruz adds with a flirty grin as he grips Lena's hips firmly and pulls her against him. She laughs, wrapping her arms around his neck before pressing her lips against his.

"Later, Baby Shaw."

I roll my eyes, turning my back as I wave them off and head back to my trailer.

Fucking jokesters.

"Oh, fuck yeah. Just like that, babe," I groan as my head falls back against the couch. Bex grinds her hips, taking my cock deeper and deeper as she rides me. Her hands grip the thick gray fabric of the couch behind my head. When I got back from Cruz's trailer and found out Talon had passed out, I wasted no time. Like an addict itching for their next fix. I needed her in my arms and against my skin.

Especially after Christian's little fit.

Fuck I needed to be inside her. To remind her just how good I feel.

The strap from her sundress falls down her shoulder, exposing one of her sexy goddamn tits. It's tiny barbell glints in the dim trailer lights. Pulling my hand from her hip, I cup it with my hand before bringing it to my mouth. Swirling my tongue around the metal bar. Soft moans slip from her pouty lips as she rides me. Slowly and deeply. Taking every inch of my hard cock inside her. Her tightness clenches down around me when I take the hardened peak of her nipple between my teeth, gently pinching it.

"Oh, fuck," she moans. I smile, looking up at her as I nip and suck at her tit some more.

"Fuck, you're so goddamn beautiful, Bex. Look at you, riding my cock like a fucking goddess. You take it so fucking good, baby," I add with a praising tone. "You're in control. Take what you need from me. Fuck, I can't wait to feel you make yourself come on my cock."

"Sayshen," she moans as her pace increases. I free her tit, placing both my hands on her hips as I guide her motions, pulling her in deeper and harder. Her arms wrap around my neck, pulling my head against her sweat-covered chest. I lick and lap at her exposed skin.

The wet sound of our bodies coming together fills the small space. "That's it. Fuck, you're so fucking wet for me. Does my cock make you feel good, Bex? Yeah? Ride my cock till your cum is dripping down my balls."

"Oh fuck. I can't," she cries out with panted breath. I smile, knowing she can and she fucking will. Gripping her ass in my hand, I hold her up while I stand and quickly flip her onto her back on the couch. "Sayshen!" she shouts, but I ignore her and slam my cock into her. Her back arches and her nails dig into the back of my neck. "Oh, god. Sayshen, I'm going to—"

"That's it, Bex. Come for me. Come all over my fucking cock," I reply as I pound into her. Hard and fast. Relentlessly pumping myself in and out of her while her body begins to convulse, and her eyes roll into the back of her head. Her pussy clenches down around my throbbing cock. Squeezing and milking it as my own orgasm hits me, and we come together. We lay like that for a few minutes. With cool sweat coating our skin as exchanging panted breaths.

"I'm kind of surprised we didn't wake up your brother," she whispers with a giggle.

Slowly I pull myself out of her, and slide my shirt over my head before using it to clean Bex up. She watches me. Biting down on her bottom lip, before sitting up and fixing her dress. After I clean myself up, I toss my shirt into the laundry bin, and tuck my dick back into my pants before plopping down on the couch next to her.

"I'm not. That guy could sleep through a fucking hurricane," I reply, pulling her into my arms.

"Oh," she adds, fiddling shyly with her dress. The moment she and Talon shared earlier today at the beach house flashes back to my memory, and I decide to use this opportunity to see how Bex feels about Talon.

"Besides, he would've just joined in if we had woken him up," I reply semi-sarcastically.

"Yeah, right," she laughs as her eyes meet mine.

"What? He's into you."

Hearing my admission, her eyes widen with shock, and her jaw drops. "Don't pretend to be shocked. You think I don't see what's happening between you two?"

She smirks, "If you mean him hating me, then I think everyone sees that."

"Nah. He'd never have stepped in with Christian that day if he hated you. I saw you guys today, back at the beach house. Something is happening between you guys."

"I don't know what that was," she replies. Her tone is quiet and guilt-ridden.

"Bex," I add, gripping her chin and forcing her eyes to mine, ensuring she knows how true my words are. "You don't have to hide your feelings for Talon from me. We've shared girls before, and if you guys feel something for each other, then I am more than happy to do it again."

"You've what? Shared girls before?" she asks with a shocked expression. Her hazel doe eyes lock with mine, searching for the truth behind my words.

"Yes, we have, but none of them meant anything. It won't be the same with you because, though Talon may not want to admit it yet, you mean everything to both of us."

"Okay... as shocking as all of this, well, as interesting this information is, I think you're getting your brother confused with someone else."

A laugh erupts through me. "Well, I guess we'll see then, won't we," I add, pressing a gentle kiss to the top of her head. I don't blame her for not believing it, just like I don't blame Talon for working so hard to hide his feelings.

It's only a matter of time till they both accept that there is something between them.

Something they both need.

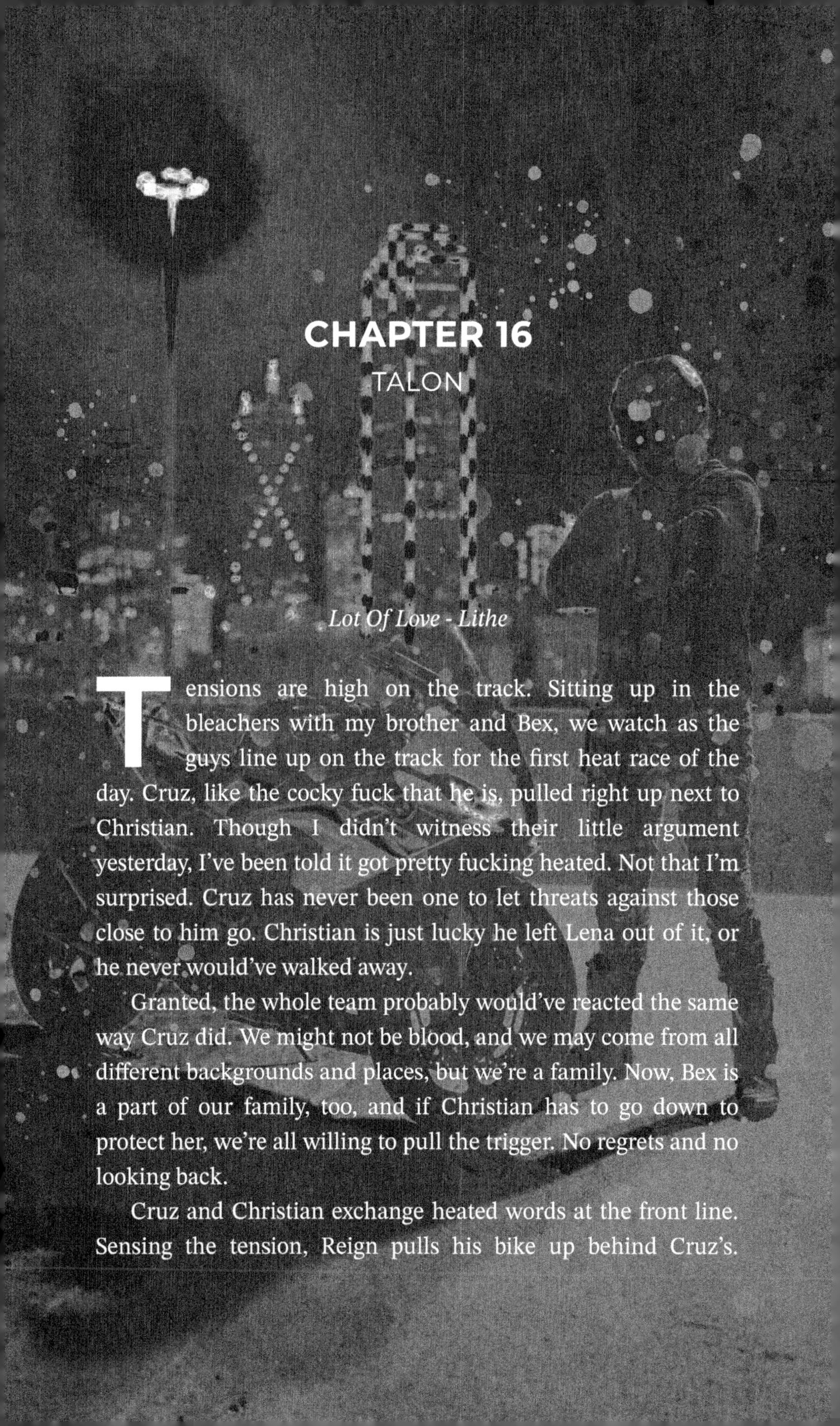

CHAPTER 16

TALON

Lot Of Love - Lithe

Tensions are high on the track. Sitting up in the bleachers with my brother and Bex, we watch as the guys line up on the track for the first heat race of the day. Cruz, like the cocky fuck that he is, pulled right up next to Christian. Though I didn't witness their little argument yesterday, I've been told it got pretty fucking heated. Not that I'm surprised. Cruz has never been one to let threats against those close to him go. Christian is just lucky he left Lena out of it, or he never would've walked away.

Granted, the whole team probably would've reacted the same way Cruz did. We might not be blood, and we may come from all different backgrounds and places, but we're a family. Now, Bex is a part of our family, too, and if Christian has to go down to protect her, we're all willing to pull the trigger. No regrets and no looking back.

Cruz and Christian exchange heated words at the front line. Sensing the tension, Reign pulls his bike up behind Cruz's.

Bumping his back tire to draw his attention. Cruz looks back at him, clearly agitated. Reign shakes his head at him to stop.

"What do you think that's about?" Sayshen asks, leaning his back against the metal seat behind us.

"Christian's attempt to get Cruz's head out of the race," I explain. "Odds are Cruz is still pissed about last night, and because Christian knows he doesn't stand a chance of beating him fairly, he wants to distract him. Piss him off so much that it's not about the race anymore, it's about beating Christian."

"Wouldn't that be a good thing?" Bexley whispers as she pulls her knees into her chest to keep warm. It's overcast here today, leaving it chilly and cool. Pulling my *Now Or Never* hoodie over my head, I hand it to her.

"Here, put it on," I explain. Her eyes meet mine as she smiles.

"Thanks," she replies softly before putting it on. It's huge on her, as I expected. But fuck if she doesn't look adorable wearing it. Her dark hair is pulled back from her face into a high pony today, showing off her high cheekbones and gorgeous neck. Especially now that there's no sign of bruising on it. She isn't used to showing off much skin, probably due to always having marks on her body that she's forced to hide. Sayshen's eyes meet mine, and his lips pull into a shit-eating grin as he crosses his arms over his chest.

Cocky fuck.

"No problem," I add just as the horn blows, signaling the start of the race. All our eyes snap to the track, watching as the bike revs before taking off. After the first lap, Cruz is still in the front, with Christian close behind him. Reign is trying to keep up but it's clear to everyone in the bleachers that something is happening. Neither of them are using their heads. They're taking corners at dangerous speeds.

"What the fuck is he doing?" Sayshen's voice does little to hide his concern. Cruz takes the last corner before the straightaway, zipping past us with Christian right on his ass. As

Reign passes, he looks up at us, shrugging his shoulders. Even he doesn't know what's going through Cruz's head.

"I don't know, but Cruz better slow it down. Beating Christian isn't worth the risk," I spit. Cruz and Christian tear down the straightaway, approaching the next turn before the third lap. Christian increases his speed, coming up alongside of Cruz, trying to force him out. But Cruz doesn't back off. Instead, he pushes back, trying to use the upcoming turn to his advantage. The crowd panics. Gasping with terror, they watch the race before them.

Fucking idiot.

Pissed off that Cruz isn't giving up so easily. Christian inches closer, but at the speeds they're going, the bikes are barely controllable. Approaching the next turn, Christian tries again, pushing up on Cruz just as they're about to turn, but his front wheel wobbles just when they're taking the apex, and he hits Cruz's back tire. The impact causes Cruz's tire to lose its grip on the tarmac. Cruz's bike goes down, and he's thrown over the handlebars. The force sends him violently rolling across the tarmac. I watch. Unable to tear my eyes from my friend and teammate as his body is thrown around like a rag doll, rolling and tumbling across the track until it stops. His bike skids and cartwheels behind him before landing on top of him.

Crushing him.

The riders behind them don't have enough time to react. Reign tries to swerve but ends up going down right behind Cruz. He's thrown off and follows his bike as it slides across the tarmac. His bike ends up right in the path of one of the Nomads, who also goes down when trying to avoid it.

My heart stops. Around us, the people in the bleachers are all freaking out. Some running down the narrow metal stairs to get to the track. Others sobbing as we're all forced to watch the sheer carnage before us.

The Corner Marshalls begin waving their red flags

simultaneously, signaling to the other racers to stop and exit the track. Sayshen takes off down the bleacher stairs. He finds Thorne at the bottom, and together they head out to the crash site on foot. Debris covers a large section of the track, some of which is completely engulfed in bright orange flames.

High-side crashes are always brutal, but the moment I saw Cruz's bike come down on him. My stomach twisted, and the world around us seemed to freeze.

The Nomad racer is up, walking around but clearly shaken up. Reign is moving, but even from here, I can tell it's not good. He's sitting up, rocking back and forth, holding his leg in his hands as he cries out in pain.

Cruz hasn't moved. His bike, still laying across his torso as thick black smoke billows out from it.

"Fuck. This isn't good," I mutter and I stand. Christian approaches the exit lane of the track and stops. He flips his visor open, and looks back over his shoulder at the chaos he created, before turning his eyes to where Bex and I are standing in the crowd. Even with only his eyes exposed, I can tell behind his helmet he's smiling.

"Go," Bex whispers from beside me. Her voice pulls me back to reality. "What are you waiting for? Get down there," she adds. But I know I can't. We all do. As much as I want to be down there checking on the guys, I can't leave Bexley alone. I can't leave Christian an opening to fucking touch her, and even if I went down there, there is nothing I can do for any of them that Sayshen and Thorne can't handle.

"No, I'm not leaving you," I reply as I watch Christian pull off the track and head back into the pits. *Piece of shit.* If having his blood on my hands was a possibility before this, it's an absolution now.

Christian Cordova is a fucking dead man.

Red and white lights, followed by the loud siren sound, signal the ambulance as it heads out onto the track just as Sayshen and

Thorne reach Cruz. Working together, they quickly pull the bike from his body, and the second they do, I know from my brother's reaction that it isn't good.

Thorne collapses, pulling Cruz's limp body into his lap before trying to wake him up with no success. Sayshen's hands find their way to his head as he paces about frantically before waving down the ambulance.

The paramedics rush to Cruz. Checking his vitals before pulling off his helmet and cutting open the chest part of his suit. One of the paramedics makes his way over to Reign and tries to help him, but he refuses, telling the medic to focus on Cruz.

"I—I can't watch this anymore. I'm going to go find Lena," Bex adds. I grab her arm with my hand, and her eyes snap to mine.

"I'm coming with you," I reply. The last thing I want to do is leave my boys, but Bex is right. We need to find Lena. She nods, slowly taking my hand in hers as she guides me down the stairs.

As we head back to the pits, I take one last look over my shoulder to find black smoke billowing up into the air, and something inside me just fucking knows that today, we lost our brother. That our Demons family just lost a member. Though I'm not showing it on the outside, on the inside I am in fucking pieces.

Visions of the bike coming down on Cruz replay in my head as Bexley leads me through the pits. The sound of a chopper hits my ears before it comes into view, flying over the pits and campsite on its way to the track.

When we reach Lena and Cruz's trailer, the screen door is wide open, and the wind is banging it off the side of the trailer. Bex quickly releases my hand and heads inside in search of Lena. My hands find their way to my hair, gripping and pulling tightly at my roots.

"She's not in here," she explains as she emerges. "Do you

think she would've gone out onto the track after hearing all the commotion?"

"Fuck!" I shout, kicking one of the lawn chairs set up under Cruz's tent. Bex rushes to my side. Taking my hands in hers, she wraps them around her small frame before pulling me into a hug. "I can't believe this is fucking happening. He's fucking gone."

"Shh. I know it's hard, but don't think like that. Not yet. Cruz is tough. He's a fucking fighter and we don't know all the facts yet, okay? The paramedics are with him, they'll help him. Just breathe. Stay calm. The team is going to need you, Talon. You have to be strong."

"I can't. Not right now." The helicopter flies overhead again on its way back to the hospital just as Andre pulls up to Cruz's trailer on a golf cart with Sayshen and Thorne. Bex releases me, and we both turn toward them as they park.

As he steps off the golf cart, my brother lifts his swollen and tear-stained eyes to mine.

"He's gone."

CHAPTER 17

BEXLEY

See You Again - Wiz Khalifa & Charlie Puth

If there are words to describe a type of pain you not only feel but can witness with your own eyes, I don't have them. It's been six days since that day on the track. Six days since Cruz's life came to an end, and though he was doing something he loved when we all lost him, it doesn't seem to help the cavity of emptiness that weighs heavy in all of our chests. Looking around at all the people who have come to Talon and Sayshen's beach house to celebrate his life and memory, my heart aches for each and every one of them. Knowing they all share more memories and thoughts of him than I do. I have no doubt the pain they must feel is truly immense with how close the team is, even if they don't all show it.

Sayshen's pain is undeniable. He's angry. Heartbroken and utterly gutted over the loss of his best friend. He's barely slept or spoken to any of the guys, including Talon, who, just when I thought he was starting to soften up to me, has gone back to hating me. I don't blame him.

I may not have been on the track that day, but it's Christian's fault Cruz is gone.

My fault.

It's Christian's retaliation for me being here, with the Speed Demons, that got Cruz killed. While I know most of them don't blame me by any means, I can't help but feel that Talon's cold shoulder is for the very same reason I have felt nothing but guilt since the moment the news of Cruz's death slipped from Sayshen's lips.

Thankfully, the team only lost one Demon that day. Though beaten up pretty badly, Reign woke up a few days later. His leg was badly shattered in the crash. The doctors were forced to operate on him and pin it back together. He won't be riding any time soon, but at least he's alive and overall in good spirits. All things considered.

Sayshen and I have spent the last few days hiding away in his room. The team was given a week off without losing points to grieve before returning to the track.

A week.

Like that's all it takes to heal someone's heart from a loss as traumatic as this. Sayshen has told me that's just how it is. That the world, racing... it all carries on—without Cruz—like he never existed.

Cruz wasn't the first to lose his life on the track, and he won't be the last.

He's told me so many stories the last couple of days about him and Cruz over the last few years and how he was always the comical one who always wanted to make light of tough situations and mess around. I've expressed my feelings of guilt to him, and though he's struggling and working through pain of his own, he's made it his mission to reassure me that Cruz's death isn't my fault. That Cruz was always a hothead. One that would never go down without a fight.

And he didn't. He fought to the very end.

Christian's role in his death is something that everyone, including the league, recognized. Though his punishment was nothing short of pathetic. A slap on the wrist, if you can even call it that. Christian was suspended for one race, and his team lost ten points. Nothing that they can't make up next weekend, especially with the Speed Demons sitting it out to mourn the loss of their friend.

Our friend.

"Are you okay, Bex? Do you want me to get you some water or something?" Cece asks as she softly runs her hand up and down my bare arm. The touch startles me and pulls me from my thoughts back to the growing crowd of people around us.

Cece's gentle and concerned eyes lift to mine as she awaits my response. She's been hanging around more lately, helping out wherever she can. She and Sayshen have gotten along fine, not that I'm surprised. They may not have been friends in high school, but they aren't exactly strangers either. Thankfully, even though it's clear Talon isn't a fan of her being around so much, he hasn't said anything about it.

"No, I'm okay. Thanks, though," I reply, offering her one of my first genuine smiles in days.

"Quite the crowd, huh?" she added, bringing herself to stand next to me. Together, we scan the sea of people all wearing black, who came today. Talon and Sayshen's large deck is packed full of people who loved Cruz. Nomads and Heathens make their rounds, shaking hands and giving their condolences to the Demons for their fallen brother, before finding seats around the outdoor space. If anyone here can relate to the pain the team is feeling, I have no doubt it's them, so seeing them here brings me a slight smile.

Lena, Wolfe, and Thorne—who is pushing Reign around in his wheelchair—begin making rounds. They greet everyone and guide them to the deck as they enter. Talon and Draygon are at the grill, cooking up a feast of grilled meat and veggies for anyone who wants them. Large white tables are lined up along the railing overlooking the beach, and each person who shows up seems to add another dish of food to it: salads, chips, mini sandwiches. If you can eat it, odds are it's on that table.

Watching Lena, my heart breaks for her. Sayshen told me about her and Cruz, how they met as teenagers in a group home. Both being orphans, they literally had no one except each other and the team. The guys have been trying to express to Lena that she'll always be a Demon even without Cruz. She'll always be family, but even looking at her now, I can tell it will never be the same for her.

She lost her person. Her other half. While everyone here today is feeling the loss of Cruz, no one is feeling it on her level. Not even close. Her long blonde hair hangs down her back in bouncy curls that Cece and I helped her style early this morning, and she's wearing a cute black summer dress that hugs her tight-frame body perfectly, showing off her newest ink. A tattoo on the upper part of her rib, near her breast.

'#88 Cruz VanDoren'

Noticing there is one Demon I haven't seen, I search the dense crowds of people for his familiar dark hair and daunting brown eyes. "Yeah, it really is. Have you seen Sayshen?"

"Did someone say my name?" he whispers softly against the shell of my ear as he comes up behind me. He wraps his arms around my waist and pulls me into him before pressing a soft kiss to my cheek. A small giggle escapes me, and the moment I'm in his arms any unease I feel melts away. Tilting my head up to look at him, I find him nodding toward Cece. "Hey, Cece. Thanks for being here and for all your help setting up."

"Oh, it's no problem at all. I was glad to be able to help. Really," she replies reassuringly. Her lavender hair is pulled up and out of her face today. Resting in a messy knot bun on the top of her head. She wore a cute black lace top, with black leggings. Simple, yet somehow pretty, as always. "Speaking of help, I should go help the guys get all that food plated and on the table. I'm sure people are getting hungry," she explains before excusing herself and heading off toward Talon and Draygon.

Sayshen leans against the wall behind us and pulls me into his chest as he exhales deeply.

"Are you okay?" I whisper, pulling his arms around me tighter before gently trailing my fingertips along them.

"Yeah, I think so. I mean, overall, no. I'm a fucking mess. I'm broken in so many ways I don't know how to put them into words to explain to you. But I also know Cruz wouldn't want that. For any of us. He'd want us to celebrate his life, not mourn his death, and as hard as it's going to be, that's what I intend to do. For him."

"Well, I think Cruz would be proud of you for that, especially knowing how hard it must be. I know I'm proud of you."

"Thanks, baby," he whispers as he rests his chin on the top of my head. "It's nice, though, to see all these people coming together to remember him," he adds.

An older man wearing a Demons shirt approaches us. He's tall, lean and though I've never seen him before, I can tell by his dark and familiar features exactly who he is.

Mr Shaw.

My body tenses, and Sayshen laughs, clearly sensing my unease. His chest rumbles against my back as he bends down to whisper in my ear. "Don't worry. It's going to be fine." His reassurance does little to help my racing heart. I've heard so much about their father, mostly from Sayshen telling me about how much of a hard-ass he is, but also things from the team about how he works with Andre to train them a lot through the off-season and how he isn't one to mess around with.

A take no shit kinda guy.

Knowing all that, I find it hard to believe he's not going to tell me just how much he disapproves of Sayshen spending time with me and not training, especially after our little getaway to the beach house after Talon saved me from Christian. Now, with Cruz's death being a direct result of the Demons all going to bat with my ex, I wouldn't be surprised if he, like Talon, blamed me for that, too.

Reaching us, he looks down and nods his head at me before lifting his eyes to his son's and placing a hand on his shoulder. "I'm proud of you, boy. Everyone knows how hard this must be for you, but you're here and did all this for him. He'd be proud of you. So, take this time for yourself, for your team. Be there for each other, mourn together, and then get back out there and make them pay. Make him pay," he whispers before lifting his beer to his lips.

His eyes drop back to me as he swallows his beer. "I hate that this is our first time meeting, Bexley. I have heard a lot about you, from the team, and my sons. I know I may not be around much, but just know I do see what you've done for both my boys, and I want you to know I am thankful for it—even if I don't show it. You're a Demon now, don't ever forget that."

My stomach catches in my throat, and I find myself caught off-guard by his kindness. It's the complete opposite of what I was expecting. I manage a small smile and nod as Mr Shaw pats Sayshen on the back before heading off toward where Cece is helping Talon and Draygon plate up the food.

"See, I told you it would be fine. I will say though, watching you squirm was fucking hot," he adds with a soft seductive tone as he gently ghosts his lips over my exposed neck and shoulders. Keeping with the black theme that everyone wore, I chose a strapless floor-length dress. Looser than I'd usually wear, but in the heat of the Tampa summer, I felt like one with some flow was a better option.

Goosebumps prickle along my skin.

"Stop it!" I shout playfully as I elbow him in the stomach. Spinning around in his arms, I wrap my arms around his neck and tilt my chin to look up at him. "Me squirming should be the last thing on your mind right now."

"Should it, though? With everything going on, I think I'd much rather drown myself in every inch of you. I mean, it would help take my mind off everything else," he adds with a coy smirk as his hands find their way to my ass, and he squeezes. "Besides, I think Cruz would get a kick out of it. He wouldn't want all this seriousness."

Even though I didn't know Cruz long, I have a feeling Sayshen is right.

My eyes meet his, and my body tingles as his hungry eyes flicker with mine. I roll my eyes and pull my bottom lip into my mouth with my teeth.

Fuck, I am such a sucker for Sayshen Shaw.

CHAPTER 18

BEXLEY

Your Guilty Pleasure - Henry Versus

The celebration went smoothly. People gathered, we ate, we talked, but most importantly, we remembered. We remembered Cruz not for the way he left but for the way he lived. It was everything he would've wanted but also everything I think the team and Lena needed. The Demons, Lena and Cece stayed later to help us clean up, but Sayshen and I told them all to head out and that we could handle the rest. It was getting late and honestly, I think we were just 'peopled' out.

Talon took off to his room the moment he could. I watched as he stormed off down the hall and the stairs. Confusion building in my stomach and the moment I heard his bedroom door slam shut, I jumped.

I sigh. One moment, I feel like he's about to kiss me, and the next, it's like he can't stand to be in the same room as me. I wish he'd let me be there for him, the same way Sayshen is. After all, I was with him when it all happened. I saw the look on his face when Cruz went down. I watched the concern grow when Reign followed him.

He was afraid.

We all were.

"Let's call it a night. The rest can wait until morning, babe," Sayshen adds as he gently takes my hand in his and pulls me over to the large sectional couch. His large hand encases mine ever so carefully as he guides me to sit down with him. We both plop down, and he wraps his arm around my shoulder, pulling me into him.

"It was a good day. I think, anyway. I think Cruz would've loved it. Seeing everyone together."

"Oh I'm sure he was looking down on everyone. Shit that fucker was probably cussing us out over all the wasted food," he laughs lightly.

"He definitely was," I add with a smile.

"My favorite part though, was easily watching the terror in your face when my dad came over. The way I could feel your body tense against mine. Your little squirm—" he whispers as he leans over me and lowers his lips to the crook of my neck. Slowly he peppers kisses down my shoulder. Nipping and sucking at my sun kissed flesh. "Fucking almost did me in. If it weren't a memorial for my best friend, I'd have thrown the food to the floor and taken you right there. Bent over the fucking table."

I giggle, "Oh, I bet Cruz would've loved that."

"Shit, I bet he'd be happy to watch even if it cost a few cheeseburgers and salads their lives. Besides, who needs real food when you taste so much better," he purrs.

Slowly, I shimmy out from under him and slide my body down to the floor. His eyes darken as he looks down at me. Watching as I position myself between his legs.

"Speaking of tasting," I whisper with a hushed tone. Unbuckling his black skinny jeans, I slide my hand inside and wrap it around his hardening girth before carefully guiding it through the hole in his boxers. Holding his gaze, I lower my mouth, gliding my tongue across the tip of his cock.

A slight hiss slips from his lips as his hands find their way to my hair. He threads his fingers through the strands as he positions himself more comfortably on the couch. I repeat the motion, still holding his stare. His jaw falls open, and my lips pull into a smile.

Placing my flattened tongue on the base of his cock, I run it up along his shaft before circling my tongue through the beads of precum around the tip. His head falls back against the couch. His hold on my hair tightens briefly as his body melts into the couch.

I take his cock into my mouth. Bobbing my head up and down as I suck and lap up the excess saliva that drips down. With my hand firmly holding the base, I match the motion of my mouth and begin to stroke him slowly.

"Fuck, Bex," he groans.

He needs this. We both do, but mostly him. Though we've spent every day together since Cruz's death, we haven't actually been together. Truthfully, I think we both wanted it, but felt guilty if our thoughts became sexual and we actually acted on them. But honestly, I think this is exactly what we've both needed all along to drown ourselves in each other and forget about our pain and our loss, even if only for a little while.

The floor creaks, drawing my attention. Looking over, I find Talon leaning against the hallway frame. His eyes zoned in on me as I take his brother's cock into my mouth. I freeze briefly. Unsure of how I should react to the situation.

Talon is shirtless, wearing nothing but a pair of gray sweats that do little to hide his arousal as he stands there watching. His sweat-coated, toned chest glints in the dim lighting of the living room.

"Bex," Sayshen whispers. Sliding his cock from my mouth, I turn my eyes to his. "It's okay," he adds softly before guiding me to continue. "Let him watch, babe." A familiar need builds between my thighs.

A tingle that craves to be touched.

Rubbed.

My tongue glides across the pulsing veins protruding from Sayshen's hard cock. Working its way up his shaft until his tip is once again sliding between my swollen lips and into my mouth.

My eyes find their way back to Talon as he pushes himself off the wall and slowly saunters across the room toward us. He holds my stare with each step he takes. His piercing blue eyes follow the movement of my mouth as it glides up and down his brother's cock. Taking it deeper and deeper into my throat each time. Talon takes a seat across from us before rubbing his hand along his cock over his pants.

"Fuck, Bex. Just like that, baby. God, your mouth feels so fucking good." Sayshen moans, as he guides my head. Keeping my eyes on Talon, I watch as he slowly rests his arm on the back of the couch, while sliding his other hand into his pants. He pulls his cock out, and for a moment, I gasp. Taking in the sheer size of him. Sayshen always told me the Shaw brothers were blessed, and fuck, he was right.

Talon spits in his hand, before wrapping it around his cock and pumping himself to the view of us before him. He watches. His hand matching the pace of my mouth on his brother's cock. His chest rises and falls with heavy panted breaths. Needing to find pleasure of my own, my free hand reaches between my thighs, bunching up the black fabric of my dress to reach my panties.

The moment my hand grazes my wet panties, a shudder runs through me. Fuck. Pulling them to the side, I circle my clit slowly and a soft moan slips from my lips. Vibrating down Sayshen's cock.

"Fucking hell, Bex," he whispers. "That's it. Just like that. You look so goddamn sexy with your lips wrapped around me."

"That's right. Touch yourself while you suck my brother's cock," Talon adds. His tone deep and husky. Just hearing his voice adds to the need building between my legs, and I carefully slide a finger inside myself. "Fuck. Just like that, Princess. Ride your fucking fingers while you watch me stroke my cock. Imagine how fucking good it would feel inside you. Filling you. Stretching your tight cunt," he grunts, as the speed of his hand increases. "Or maybe I should take your ass, hmm. I bet its fucking ripe. Tell me, Bex. Have you ever been shared before?"

Pushing my fingers deeper inside me, my body trembles as thoughts of them sharing me fill my head.

"Bex, baby. I'm going to fucking come." Sayshen's voice causes my eyes to snap back to his. My finger continues to slide in and out of my pussy as I take his cock to the back of my throat. I moan against him, and he quickly pulls out. "Show me those pretty tits, baby. I'm going to paint them with my fucking load," he says, as he takes his cock in his hand and begins to stroke himself. Pulling my finger from my pussy, I slide the top half of my dress down, exposing my pierced nipples to both of them. Talon growls from where he's seated on the couch, his pace increasing as he watches. Sayshen stands, pointing his cock at my tits as he jerks himself faster.

Kneeling before him, I ready myself. Wanting and craving every fucking drop of his delicious release. Within seconds, jets of white cum land across my chest. Some hitting my jaw and neck.

"Ahh, fuck yes," he groans as he empties himself. When he's finished, he falls back down onto the couch, clearly spent. Taking my fingers, I run them though the cum coating my chest. Scooping it all up before lifting my eyes to his, and licking my fingers clean. "Fucking hell that was hot, Bex," he adds with a cheeky grin.

The praise adds to my hunger, and my attention finds its way back to Talon.

"Go on," Sayshen whispers, nodding his head toward Talon. "Go show my brother what that pretty fucking mouth can do."

Talon's hand continues its motions. Gliding up and down his engorged shaft. He watches my every move with hunger filled eyes as I lick his brother's cum from my fingers before slowly crawling toward him. I hold his stare the entire way, until I'm kneeling before him. The way he looks down on me has my pussy throbbing. Begging to be touched.

Leaning back, I spread my legs, and lift my dress up over my knees, giving Talon a clear view as I once again pull my panties to the side and slowly begin to circle my clit with my fingers. His jaw drops, his eyes following the motion of my fingers in their circular assault.

"Fuck, Bex. You're such a goddamn tease," Sayshen adds jokingly from behind me.

His comment brings a smile to my face. "Do you want to watch me touch myself?" I ask. My voice barely a whisper as I slowly slide one fingers inside me. My back arches as I pull it back and repeat the motion. This time adding another finger. My pussy is slick with my arousal, allowing my fingers to slide in and out with ease. Carefully I pull them out, bringing them to my lips and sucking on them. Tasting myself before returning them to my pussy and continuing to fuck myself.

Talon's eyes darken, and a pleasure-filled groan escapes him. "Want to watch me ride my fingers? See how tight my little pussy is, so you can imagine how fucking good it would feel to slide your cock inside me," I add with a seductive tone.

"Do it, Princess. Make yourself come for me," he replies.

"I want you to watch me. I want you to watch me come while you fuck yourself, Talon, and then, I want to look you in the eyes while you fill my fucking mouth with your load."

He freezes at the sound of his name on my lips. His body tenses and the hunger in his eyes fades. Replaced by disgust as he quickly tucks his cock back into his pants. Rising from the couch, he knocks me over and storms off back down the hallway and up the stairs. The sound of his door slamming startles me and I jump.

Sayshen rushes to my side, his skinny jeans still undone as he kneels down next to me. "Bex, are you okay?" he asks, clearly concerned.

"Yeah, I'm okay. Just confused. Did I do something wrong? Did I cross a line?" I ask as I lift my eyes to his. It's clear that there is something between Talon and I, and though that situation was a first for me, I can't say I was uncomfortable. If anything, I was the most comfortable I've ever been in a sexual situation. Talon seemed to want it, I thought we both did, but after seeing the way his eyes changed before he stormed off. I suddenly find myself feeling self-conscious and unsure.

Maybe it is all in my head.

"No, baby. You didn't do anything wrong. Shit you were hot as fuck, and the moment my cock is ready for round two, I can't even tell you all the shit I want to do to you. Talon is just, well, Talon. He'll come around. Just give him some time." he explains as he helps me pull my dress back up.

"Maybe we were both wrong. Maybe he doesn't like me, at least not like that."

"You're joking. Right? You can't fucking tell me you actually believe that. I may not be in on whatever it is the two of you have, but from the outside looking in, whatever the fuck just happened between you two, trust me. He more than likes you, Bex," he explains as he helps me to my feet. I carefully pull my dress back down, feeling embarrassed. "Come on, let's head up to bed. I promise shit will be better in the morning, okay?"

"Right. Okay," I whisper, not fully believing him. Sayshen guides me up the stairs, flicking the lights off along the way until we reach his room. I don't fully understand what just happened, but I do know that there's no doubt left in my mind.

I have feelings for both of them.

I want both of them.

CHAPTER 19

SAYSHEN

War - Phix

The sound of my phone vibrating on my nightstand beside the bed wakes me. Forcing my eyes open, I find Bexley sound asleep beside me. Her back curled into the crook of my arm, and her thick raven hair fanned out across my pillows. My phone vibrates again. Groaning, I reach for it. Draygon's name is lit up across the glowing screen, and I swipe to answer before lowering the phone to my ear.

"What?" I ask. My voice cracked and husky.

"Yo, Baby Shaw," Draygon replies. "Why do you sound like death reincarnated? Were you asleep or some shit?"

"Yeah, actually, I was. It's what—" Pulling the phone from my ear, I check the time, finding it's barely eleven pm. Fuck. *When did I become an old person?*

Draygon's laughter echoes through the phone. "Alright, I see how it is. That girl got a tight leash on you, yeah, huh? Good, you need it."

"Shut up. What the fuck did you call me for?"

"I wanted to see if you were up for a little race. On the strip."

The strip. For years, bikers have been meeting up along Morris Bridge Road, on certain days throughout the month to race. It's hugely frowned upon by the league and, of course, our coach. Though we don't usually take part, that doesn't stop the team and I from hanging out to watch the races. You see, out there, there are no rules. There's no control, and everyone is fair game, meaning everyone is going to play dirty.

It's rarely worth the risk.

"Are you stupid? You know that shit isn't allowed. We're already down two team members compared to everyone else. You really think I wanna risk getting suspended for the rest of the season?"

"Christian is racing."

My body tenses with the sound of his name. Quickly, I sit upright in the bed, my eyes finding their way back to Bex. Even in sleep, she's fucking beautiful. Scanning every inch of her exposed body with my eyes, I find myself still struggling to believe she's actually mine.

Finally fucking mine.

There isn't a single sign of the marks he left on her body. Not a single bruise. Now, she's thriving. Healing, and in the process, healing some part of myself and my brother. Even if he's not as willing to admit it, I know she thinks he blames her for Cruz's death and Reign's accident. It's eating her up inside, especially with how he suddenly turned on her. But it has nothing to do with her.

Talon has never handled emotional pain well. He shuts down and blocks out everyone who wants to help him. I've seen him do it a hundred times, but he'll come back around when he's ready. Bex just needs to be patient with him and let him grieve in his own way. Tonight was a small step in the right direction—one I didn't see coming.

"Baby Shaw, you there?" Draygon's voice shouts through the phone, pulling me from my thoughts.

"Yeah, I'm here," I reply.

"So? Are you coming or what?" he asks loudly. I can hear crowds of people in the background, music blaring, and bikes revving. My head is telling me not to go. To stay here, in bed with Bex. But my heart hurts for the friend I lost. It hurts for Bexley, and in some fucked up way, I feel like I need to go. I need to beat him, even if it is an unofficial race. Christian needs to be put down, both on and off the track. Beating him at the strip would be the perfect little slap in the face until I can beat him on the track this season.

I could beat him for Cruz, Reign, and Bex.

"I'll be there in ten," I add before ending the call. I press a soft kiss to Bexley's head, allowing myself a minute to inhale her sweet scent before carefully sliding out of the bed. Heading to my walk-in closet, I pull on a pair of jeans and a white tee, slide on my race boots, and quietly open the bedroom door. Taking one last look over my shoulder, I look at the beauty sound asleep in my bed. I softly close the door and head downstairs. Grabbing my jacket and keys I head out, locking the door behind me.

The cool night wind coming in off the ocean assaults my nostrils with salty air as I head down the deck stairs to the driveway. Picking up Bexley's helmet, I place it on Talon's S1000 bike seat before climbing on my own bike and starting up the engine.

Tonight, Christian gets to find out what happens when you fuck with my family. It's a lesson he'll never forget. He's already taken one too many people from me, and I will fucking die before he touches a single hair on Bexley's head again.

Morris Bridge Road.

This is the hangout spot for all the underground street races and stunt performances. It's a long straight away with a slight curve in the back roads of Tampa. Not a very popular spot, even for locals. It's why it's the perfect place for this shit.

I pull down the street, slowly swerving through crowds, searching for Draygon. The sides of the road are full of dense crowds of people, all watching and placing bets on the races. Some riders are ripping it up and down the straight, doing stunts and tricks while crowds cheer them on.

Flipping my visor up, I stand on my bike, getting a better view of the people up ahead. Finding Draygon, I slowly make my way over, greeting people with a bump of my knuckles as I pass them.

Pulling up next to Draygon's red S1000, I find him chatting up with the guys hosting the races. He's the one who takes the bets and ensures everything goes smoothly. Draygon's onyx-black hair is slicked back, and he's wearing a white muscle shirt that shows off all the ink across his arms and chest. A thick silver chain dangles around his neck. A perfect match to the silver Rolex around his wrist. Draygon has money. A lot of it, and he loves to show it off. Always has. He's a fan of the finer things in life, and if he can flaunt it to get ahead in life, he sure as fuck will.

A few girls are crowded around his bike, which is not surprising. Draygon has always been a fan of having multiple girls at once, and I can't say I blame him. I've had my fair share of fun nights, but now, the only girl I want in my bed is still there, sound asleep, and I can't wait to get back to her.

"Hey, Sayshen," one of the girls say as she pushes off Draygon's bike to greet me. She struts toward me with intent, and I know immediately exactly what she is looking for by how she sways her hips and bites down on her lip. I've probably given it to her before, and if I didn't have my perfect girl in my bed at home waiting for me, I might do it again.

"Not interested," I snap. She stops, and I watch as her expression changes with the rejection. Giving her my back, I turn toward Draygon. "Yo, we doing this shit or what?" I shout, drawing Draygon's attention. He smirks, handing the guy a couple hundred-dollar bills before sending him off and approaching me.

"Took you long enough. Does your brother know I called you?" he asks, narrowing his dark brown eyes at me.

"Do you think I'd be here if he did? Stop with the stupid questions. Where is he?" I snap, my tone sounding colder than I intended, but I know Draygon can handle it. He's probably expecting it.

"Over there, listen though. He will be gunning for you as badly as you're for him. Are you sure you want to do this?"

"Are you fucking with me? You literally woke my ass up to come here, and now you wanna play good guy?" I laugh.

"Listen. I know you're fucking pissed, okay. We all are. But it's different with you. It's not just about Cruz and Reign for you, it's about your girl. That's why I fucking called you. If anyone is going to take Cordova out, I think it should be you, and I know you want it to be you. I'm just making sure you know what you're getting yourself into." he explains. "This ain't the track. Theres no fucking rules, Baby Shaw, and we both know he's not going to go down without a fight. So I'm asking, are you ready?"

"How much did you place on my head?" I ask, cocking a brow.

"Too fucking much. So you better not let me down fucker," he laughs.

The fog horn blares, signaling the racers to line up at the start.

"I got this," I reply, doing my best to reassure him. "Here, hold my piece," I add, pulling my gun from my waistband and handing it to him. He tucks it in the back of his jeans, and nods. I don't flaunt it, but I never leave home without my gun. Tampa isn't the safest of places, especially when you're meeting up at an illegal race in the back roads where just about anything can happen. I'm not the only one here who's packing either, even Draygon has his own piece tucked into his jeans right next to mine.

Flicking my visor closed and revving the engine I follow the line through the crowd of people right to the starting line and pull up right beside Christian. Stopping with my front tire on the line, I turn my sights next to me, where Christian is already staring me down.

His eyes are smiling with amusement as if he's so sure of himself about this race—about beating me. He flips his visor closed before returning his attention on the empty road in front of him.

A tall brunette in short denim shorts and a low-cut crop top heads out onto the road with a red bandana in her hand. Her long, straight hair blows around in the wind as she turns to face us. Besides Christian and me, there are two other racers: a girl I've seen around riding a bright pink GSXR 750 and a guy I don't recognize revving up his little Honda CBR like it stands a chance against the bigger bikes.

Draygon makes his way to the front of the crowd, nodding his head at me before the brunette waves the flag, signaling the start of the race.

All four of us take off down the straight.

At first, the pink GSXR takes the lead, leaving the rest of us behind her. I hold the same pace as Christian, not wanting to give it all I have too early.

He looks over at me, and I meet his glare before we both twist the throttle. Each second seems to last forever as the crowds of people around us blur together. My head fills with thoughts of Cruz—the empty hole in my chest that his death has left behind. I think of Reign. Left to finish out the remainder of the season from the pits with a shattered leg.

Christian speeds up, taking the lead by a few feet in front of me and tries to cut me off. I'm forced to back off to avoid him hitting me. Dirty fucking move, but I knew it was coming. I expected him to use the 'no rules' bullshit to his advantage. After all, it's what I plan to do too. Call it revenge, or retaliation, I don't give a fuck. All I know is by the time this race ends, Christian will be laying on the pavement and I'll be stuffing my pockets with some extra cash.

Twisting the throttle, my bike picks up speed. I sway, left and right, before deciding to make the move and pass him on the left side. When we're parallel to each other, the sound of my phone ringing blasts through my Bluetooth headset in my helmet. For a split second, I glance down at my phone mounted on the front of my bike to find Bexley's name.

And then I realize, I fucked up.

All it takes is one split second. One fucking moment where eyes stray from the road in front of me, from Christian, to fuck everything up.

Christian's tire hits my front tire with his, causing me to lose control. The front brakes lock up, and the bike slides out from under me. I follow it, sliding across the pavement. My helmet goes flying the first time it smacks off the ground. The second time sends a shooting pain across my skull, causing me to cry out.

Fuck.

I wrap my hands around my head in a last-chance effort to try and protect myself from further injury. My body rolls around, smacking off the hard ground along the way. It isn't until my body finds its way to a grassy ditch on the side of the strip that I finally stop. The first thing I notice as I lower my arms is that I can't feel anything. My body is completely numb, and no matter how hard I try to force my eyes open. I can't.

My thoughts fill with Bexley.

I can picture the gold flecks in her hazel eyes and the way she smiles when I kiss her forehead. Suddenly, a sharp pain radiates through my head, and slowly, the images begin to fade.

Then everything goes black.

CHAPTER 20

TALON

Phases - Chase Atlantic

The alarm ringtone sound of my phone echoes around my room, waking me from a deep sleep. Quickly, I reach for it off the table and swipe to answer it.

"Talon? Talon, you there?" Draygon's panicked voice muffles through the speakerphone. Jolting upright, I click on the small lamp on my bedside table. I rub my eyes with my index finger and thumb, allowing them a moment to adjust to the light before responding. Pulling my phone from my ear, I check the time on the glowing screen.

1:24 am. Draygon would only call me this late if it was something important. He can be a fuck head when he wants to be, but when it comes down to it, the guy doesn't fuck around. Especially not after spending the day saying our goodbyes to our friend. To Cruz.

His breathing becomes rugged and coarse against the phone.

"Draygon? Yeah. What's going on?" I reply, sensing his distress. "Are you okay?"

"Yeah, I'm fine, it's just—fuck!" he shouts.

Rising from the bed, I begin to pace around the room with anticipation. The cool ocean breeze billows in through the window, but it does little to calm my nerves as I wait for his reply. "What are you talking about? What happened?" I ask, running my hand through my thick hair.

"It's Sayshen, man." He shouts. "They just took him to TGH. Fuck man, this is all my fault. I knew this was a stupid idea."

His words replay in my head. TGH, Florida South Tampa General Hospital.

I freeze. My back stiffening with the mention of my brother's name. "What are you talking about? Who is taking him there? And why? What the fuck is going on?"

"He went down, bro, at the strip. It's not good. They said he suffered a lot of head trauma, man. His head was all fucked up. I'm so fucking sorry, fuck."

"What do you mean you're sorry? Why the fuck was he even at the strip! Why are either of you?" Draygon tries to explain, but I snap. "Fucking forget it, you can explain later. I'm leaving now," I add before ending the call. Grabbing my gray sweats from the floor, I quickly step into them and throw on the first T-shirt I can find.

Heading out into the hall, I first rush right past Sayshen's room, but once I reach the top of the stairs, something in my gut stops me.

Bexley.

I've avoided her as much as possible since that day at the track. Not because I'm angry with her, though I know that's what she thinks. She thinks I blame her. She probably assumes that my rejection last night was because of her, and I have no doubt that she believes Christian's wrath is because I saved her that day. But I don't, at least not fully.

Fuck, rejecting her took everything in me. Watching her crawl toward me with that look in her goddamn eyes did something to me. Something no other girl has ever done. She was so eager to please, even with my brother's cum still coating her lips, and every fucking fiber of my body wanted to let her. I wanted to sink myself inside her right then and there on the living room floor with my brother watching. To hear the sweet fucking sound I heard the other night, slip from her lips again. But I couldn't. Because right now, when I see her, I see him. *Christian.* The mother fucker responsible for all the pain my team is feeling.

And I don't know how to get past that.

I know it's not what she wanted. Cruz's death hurt her just as much as the rest of us. She didn't want this for any of us, especially him. And yet, some fucked up part of me still wants to blame her so I don't have to blame myself. In some fucked up way, when I see her, I see my team crumbling. But even though I want to grab her face and press my lips against hers until the pain coursing through my body dissipates, I won't.

Because if I hadn't saved her and brought her to my brother that night, maybe Cruz would still be here, and maybe, just maybe, Reign would still be riding... and Sayshen wouldn't be at TGH.

Opening the wooden door, I prepare to find darkness, but instead, I find Bexley sitting in the middle of the bed. Her legs are crossed and her dark hair is hanging down her shoulders in thick natural waves. The black silk sheets are pulled up over her tits as she scrolls mercilessly through her phone. The door creaks, causing her widened eyes to snap to mine.

"Get dressed, we have to go," I explain with a commanding tone.

"It's Sayshen, isn't it," she asks as she quickly rushes out of bed. Holding the silk sheet around her tight frame, I watch as she gathers clothing from around the room and heads to the ensuite.

"Did you know he left? Did he tell you where he was going?" I ask.

She quickly makes her way out of the bathroom fully clothed in a pair of black leggings and a small navy crop. She sits on the edge of the bed, frantically trying to slide her feet into some checkered vans.

"No," she replies, shaking her head. "I just woke up, and he wasn't here. I've tried calling him. It rang the first time, but after that, it just went to voicemail every time. It's not like him," she adds. "He always answers my calls."

"Draygon called me. Sayshen's being taken to TGH. He went down at the strip. It's a—"

"I know what it is. Christian races there all the time," she admits, clearly putting two and two together. "Why would he go there in the middle of the night? Why wouldn't he wake us?"

Whatever has happened to my little brother, I have no doubt, is a result of that piece of shit. "Besides street racing being illegal and getting him kicked off the team, there's only one other reason I think of that would make me go down there. I swear to fucking god if that fucking piece of shit has anything to do with this, I'll fucking kill him."

"Let's just get there and figure out what's going on, okay?" Bex adds with a soft tone as she approaches me. Taking my hand in hers, she lifts her brown eyes to mine and her expression softens. "Right now, Sayshen needs us. Everything else can wait."

Threading my fingers with hers, I lead her downstairs and through the hall to the main entrance. I grab my jacket off the hook by the door and slide it on before tossing Bexley my *Now Or Never* hoodie.

"Put this on. The ride is going to be chilly, you'll need it," I explain. She quickly lifts it over her head before heading out to the deck and down the stairs to where my bike is parked. I don't know what it is about her that has me so captivated. How one small touch and suddenly my nerves are settled, my emotions calm and I forget about my anger. My rage.

Because she's right. Right now, all that matters is my little brother.

Grabbing my keys, I lock the door behind me before heading down to where Bex is waiting. When I reach my bike, she's already got her helmet on her head and is struggling to buckle it.

"Here, let me help," I add with a hushed tone.

"Thanks," she replies. Taking the straps in my hands, she tilts her chin up. Her eyes searching my face like she's waiting for me to say something that will make her better. Something to ease the pain and worry she's feeling. But I can't. Because I don't know what we're about to walk into when we get there.

I can feel her fear for my brother. She's trying to hide it, and I'll give her credit, she's pretty good at it. But she's not fooling me.

Because I'm feeling everything she is.

With her helmet secured, I climb on my S1000, and with a twist of my key, the engine purrs to life. Bex climbs on behind me, pressing her chest against my back and wrapping her arms tightly around my waist. Slowly, I back the bike out of the driveway, and take off down the beach strip toward the city.

To find out if my brother is dead, or alive.

Though the ride to the hospital is short, the minutes seemed to feel like hours as all the possibilities of what could be awaiting us played out through my head. Pacing the waiting room, I wait for the doctor treating Sayshen to update us. Draygon and Bexley are sitting in the row of chairs along the wall. Draygon is hunched over, his fingers locked along the back of his neck as he keeps his eyes glued to the dated tile floor.

When we arrived, no one told us anything, not even if he was alive. All anyone said was that the doctor would be out to speak with us. That was three and a half hours ago, and there's still no update.

Draygon filled Bexley and me in on what happened. Told me about how he called Sayshen down to the strip when he heard that Christian was racing. Figuring he'd want retaliation, which of course he did. What he couldn't tell me was how Sayshen went down. Everyone saw Christian run him off the road after hitting his front tire, but Sayshen would've had time to dodge it, and he didn't. He didn't even move, Draygon said.

But why? What had him so fucking distracted that he didn't see Cordova coming?

"Mr Shaw?" An older gentleman in teal scrubs shouts as he enters the waiting area.

"Yeah. That's me," I reply as Draygon, Bex, and I rush toward him. My heart races. Thumping fast and hard in my chest as I try to mentally prepare for the worst news to leave the doctor's mouth. "Is he okay?"

He shakes my hand as he greets me. "I'm Dr O'Brian, and I'll be in charge of your brother's care. When he arrived, it was clear he had sustained multiple injuries, the majority of them to his head after his helmet was knocked off. Thankfully, he was smart enough to lift his arms around his head after the initial impact, shielding it from the worst of it," the doctor explains.

"He'll be okay, though, right?" Bex asks with a soft and concerned tone. She is fidgeting with the rim of the sleeves of my hoodie, keeping her attention focused on the doctor. Even like this, she's fucking beautiful. Her eyes are swollen from spending the last three hours crying. She tried to hide it from me, thinking that if she just turned away and wiped her eyes on the sleeve of my hoodie, I wouldn't notice. But I did.

It shows me she truly cares for my brother. Her feelings for him are genuine, and though their relationship may be newer, she's struggling as much as I am with the news of his crash. Part of me wants to scoop her up in my arms, console her, and tell her everything will be okay. That he will be okay. I want to wipe her tears. Replacing them with soft and gentle kisses along her rosy cheeks. But I won't. I can't.

Because the guilt is just too much, and not only is she my little brother's girl, but I don't deserve her. Not after the choices I've made have caused so many people I love, so much pain, and especially not after being so hard on her. For viewing her as a problem that needed to be fixed, erased. After thinking my brother's obsession with her would fuck with his head. That he wouldn't be able to focus on racing. On the team, but since she's been here, I've seen a whole new side to my little brother and the guys on the team.

Sayshen's obsession with her was never the problem. It was me. My failure to see that some things are more important than racing.

"That's hard to say. He's stable right now, but he's been very touch and go. I expect him to improve, but he'll be heavily monitored over the next few days."

Just knowing he's alive eases some of my distress, but it does little to calm the anger flowing through me. "Can we see him now?" My fists ball at my sides, and my jaw clicks. My little brother is laying in there, fighting for his life the same fucking way Cruz did, and it's the same mother fucker who took Cruz from us that put him there.

"You can, but he is unconscious. We've put him into a medically induced coma to allow the swelling in his brain to go down. But you're welcome to sit with him in the meantime," he adds.

"How long will that take?" Draygon asks, cutting in. "For the swelling to go down, I mean."

"That's hard to say. Everyone is different, and everyone's body heals differently. But I expect to see some improvement in the next few days. I have other patients to attend to, but if you need me, have the nurses page me."

"Thanks, Doctor." I reply, before he walks away.

"Draygon, you should go home. Get some rest. Bexley and I will stay with Sayshen."

"I'm not leaving him. He wouldn't have even been there if it wasn't for me. This is my fucking fault, I'm going to be here to help him when he wakes up."

"It's not your fault, even if you did call him down there. Sayshen knew better than to let anyone or anything distract him. He knew not to take his eyes off the road and give that piece of shit the chance to do anything." I reply, though part of me agrees with him. Had he not called Sayshen down there, we would not be here right now. But Draygon didn't do it with the intent on hurting my brother. Not like Christian did. He's the one I'm angry with, and myself.

Not Draygon. Not Bexley. Not even Sayshen.

Though I should be. He's a fucking idiot for being so reckless.

"Doesn't mean I don't feel guilty, man. He wouldn't have even been there if it wasn't for me." He's not wrong, and I share the same guilt he feels. Bexley wouldn't be here if I hadn't stepped in that night, and Christian wouldn't be so set on destroying Demons, one by one.

"Maybe so, but even you couldn't have predicted this would happen, so don't beat yourself up over it. He's alive, he'll pull through, and Christian, he'll get his," I explain doing my best to sound sincere.

"Alright, fine. But I'll be right back here, first thing in the morning," Draygon agrees, nodding. Sensing his concern and guilt. I pull him into a hug, tightly wrapping my arms around him. "Here," he adds, pulling Sayshen's gun from the waistband of his jeans and handing it to me, "he asked me to hold this before the race,"

Quickly, I take it, tucking it in my pants before it draws unwanted attention, "Shit will work itself out, and Sayshen will pull through, alright. This isn't your fault," I whisper again as I pat him on the back for reassurance.

As his name slips from my lips, my eyes reach Bex. Her arms wrapped tightly around herself as she watches us.

Releasing him, he lifts his eyes to mine, "Appreciate that man. I really never meant for none of this shit to happen. You're right about one thing though, Cordova is going down for it," Draygon spits. "We're not losing another fucking Demon to him. I won't let it happen. He has fucked with our family too many times."

"Fucking right he has. He may have gotten away with the first two. But not this one. Once I know Sayshen is good and clear, I'll be coming for him."

"We'll be coming for him. All of us. Christian is going to see what happens when you mess with Demons, and I'm not stopping until he's rotting in fucking hell."

"That makes two of us," I reply. "Now, get home. Get some rest, and fill the guys in. We'll check in tomorrow."

He pulls Bexley into a consoling hug and nods his head at me, "You got it." With that, he heads out of the hospital through the sliding doors, leaving Bex and me alone.

"Why would Sayshen have had a gun?" she questions with a hushed tone as she looks around the room.

"Everyone carries a piece when they're going to the strip. The street bike scene isn't like the track, Bex. There's no authority, no rules, and everyone plays dirty. It's why Sayshen going there was so fucking stupid," I explain.

She wipes her flushed cheeks on the oversized sleeves of my hoodie one last time before stepping toward me and taking my hand in hers.

"Let's go," she whispers as her dark eyes lock with mine.

"You don't have to come with me if you don't want to. It could be hard to see him like this."

"I'm not leaving you to do this all alone, Talon. I want to be here, for both of you," she explains as her hold on my hand tightens.

"Alright, have it your way," I reply before we head down the hallway toward Sayshen's room.

The moment we walk through the door, and my eyes land on the bed where my little brother lays motionless, my hold on her hand tightens and my body tenses.

Suddenly, I find myself thankful that Bexley chose to stay. Because this is one situation, even I don't think I could handle alone.

CHAPTER 21

BEXLEY

Ride For Me - Daniel Di Angelo

If it weren't for all the tubes and machines hooked up to Sayshen, you'd think he was sleeping. The monitors' constant beeping, which I once found annoying, has become a comfort to me as the hours pass. They tell me he's holding on, that his heart is still beating, fighting.

It's been three days since he was first brought here, and today is the first day we actually received some good news. The doctors say the swelling has gone down, and that they can safely stop the medications keeping him in the induced coma. However, as they've explained, it doesn't mean he'll wake up. That even *they* can't determine when or if that will happen, but they have done all they can for him. The rest is up to him.

Talon is sitting in the chair across the room. The stubble covering his chin has grown longer in the last few days. It suits him. Despite the concern etched into his face, he looks handsome. Even wearing a simple pair of sweatpants and his *Now Or Never* hoodie. He's been colder than usual toward everyone, including the team. Shorter too, which is expected, especially with the stress he's feeling.

We've been staying with Sayshen in shifts, which has been helpful. Mr Shaw has been by a few times to check in, but he doesn't stay long. It's clear he's pissed with Sayshen for being so reckless, and while Talon might've forgiven Draygon, I don't think their dad will forgive and forget so easily.

The guys will be here soon to replace us, allowing us time to go home, freshen up, and eat some real food. Not that either of us wants to leave Sayshen, but we know we need to look after ourselves, too. It's what he'd want.

These last few days with Talon have allowed me to learn a lot about him. Even if he's suddenly become a man of few words. I've spent a lot of time watching him. Reading how his body language changes in certain situations, he clearly feels a lot of guilt. For what, I can't be sure, but just being near him, I can feel the weight he carries, and I can't help but feel bad for him.

I have tried to get him to open up more. To let me help. But he's less willing than Sayshen when it comes to letting me in. Just when I think I'm making progress, he shuts down completely, leaving me right back where I started.

The knob on the door twists, and the door slowly opens as Reign, Thorn, and Wolfe make their way into the room. Reign is still in a wheelchair, but he seems to be in better spirits than he has been, considering everything he's going through.

Thorne greets Talon as he tips his chin toward him. "Bex, looking fit as ever. How are you holding up, girl?" he asks in a hushed tone as he leans down to pull me into a hug.

"I'm okay, thanks," I reply, offering a soft smile. The guys have been great. They constantly check up on me, making sure I'm doing okay and that if I need anything at all, I have it. It's clear they all want to be here for Talon too, and support him in any way they can, but he won't let them. So they've turned to me when it comes to asking about how he is doing. Some days, like today, I don't even know what to tell them. It's hard to determine how he's doing when he holds everything in.

"Good. That's good, and our boy?" Wolfe asks as he pulls a chair up next to Sayshen's bed. "Any updates?" His shaggy golden hair is pulled up into a bun on the back of his head today. My eyes are drawn to the beautiful ink that covers his muscular arms—the thick black lines that make up different totem poles and other native symbols that represent his father's heritage.

"They stopped the meds that were keeping him in a coma, but they don't know when he'll wake up," Talon adds with a stern tone from his chair across the room.

"That's good then, right?" Reign asks as he wheels himself up next to Wolfe at Sayshen's bed. "It means whatever they're doing, it's working. He'll be alright, he's got that Shaw blood in his veins."

"Yeah, I mean, they said the swelling has gone down. Which is good, but I won't feel better until he opens his fucking eyes, though," Talon replies.

"Well, if he does, you'll be the first one I call," Wolfe admits. "Now, go get some rest—both of you. We'll be here if anything happens."

"Thanks," I whisper, pushing myself to my feet. My legs are numb and shaky from sitting for so long. Slowly making my way toward Sayshen's bed, I brush his thick hair from his face and kiss his forehead softly.

"Here, take my hoodie, girl," Thorne adds, pulling it over his head. "It's chilly out there, and by the looks of it, there's a storm—"

"No." Talon snaps, cutting Thorne off mid-sentence. Pushing himself from the chair by the window, he strides across the room, pulling his *Now Or Never* hoodie over his head. "She'll wear mine," he adds.

"Okay then, big man," Thorne replies with a smirk.

Standing before me, Talon's expression softens as he hands it to me. His piercing blue eyes watch my every move as I slide it over my head. It's huge on me, with the bottom reaching my mid-thigh, and the moment it's on me, I'm comforted by his familiar scent. Oak, sandalwood, and something else I can't quite pin, but it's intoxicating.

Looking over his shoulder at the guys, his eyes slowly find their way back to Sayshen before Talon clears his throat. "Call me the minute anything changes."

"You got it," Reign replies. "Go get some food, man. He'll be alright, and we won't leave his side."

Talon nods before hesitantly leading me out of the room.

When we get outside, the sky is overcast. There's no sign of the familiar Florida sunshine or warmth as the cool wind billows around us. Pulling my hands into the long sleeves of Talon's hoodie, I wrap my arms around myself as we approach where Talon's bike is parked. He scans the sky with his eyes before grabbing my helmet off the back seat of his bike.

"It's going to be a rough ride. I doubt we'll outrun the storm, and if it gets too rough, I'll have to pull off to the side. I'm not risking going down with you on the back," he admits. I lick my lips, and his eyes fall to my mouth as he pulls the helmet over my head. His eyes lock with mine and he holds my stare before he gently tilts my chin up and takes the straps in his hands.

A lump forms in my throat, as his fingers graze the sensitive skin around my neck. My body vibrates before he quickly pulls away and climbs on his bike.

My lungs empty themselves, and my eyes find their way to the gray sky as I sigh. Something about these Shaw brothers drives my body absolutely insane.

I climb on behind him, wrapping my arms firmly around his waist, as I have done multiple times over the last few days. Once his helmet is secure, he starts up the bike and slowly pulls out of the parking lot onto the main road.

In minutes, Talon is turning off the main road and onto the

back roads to avoid traffic. Looking behind us, the tall hospital building slowly begins to fade into the background until I can no longer see it.

I hate leaving Sayshen. My heart wants to stay here. To never leave his side until he wakes up, but I know as much as I want that…I can't. I need to take care of myself too, and Talon. If it weren't for me, his stubborn ass would have gone the last few days without food, and most likely a shower. At least now he'll actually leave for a bit. The first day was the roughest, but he's come to see he isn't alone in this. We aren't alone.

We all care about Sayshen and want him to wake up, and together we'll get through this—like a family, like a team.

Thunder booms in the sky above us before rain begins to pour down, making the seat on Talon's bike slippery. My hold on him tightens, and I'm forced to constantly readjust myself to keep from falling off. Talon swerves. Weaving back and forth along the road to keep his tires warm so we don't lose traction on the road, but even I know that it will only work so long. The cold rain increases, and within minutes the two of us are completely drenched. I tighten my grip around his waist and clench my thighs tightly on the bike as the wind whips around us. Pressing my chest firmly against his back. Somehow, his body is still warm when pressed up against me.

What I'd give to have that warmth wrapped around me right now, to feel it against my chilling skin. Taking one hand off the bike, he guides my hand to wrap around his torso tighter before resting it over top of mine for a few seconds. Finding a small tree-covered grassy area off the roadside, Talon pulls off and brings the back to the dry area beneath the trees.

Turning the bike off, he climbs off and lifts his helmet off his head. I flip open my visor as he turns toward me. Gasping, I take in the sight of him. His soaked white tee is glued to his toned chest, and sucked into every dip and curve of his abs. He runs his hand through his hair, as he looks around the area and places his helmet on the seat before turning his eyes on me.

A smile forms on his face, "Are you going to get off the bike or what?" He laughs as he leans against a tall tree, clearly having noticed I was checking him out. My cheeks flush with embarrassment. He offers me a hand, and I take it as I climb off the bike. Pulling the helmet over my head, I place it on the seat next to his, before patting down my damp hair.

"What is this place?" I ask, as my eyes scan the area around us. The scent of wet earth fills my nostrils, and the sound of the heavy rain hitting the trees is loud, yet relaxing. Noticing Talon hasn't answered, I turn my attention back to him, finding his hungry eyes raking across my body and the way his soaked hoodie hugs my curves.

A familiar heat builds between my thighs as I watch him. Feeling brave, I step toward him. The movement causes his eyes to snap to mine, but I don't stop. Holding his gaze, I take another step toward him and another until I'm standing mere inches from him.

Lowering my eyes, I raise my hands, placing them flat against the ridged curves of his chest before slowly trailing my fingers down it.

His breathing slows under my touch, and his body stiffens.

Within seconds, he pushes me away and brushes past me as he heads back to the bike.

Fuck this.

"Seriously!" I shout. My voice echoing around the rural area.

Talon stops a few steps away from his bike, keeping his back to me.

"Whatever game you think we're playing, I'm done. You think I don't see how you look at me? How your body reacts when I'm near?" I spit, stepping toward him. "You think I don't know you want me, Talon?"

"Game? I don't know what you think is happening here, but I can assure you, you're wrong," he replies.

"Bullshit." I snap, taking another step toward him. Everyone who pays attention to us knows there is something between Talon and me. You'd have to be blind to fucking miss it. Sure, I understand being cautious and unsure of how to approach this, but to lie to me about it... and to tell me I'm imagining it? *Fuck that.* "I'm over this hot and cold shit. You feel something for me. Admit it. I've fucking seen it. I've felt it. So stop being a fucking coward and own up to it, Talon."

Talon steps toward the front of his bike before turning to face me. His darkened eyes lift to mine as he slowly runs his hand across the bodywork.

"Look at you. Typical princess behavior. Having a little fit about not getting what you want," his tone is husky and cold as he trails his fingers across the bike.

"You don't know what I want," I reply, crossing my arms over my chest as my eyes follow the path his hand takes along the curved plastic bodywork of his bike.

"No?" he asks, "so you don't want me to touch you like this?" I clench my thighs. Unwilling to show him just how fucking badly I do want everything he's saying.

"Or like this..." he adds, trailing his fingers along the seat on his way to the back of the bike. "You don't crave my fingers. Wishing they'd touch your pretty little cunt, just like this?" His words send a shiver up my spine, and I shake my head to say no, as I watch his hands travel along the bike until they're circling the tail end of his bike. "Such a fucking little liar you are, Princess."

The hunger building between my thighs is nearly unbearable. My body is desperate for release. He's right about everything he's saying, and the longer I watch him, the more my body aches for him and his touch. But I won't give in. Not now.

Not after all the bullshit he's put me through. Confusing me and making me feel like my feelings are completely one-sided.

"Fuck you," I snap as I stomp toward him. My still-wet hair sticks to my face, and the long sleeves of Talon's hoodie dangle at my sides as I cross the small space between us until I'm standing directly before him. Tilting my chin, I lift my eyes to his, "You think because you're taunting me about things you think I want, that I'll just bend over and let you have it? Ha!" I smirk, "Think again," I add, before pushing past him.

His hand wraps around my forearm, while his other hand is on my back roughly slamming me down on the bike so I'm bent over the seat. The helmets are knocked off in the process, falling to the grassy floor beneath the trees. Talon pins one of my arms behind my back before lifting his hoodie up my waist. I squirm under the weight of him. Unsure of how I feel about being pinned down and unable to free myself. My heart begins to race, panic slowly setting in as my eyes scan the area around us, and I realize just how alone we really are.

"Talon," I whisper.

"Relax, Bexley. I'm not him. I'm rough, but I'd never touch you the same way he did," he explains before gently sliding a finger into the waistband of my biker shorts, pulling them down until they pool around my ankles, giving him a clear view of my ass.

His admission settles my nerves. Though I know he and Sayshen would never hurt me, some situations seem to trigger memories. Scars on my soul that have yet to heal despite having spent so much time with both brothers.

Before I know it, Talon is on his knees behind me, and his hot tongue is running through my folds. It catches me off guard.

"Oh my god," I cry out. My toes curl, and my back arches as his tongue's warmth licks and laps across my sensitive flesh.

"Fuck. I knew you'd taste good, but goddamn," he groans. His hand slowly releases its hold on the arm pinned behind me as he grips my hips firmly and lowers his mouth to my pussy again. Bent over the seat of his bike, I tilt my hips and grind against his face in a desperate search for more. His tongue circles my clit, before he runs it from my pussy to my ass one last time.

He rises and leans over me to brush the hair from my face before lowering his mouth to my ear. His erection presses against my ass, and I instinctively grind my ass against its hardness.

A hunger laced laugh vibrates through his chest, "Just remember, Princess. You fucking asked for this," he whispers with heated breath. Standing, he shoves his knee between my legs, forcing them apart before he pulls his cock from his pants, and lines it up at my opening. He swirls his swollen head around my opening. Mimicking the way his fingers circled the tail of his bike, before slamming into me fully.

"Oh fuck!" I shout. His sheer size threatens to tear me in half as he holds himself in the deepest parts of me. My pussy clenches around his girth. One of his hands finds its way to my hair, threading its fingers into my thick locks before gripping and pulling my head back.

His cock remains still inside me as his other hand grips my chin tightly, forcing my mouth wide open. He spits in my mouth. His warm saliva coating my tongue.

"You're Shaw property now. Only ours. Only fucking ours. Do you hear me?" I nod in agreement, my pussy quivering around his cock. "Good girl, now swallow and tell me who this pussy belongs to," he adds, slamming my mouth closed.

I do as I'm told. Swallowing down every drop of his spit before slowly trying to grind against him. His hand comes down on my ass. Hard, firm, and fast. The impact stings and my body jolts to life.

"I said, tell me whose fucking pussy this is," he snaps.

"It's yours. Yours and your brother's." I cry out.

Slowly, he begins to move. Sliding his cock in and out of me.

"Such a good fucking girl, Princess. This is my pussy.

Fucking Shaw pussy." He groans. He thrusts into me mercilessly as he holds me still. One hand firmly gripping my hair at the root and the other pinning me down by my hip. I am completely at his mercy and I fucking love it.

His balls smack off my clit as he slams into me, and already I can feel my orgasm building. My body begins to tremble beneath him.

"No. Don't you fucking come yet! Not until I tell you to," he grunts.

"Fuck. I can't—" I mumble.

"You can, and you will, Princess. You don't get to fucking come until I tell you," he adds with panted breath. "Fuck you're so goddamn tight." Releasing his hold on my hair, he grips my ass cheeks with both hands, parting them so he can watch his cock as it sinks into me. "Look how fucking good your pussy stretches to take me, baby," he explains.

Each thrust of his cock inside me sends me closer to the edge. Making it nearly impossible to hold off my orgasm.

"Talon, please," I beg. Desperate to finally allow my body the release it so badly craves.

"Not yet. Not fucking yet, Princess," he pants. "Don't you fucking come."

My body is close to betraying me. Each second making it harder to fight off my building orgasm. Specks of stars blur my vision as Talon slams into me again and again

The sound of our wet bodies coming together is drowned out by the pouring rain around us. I grip the frame of his bike as he thrusts into me harder and deeper. The sound of his breathing behind me tells me he's nearing his own release. His cock thickens and throbs deep inside me.

"Now, Princess. Give it to me. I want to feel that pretty cunt of mine squeezing my cock while I bust inside you," he moans. My body crumbles as my long-awaited orgasm finally rocks through my body.

"Oh yes. Fuck." I moan. "Deeper, Talon."

"That's it. Fucking take it all. This is Shaw pussy now," he groans.

Talon's cock slams into me hard one last time before his own orgasm hits him. His cock, filling me with warm cum as my pussy clenches down around him. Milking him of every drop.

When we've both come down from the high of our orgasms, Talon slowly pulls out, scooping up the cum that trails out with his fingers and pushing it back inside me. I flinch at the touch of his rough fingers on my sensitive skin, and he laughs.

"Shaw pussy, Princess. Don't fucking forget it," he adds. He tucks his cock into his pants before helping me back into my shorts and standing me up, and pulling his hoodie back down over my body.

Around us, the rain seems to have calmed. The storm passed.

"Let's get home while we have an opening in the storm," he explains as he circles to the other side of the bike to pick up the helmets from the ground.

"Storm, right," I mutter, still trying to process everything that just happened. My body aches but in a good way. He smirks before pulling his helmet over his head and helping me with mine. Looking in his eyes, I know there's no going back from this. That now, each of the Shaw brothers holds a special piece of me. A piece I'll never get back.

Not that I'd ever want to.

Within minutes, we're back on the road. My arms wrapped firmly around his torso as he opens the throttle, speeding up as we make our way to the beach house. As the cool wind whips around us, carrying Talon's comforting scent, I find myself feeling like for the first time in a long time, I can breathe.

And it feels fucking great.

CHAPTER 22
BEXLEY

While You're At It - Jessie Murph

The next morning, my head is still filled with thoughts of Talon and how his rough hands felt along my skin when he took me over this bike. My pussy is still swollen and raw from how hard he fucked me, and yet I can't help but want more.

I flip the eggs in the frying pan before picking up my cell and shooting a text off to Cece about last night. There's no way I'm not telling my best friend about what happened between Talon and me.

Surprisingly, she's been supportive of whatever is going on between the Shaw brothers and me. At first, I wasn't sure how to tell her I had feelings for both of them. I wasn't even sure how I felt about admitting it. It's not like it's exactly a common thing, having brothers *share* you. Yet I wouldn't have it any other way. It's been a long time since I was this happy, this content, and though Sayshen is still unconscious and in the hospital, I know in my gut that he's going to pull through and be okay. He has to.

So, you got railed...in the woods...over a motorcycle by the incredibly hot older brother. Fucking hell, I wish I had your life...but since I can't, I need details so I can live through you. Was he big? Fuck I bet he was huge, I've seen his shoes.

My lips pull into a small smile as I read her text.

Let's say I'm still hurting this morning...

I reply before laying my phone down and turning the burner off. Grabbing the plate from the counter, I slide the eggs onto it next to the bacon and toast I made for Talon. He's still in bed, but I felt like surprising him with some breakfast before we head back to the hospital to check on Sayshen. My phone vibrates on the counter, the screen lighting up with Cece's name and her reply.

Fucking Puta. I hope you know I'm officially jealous of you.

"Was it the guys?" Talon's voice cracks from behind me. Startled, I spin around, the plate with his breakfast still in my hand. He enters the kitchen, stretching his arms behind his back, wearing nothing but a pair of black Calvin Klein boxers that leave little to the imagination.

My mouth waters as I watch him saunter across the kitchen to the coffee pot. He grabs a mug from the cupboard and fills it as he eyes me. I swallow the lump in my throat, realizing I hadn't answered him yet, "Oh, no. It's just Cece," I choke out. "Here, I made you some breakfast. I figured you should probably get some food into you before we head back into the city."

"Thanks, but I'm not hungry," he replies. His tone is cold and dismissive as he places the pot back on the burner without even looking at me. My brow furrows with confusion as I watch him brush past me to return to his room.

Fuck this. I'm done with this bullshit.

I drop the plate of food. Sending pieces of cream-colored ceramic shattering across the kitchen floor.

"You know what, Talon? Fuck you," I snap. "I don't know what your problem is, but—"

He laughs and spins to face me, "You! You're the fucking problem. Everything that's fucking happened is because of you!" he spits as he steps toward me. "How can you not see that?"

"You can't be serious."

"Oh, I am. Think about it. Why is Christian out for Demon blood? My fucking friend is rotting in the ground right now because your ex was so fucking bent out of shape about you being with my brother. My brother, who is now lying in a hospital bed, and we don't even know if he'll wake up."

My fists clench at my sides defensively. To blame me is unfair, especially considering he was the one who brought me to Sayshen in the first place. Not that it would've mattered. Cruz's death is no one else's fault except Christian's, and Sayshen snuck out in the night. I had no idea what he was doing or I would have tried to stop him.

I step toward him, and tilt my chin to meet his stormy blue eyes, "He will wake up!"

"He wouldn't even be there if it wasn't for you! IF IT WASN'T FOR YOU!" he adds. His tone is laced with pain. A pain I understand, but that doesn't make the way he's talking to me okay. I always knew Talon had it out for me, but I guess I thought because there was something building between us, that maybe, just maybe, we were past it. Then after yesterday, I thought things were finally okay. That we were okay.

Stupid. I was fucking stupid.

My stomach twists at the thought of how he touched me.

How he felt inside me just hours ago. How can someone change so quickly?

"You know, you make it really easy for me to hate you." I whisper. Knowing full well it's a lie the moment it slips from my lips.

"Hate me?" he laughs. "You don't hate me. I've tasted you. Touched you. Shit I've been inside you, Princess. You can't escape that reality, no matter how much you want to pretend you hate me."

"Fuck you!"

"Sorry. That was a one-time thing. A moment of weakness. It will never happen again," he adds coldly. His eyes darken as he looks down on me with pure disgust in his eyes.

"You can lie to yourself all you want, but I see how you look at me. I've seen and felt just how much being near me affects you. I get that you're hurting, but that doesn't give you the right to throw blame where it isn't deserved. I have done nothing but care for your brother. I have been there for you and your team."

"I didn't ask you to be there for any of us, Princess. I didn't ask you to come into our world and fuck everything up, did I?" His head falls back, and he rolls his shoulders before lowering his eyes to mine. "I should've fucking left you with him that night. I should've walked away."

Well, that's a low blow. His words hit me straight in the chest.

"Yeah, well, you didn't," I snap, holding his stare. I know he doesn't mean it, but that doesn't make the sting any less intense —especially after yesterday in the woods.

"Well, then, I guess you aren't the only one to blame."

Tears brim along my eyes, "You know, for someone who hates Christian, you act an awful lot like him." I whisper before I push past him. Not caring as the small shards of ceramic stab my feet along the way. I can't stand to be near him a moment longer. I refuse to allow yet another man to watch me fall apart because of him.

TALON

Never has someone's words hurt me the way Bexley's just did. Laying on my bed with my eyes following the circular motions of the ceiling fan, the look in her eyes and the pain in her voice is all I can think about. I knew my being cold and pushing her away was hurting her, but never did I think it was hurting her to that extent. To know she feels like there is any similarity between Christian and me has me fucked up more than I could've ever imagined.

What's worse is she's fucking right. About everything. Not only do I know that none of what's happened is her fault, but I actually blame myself for it.

Yet, after everything that's happened, I still would have never left her with him that night.

Never.

Bexley never meant for any of this shit to happen. None of us did. At first, I thought she was a distraction, a problem I needed to get rid of. But as the days have passed, I've come to see that she's actually good for my brother. For both of us.

She calms Sayshen in ways my dad and I never could. He's more focused now that she's at his side than he ever was before, and that fuckboy mentality of bringing home another girl every night is nowhere in sight.

Bexley fucking Larson has balls on her. Which is unexpected after what she's been through. But fuck if I'm not thankful for her being brave enough to call me out on my shit. Not many are.

Maybe that's part of what draws me to her. Why she fills my every thought and why even though I know her and my brother have something, I can't help but want her too. Not that I deserve her. Especially after the way I've treated her. I can't even blame her for the way she reacted today. I had it coming.

I sigh, rubbing my face with my hands as the regret begins to settle in my stomach. We only have a few more hours before we're set to head back to the hospital to check on Sayshen and I refuse to leave here with this tension between the two of us. Meaning, I have to find the right words to explain to her everything I'm feeling.

Which is something I've never been good at.

My phone vibrates on the bed next to me. Thorne's name lights up on the screen with a picture of his black and blue Yamaha, and my heart begins to race as I jolt upright. Knowing Thorne is at the hospital with my brother, I can't help but worry he's calling with bad news. I swipe to answer before bringing it to my ear.

"Yeah? Thorne? What's going on?" I ask with a concerned tone.

"Nothing, bruv, chill. It's a good call. Baby Shaw is awake. He's doing good. You should get down here."

"Fucking hell" I exhale, placing my hand flat over my chest. "Alright, we'll be there as soon as we can," I reply. "Tell my brother I'm going to fucking kill him."

Thorne laughs, "Easy bruv, let the lad breathe a bit before we go making death threats, yeah? He did *just* wake up after all."

"Yeah, yeah. We'll be there soon," I add before ending the call.

Pushing myself up from the bed, I head out into the hall in search of Bexley.

Despite the shit going on between us, I know she'll be happy to hear this news, and knowing that makes me excited to tell her.

As I pass by the bathroom, steam begins to pour out into the hall through a crack in the door. Peering inside, I find Bexley standing naked in front of the mirror, about to step into the shower.. Her long, inky black hair cascades down her back in thick, dark waves as she runs her neon green brush through it. Placing her brush on the vanity, she runs her hand through the thick condensation that's built up on the mirror from the steam.

The moment she does, her gaze finds my reflection in the

mirror behind her. Her beautiful brown doe eyes snapping to mine. She freezes and stiffens briefly before she slowly turns to face me and drops her towel to the tile floor.

Fuck.

Even in the dim lighting of the bathroom, her body is undeniably fucking beautiful. Every inch is pure perfection. Placing my palm on the wooden door, I push it open more before taking a step inside. My cock hardens as I follow the curves of her body with my eyes. What I'd give to take her perky pierced tits in my mouth, swirling my tongue around the piercing while she's straddling me. Taking my cock into that sweet goddamn pussy of hers.

As if sensing my thoughts, she takes a few steps toward me and I can tell by her expression she hasn't forgotten about earlier and has no intention of letting it go. Meaning I have a lot of groveling to do. Good.

She *should* make me earn it.

I clear my throat, "Thorne called. Sayshen is awake. I told them we'd head over as soon as we could."

"That's great news," she replies. "I can be out in just a minute," she adds, placing her palm flat against my chest. She tries to shove me back out into the hall, but my hand slams down on the door frame, stopping her.

Here goes nothing.

"Can we talk, Princess," I ask with a soft tone.

She rolls her eyes, popping her hip as she crosses her arms over her chest. "Why? Pretty sure you said everything there was to say. You hate me, I get it. You blame me for everything, cool. Got it. Now, can I shower? I'd really like to get back to your brother. At least he isn't a raging confusing asshole."

"I deserve that," I reply. "I never should have spoken to you the way I did. None of what's happened is because of you, Bex. I know that. Fuck. I just, I'm not good at this shit."

"Talon, I didn't ask for your apology, just like you didn't ask for me to, what was it you said, '*Come into your world and fuck everything up.*' I don't want to hear how sorry you are, and I honestly don't care anymore," she spits before turning away from me. I grab her wrist firmly, spinning her back around before I fall to my knees before her.

"I know I don't deserve your forgiveness. Especially not after knowing I reminded you of him. I never want you to think of me as him, nor do I ever want to be someone who makes you feel the same way he did. I just—I don't know how to process all these things I'm feeling," I plea from my knees. Resting my head on her thighs, I wrap my arms around her legs, holding her tightly against me.

"Talon, stop—" she whispers, trying her best to push me away. My hold around her legs tightens.

"Everything I said to you today was bullshit. I know none of what's happened is your fault. It's mine. I'm the one who brought Christian's wrath on the team. It's my fault Cruz is dead. It's because of me that Reign and Sayshen got hurt. Not you. You did nothing wrong. You were never the problem, Princess. You're the fucking solution to everything."

"It's not your fault either," she adds, her voice a mere whisper as she runs her hands through my hair. "No one could've known how far Christian would take things. Not even you."

Still kneeling before her, I lift my eyes to hers so she knows the next words to leave my mouth are genuine. "I'd never have left you with him. Never." I admit. The moment the truth slips from my lips, it's like a weight is lifted off my shoulders.

"I know," she replies. "I know you wouldn't have, and I know you're not like him. I never should've said that to you. I was hurting."

Rising to my feet, I brush the hair from her face, tucking it behind her ear as I look down on her. "We both are, but you know what? We're going to be okay. All of us. We'll get through all of this together." Pulling her in for a hug, her sweat-coated body clings to my bare chest as she wraps her arms around the back of my neck.

"I know we will. Now, take your clothes off. Sayshen is waiting for us, and we'll be faster if we shower together," she adds as she releases me and crosses the small space to the walk-in shower.

"Faster? Definitely not, but it's not like he's going anywhere," I reply with a cocky smirk as I slide my pants down.

The tension between us seems to melt away with the skin-on-skin contact. There's still so much to figure out between us, but regardless of how the day started, it's now turning out to be a good day.

My brother is awake and improving, and I got my girl back.

Shit is good.

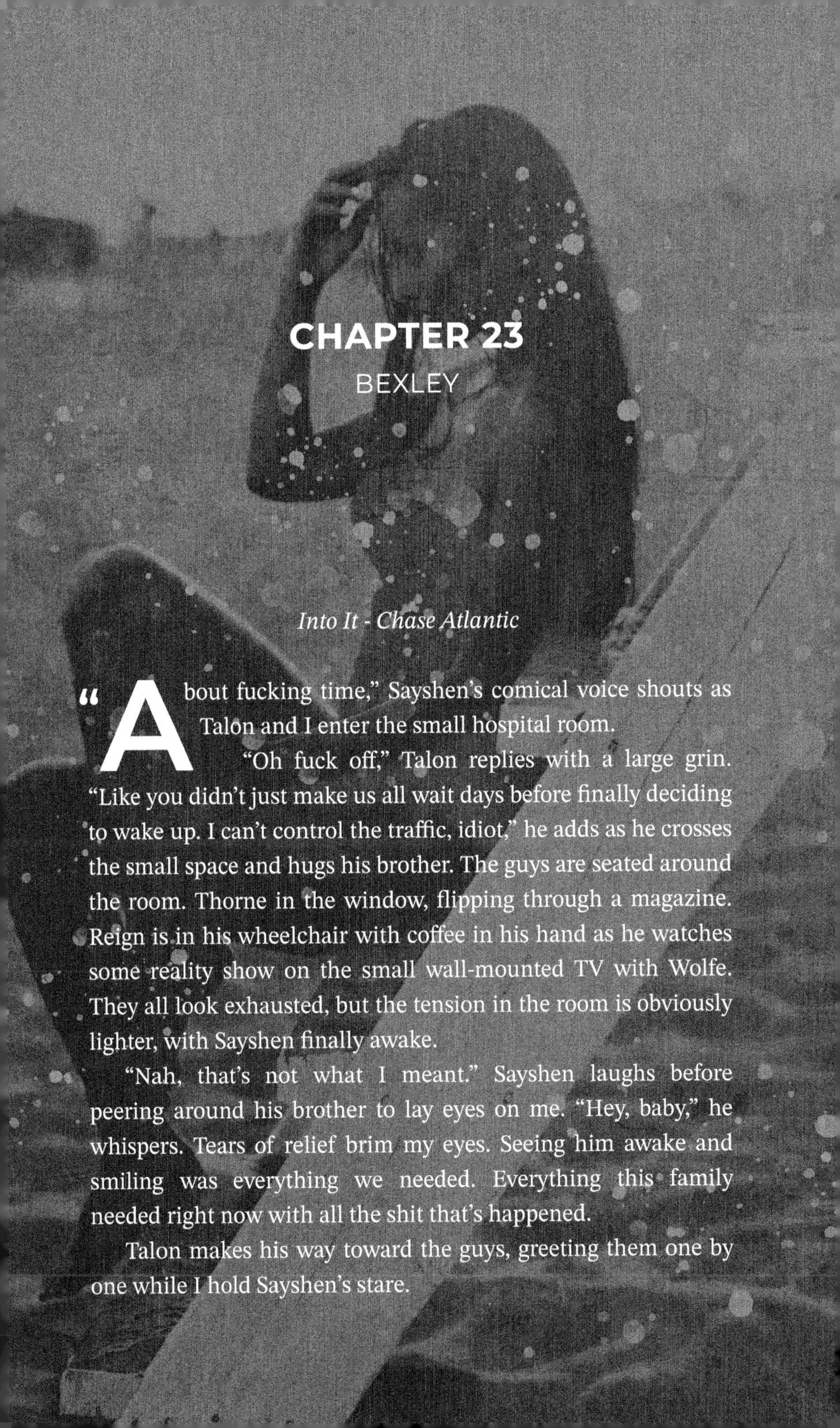

CHAPTER 23

BEXLEY

Into It - Chase Atlantic

"About fucking time," Sayshen's comical voice shouts as Talon and I enter the small hospital room.

"Oh fuck off," Talon replies with a large grin. "Like you didn't just make us all wait days before finally deciding to wake up. I can't control the traffic, idiot," he adds as he crosses the small space and hugs his brother. The guys are seated around the room. Thorne in the window, flipping through a magazine. Reign is in his wheelchair with coffee in his hand as he watches some reality show on the small wall-mounted TV with Wolfe. They all look exhausted, but the tension in the room is obviously lighter, with Sayshen finally awake.

"Nah, that's not what I meant." Sayshen laughs before peering around his brother to lay eyes on me. "Hey, baby," he whispers. Tears of relief brim my eyes. Seeing him awake and smiling was everything we needed. Everything this family needed right now with all the shit that's happened.

Talon makes his way toward the guys, greeting them one by one while I hold Sayshen's stare.

"Hey," I reply softly before eagerly approaching him. I need to hold him. To touch him. To feel his heart beating next to mine.

As if sensing my internal panic, Sayshen shuffles himself to the side of the bed before placing his feet on the ground. When I reach him, he pulls me into his arms. Holding me tightly against his chest. Wrapping my arms around his neck. I sigh, and inhale his earthy yet citrus scent. "You fucking scared me," I mutter into the crook of his neck.

"I know, Bex. I know. I'm sorry," he replies, running his hand softly along my hair. "I'm okay, though. Alright?"

"So you going to fill us all in on what happened?" Talon snaps. He leans against the window next to Thorne and crosses his arms over his chest as he waits for his brother's response.

Sayshen lifts his legs back onto the bed and positions himself on the far side, leaving me room to climb up and cuddle with him. "What's to tell? I went down, it happens."

"Bullshit," Reign shouts with agitation. Turning himself around in the wheelchair, he turns his eyes to Sayshen. "You don't really expect us all to believe that, do you? You just went down? Bro, we've seen you ride. Bikes and riders go down, that's life. But you're one of the best riders on our team. There's no fucking way you just went down on the strip. It's a fucking straight shot to the finish."

"You could've avoided him. We all fucking know it. So what is it then? You didn't see him coming?" Talon spits with an aggressive tone. His chest rises and falls with quick, panted breaths as he pushes off the wall and brings himself to stand at the end of Sayshen's bed. He firmly grips the metal bed frame until his knuckles turn white. His jaw clicks as he stares at his brother, waiting for an explanation.

He clearly agrees with Reign's statement, and I don't blame him. Even I've seen Sayshen ride. I've been on his bike, and I know how skilled he is.

There's no way he just let Christian hit him. He'd have

avoided it if he saw it coming, but why didn't he? What had him so distracted?

Then it hits me.

I called him that night.

"It doesn't matter. Can we just talk about this later? What's important is that he's okay. That Christian didn't win. Not this time," I explain in a soft tone, desperate to change the subject as the guilt begins to set in.

Talon's eyes snap to mine, and I silently plea for him to stop.

"You're right," he admits, releasing a deep breath. He runs a hand through his hair before taking a seat in one of the chairs along the wall. "Why and how, isn't important right now."

"I fucking knew it," Sayshen laughs as his eyes shift between Talon and me. His laugh is a welcome sound in light of the situation.

"Why do I feel like something is going on here that we don't know about?" Wolfe chimes in as he rises from the chair.

"Nothing is going on," Talon adds sternly, shaking his head at his brother. Sayshen pulls me in tighter against him, and I rest my hair in the crook of his arm, making myself comfortable.

Thorne's phone rings. Backstreet Boys – Shape Of My Heart echoes around the small hospital room.

"Really? That's your fucking ringtone? Fucking pussy," Reign mocks, tossing the empty coffee cup at Thorne as he hops down from the window.

"Oi listen yeah, you man, are just chatting absolute shit... you don't know about this tune, bruv!" he snaps back with a smirk as he dodges the cup and swipes to answer his phone. He brings it to his ear, "Yeah? Alright, boss man, I beg you, just give us twenty minutes, and I swear we'll be there..." he ends the call, "Coach wants us at the track, like yesterday," he adds, signaling to Reign, and Wolfe.

"Well the doc said I'd be out of here today, so no point in hanging around here," Sayshen explains.

"Really? So soon?" I ask, tilting my head to look up at him. He presses a kiss to my forehead as a small smirk forms on his face.

"Yeah, babe. Going to take more than a little wipeout to keep me in this shit hole for another day. Especially when I could be home, in bed, naked with you," he whispers.

"Okay, that's enough for me," Wolfe laughs. He grabs the handles on the back of Reign's chair, "Hit us up when you get home, yeah? And Bex, keep him in line. Don't let him get back on that bike too soon."

"Oh fuck off, I'm fine. Would you all chill out? It was one small wipe out." Sayshen rolls his eyes with annoyance.

"Don't worry, Wolfe. I won't," I add, taking Sayshen's hand in mine. "It will be home to bed with his royal cockiness," I reply, returning his kind smile.

"Good. Alright, boys, let's dip before Andre has our asses," Wolfe explains as he slowly pushes Reign out of the room with Thorne close behind him, still humming the tune of his ringtone.

When the door closes behind them, Sayshen's eyes snap back to the chair where his older brother is sitting.

"So…you guys finally fucked, huh?" his tone is playful and soft. Talon's head falls back against the back of the chair, his eyes fluttering closed as he exhales.

"Sayshen—" Talon huffs.

"We totally did, twice actually," I admit. Sayshen laughs, and Talon's eyes snap open, widening as he sets them on me. His lips pull into a smile as he shakes his head with disapproval. "What? It's not like he isn't going to find out, and besides, I rather enjoyed it."

"I fucking knew it," Sayshen replies excitedly. "Shit. All that shit-talking, to end up eating your own words, huh."

"Yeah, yeah. Is this where you tell me how wrong I was?"

Talon adds, rolling his eyes. "Cause I don't need to hear it from you too. Fuck knows our girl here gave me an earful already."

"Our girl," Sayshen replies, wiggling his eyebrows. "Ha, I bet she did." He pulls me into him playfully. "I fucking bet she did. Little spitfire, god, I missed that mouth of yours."

An uncontrollable laugh erupts through me, "Would you relax!" I snap, "You literally just woke up from a coma like a few hours ago, can you chill out and take it easy!"

The knob on the door twists open as the doctor from the other night enters. He closes it softly behind him before greeting us with a kind smile. "Well, Mr Shaw, I've gone over your chart and the recent tests, and I think you're good to head home for the rest of your recovery."

"Thank fuck," Sayshen replies. "Thanks, doc."

"So, he's all good then?" Talon adds, rising from the chair. "Is there anything we should watch for?"

"No. I don't think so. The swelling is completely down, so he is out of the woods. There is still some minor healing that needs to be done, to the scrapes and cuts, of course, and a headache in the next day or so is a possibility but nothing to worry about."

"Great. Thank you," Talon adds, shaking the doctor's hand.

"Here are your discharge papers, and you're free to go whenever you please." The doctor replies. He hands the papers to Sayshen before exiting the room and closing the door behind him.

Talon sits back down in his chair and pulls out his cell, shooting off a quick text.

"Draygon will be here shortly to pick you up and give you a ride back to the beach house," he explains.

"Bex and I will stop and grab you some supplies and some pain meds on the way home," Talon adds as he rises from the chair and begins to pace the room. The vibe in the room changes, the tension from earlier slowly returning as he clears his throat. "You know I'm not going to let this go, right? Neither will the team. Not this time."

"Good, because that fucker should've been dealt with weeks ago. Even before the shit with Cruz and Reign," Sayshen replies. "It should be him rotting in the ground, not fucking Cruz." I don't have to ask who they're talking about. I already know it's Christian, and I don't blame them for feeling the way they do.

I don't even disagree with them.

Does that make me a bad person? Maybe. Probably. But in the short time I've been with the Demons, they've shown me more respect and love than Christian ever did, so when it comes down to it, I'll support and back them, no matter what.

Sitting myself up, I comb my hands through my thick hair, pulling it up into a top knot on my head.

"What will you guys do?" I ask. The sound of my voice causes Talon to stop his pacing. He crosses the small room space until he's standing beside me on the bed. Gripping my chin firmly in his hand, he tilts my head up so my eyes are forced to his.

"Nothing you need to worry about. You're ours now, and he will never hurt you or anyone we care about again," he whispers before lowering his lips to mine. At first, I feel guilty. Having Talon kiss me while his brother's arm is still wrapped firmly around my waist. But Sayshen slowly runs his hand softly up and down my back reassuringly. His way of letting me know it's okay.

That what I'm feeling for both of them, is alright. Talon breaks the kiss, and the moment he releases my chin, Sayshen's hand grips it, turning my head to face him. His whiskey-brown eyes scan my face as his lips pull into a coy smirk. My cheeks flush.

"It's all good, Bex. Like my brother said, you're ours now," he whispers, ghosting his lips over mine. "Ours." He kisses me softly before pulling back. "You guys should get going. Draygon will be here soon anyway, and I can meet you guys back at the house."

"You sure?" Talon asks, "We can wait."

"Nah, it's all good. Get our girl home before it gets too late. I'll make Draygon stop and grab some food from his parent's restaurant too for dinner," he explains. I hop off the bed, and Sayshen taps my ass playfully as he bites down on his lip.

Talon's phone beeps, and he pulls it out of his pocket.

"Maybe we can all chill and watch a movie tonight?" I ask, feeling the need to decompress everything and hang out.

"Sounds like a plan." Talon cuts in. "Apparently, Andre wants me at the track in the morning, so it won't be a late one for me tonight," he explains. "You ready?" he asks, taking my hand in his and pulling me toward him.

"Yep," I answer excitedly.

"Alright. Tell Draygon to text me when you guys are on your way."

"You got it," Sayshen adds as Talon leads me to the door. "And don't get my girl killed fucker," he shouts from his bed as we leave the room.

"Our girl!" Talon yells back. The door clicks behind us, and Talon drapes his arm over my shoulders, pulling me into him.

A smile forms on my face. I never saw myself falling for two guys at once, let alone brothers. Sure, it's chaotic, and it's not all sunshine and rainbows, but when it comes down to it, I know there is nothing they wouldn't do for me and I for them.

Our relationship is far from conventional. It's different, and yet I wouldn't change a fucking thing about it. We're a family.

CHAPTER 24

SAYSHEN

Meneo - Fito Blanko

Climbing out of bed the next morning, I feel pretty good besides a throbbing headache, which I expected. Thankfully, that seems to be the only issue I'll have to deal with recovery-wise over the next few days seeing as by the time I woke up, most of my bruising and scrapes had already healed. The sun shines through the skylights and large windows as I make my way downstairs and through the hall to the kitchen. I grab a bottle of pain meds Talon and Bex picked up for me off the counter. Twisting the lid open, I toss two in my mouth before swallowing them down.

Opening up the screen door on the deck, the nice breeze off the ocean billows into the house. Not a single cloud in the blue sky today, and though it's barely nine A.M., and I already know it's going to be a hot one. The perfect day for the team to get together and have some fun, especially after everything that's been going on. We all need a day to let loose. To unwind and remember how lucky we are to still be here.

"You just going to stand there in your boxers all day?"

Bexley's soft voice behind me pulls my attention. Spinning around, I find her bent over as she leans against the large island in the kitchen, wearing nothing but one of my white t-shirts. Her dark hair is pulled into a large, thick braid that hangs over her shoulder. It's messy and chaotic from sleeping. "Or are you planning on coming back to bed?" she adds with a smile.

Goddamn, she is fucking hot. Even in the simplest clothing, with messy hair and morning breath, there isn't another woman who could rival her in my eyes. Ever.

Slowly making my way toward her, I scan her body with my eyes. Taking in the way my shirt hugs her tight little ass perfectly, leaving only the bottoms of her ass cheeks poking out.

"Now, why would I do that when it's such a gorgeous day outside?" I reply playfully. I know exactly what she's hinting at, and though I'm more than happy to give her exactly what she wants, I'm in the mood for a bit of fun. "I was thinking, we should have the guys over today, maybe even Cece. We could get the jet skis out, and make a day of it. I think we all could use it," I explain, peppering soft kisses along her neck and shoulders as I wrap my arms around her waist, pulling her ass against my hard cock.

"I mean, we can do that...after you come back to bed for a bit," she whimpers softly as she needily grinds her ass against me.

Fuck.

The sound of Talon's bike pulling into the driveway causes her body to stiffen. She's been with both of us, and we've told her we're more than happy to share her, but it's clear she's still unsure of how this relationship will work. Gripping her hips, I pull her ass firmly against me, holding her as she tries to squirm away in panic.

"Sayshen, stop." She giggles, "Your brother is going to walk in the door any second."

I laugh, "Good, let him." Her body stiffens, as she tries to stand. "What are you so afraid of? Do you think he doesn't know I was fucking you last night? You think he didn't hear you moaning my name? He was probably jerking off in his bed, listening to the sounds you were making." I whisper against the shell of her ear. "Squeezing his dick with his hand while he thought of how fucking good it felt to be inside you."

"Sayshen!" she shouts, slapping my chest playfully with her hand as her cheeks flush a gorgeous crimson color.

Talon walks in the door, hanging his leather riding jacket on the hook at the entrance. "You guys are up early," he says as he makes his way toward us. Wrapping his arm around Bex, he pulls her in for a quick peck on the lips, "Morning beautiful," he adds, before making his way to the coffee pot.

Bexley smiles and my heart fucking melts. "Morning," she whispers in reply as she slowly tucks a loose piece of hair behind her ear.

"Yeah, I couldn't sleep anymore. Besides, it's fucking gorgeous out, no point in wasting yet another day. How was the track? What did Andre have to say?" I ask. Bexley heads over to the coffee pot, filling up two more mugs with the dark liquid before handing one to me.

"Nothing much," Talon replies, before taking a sip. "Asked how you were. He was happy to hear you are on the mend. Said he plans on having a little chat with you about the Strip and what the hell you were doing there."

"Oh fun," Sayshen adds, rolling his eyes. "Guess I should've seen that one coming."

"Well fuck, I would think so. How are you feeling anyway? Any better?"

"Honestly I feel fucking great. Bit of a headache, but that's it. I was thinking we should get the team over here, take the jet skis out for the day."

"I mean, sure I'm down. It's fucking hot as shit out there. Are you sure you're up for that so soon?" he explains, as he wipes the sweat from his brow.

"Yeah. I think I need it. Bex, why don't you go give Cece a call, and see if she wants to come by too? We'll make a day of it, drinks, food, and fun."

"Okay, sure," she replies softly, before taking her mug and heading back to my room. I watch as Talon leans over, checking out her ass as she makes her way down the hall to the stairs. Furrowing my brow, his eyes snap to mine and he grins.

"Fucking guy," I laugh.

"Oh fuck off. Can't even blame me, you little shit," he adds before tossing back the last of his coffee.

"Nah, I can't. Bexley is something else. Girls got me wrapped around her pretty little finger," I explain, before bringing my mug to my lips.

'That makes two of us. Fuck I was wrong about her," he admits. His tone is sincere, and I know though Talon isn't one to show much emotion, he cares about her. A lot. "You sure you're up for today?" he asks again.

"Yeah, bro. Honestly, I'm excited for it," I reply.

"Alright, I'll hit up the guys," he adds as he eyes me. "You go hit the showers, you smell like sex."

A laugh erupts through me, "Aw, don't tell me you're jealous."

Pulling his cell out, he types in a name before putting it to his ear, "Nah, the day is still young. I'll get my time with her later, little brother, don't even worry about that," he adds with a smirk as he heads outside to the deck.

Placing my mug in the sink, my lips pull into a smile and I find myself eager to get this day started.

"Today is going to be fucking epic," I whisper to myself, before heading upstairs to my girl.

BEXLEY

Sigue – J Balvin, Ed Sheeran

The ocean's salty air blows through my hair as Sayshen takes us further out on his jet ski. The turquoise waters are crystal clear, and the sun is shining down on her. It's a gorgeous day, and as I watch Talon, Wolfe, and Thorne, who has Cece on the back of his jet ski, take off ahead of us, I have to admit, Sayshen was right. This is exactly what we all needed.

Things have been so tense and stressful lately, and while we still have a lot to figure out and get through, today's break will at least help. Wrapping my arms around his torso, I laugh and smile as he crashes against the waves, sending cool water spraying into the air around us. There's something relaxing about the ocean. Healing. No matter what you're doing, the moment the ocean's water comes in contact with you, it's like it washes away any stress or bad energy clinging to you.

Sayshen slows down as we watch Talon, Thorne, and Wolfe all head further out. They're racing each other. Cece shouts and cheers Thorne on as he takes the lead. Her lavender hair blowing about in the wind as they take off.

"I want to take you somewhere," Sayshen explains as he looks over his shoulder at me. I nod in response and tighten my grip around his waist.

We ride for a few minutes before he stops in a small cove of mangrove trees near a tiny, secluded island. It's beautiful. He pops open a small compartment on the back of the jet ski, pulls out the anchor, and drops it into the water next to us.

"Come on then," he smiles, taking my hand in his as he carefully helps me stand. The jet ski wobbles side to side with the waves. Sayshen takes off his life jacket and leans it over the front of the jet ski before driving into the water.

Following his lead, I slide out of my life jacket, laying it over top of his before jumping it. The cool, clear water is a shock to my heated skin at first, but it quickly becomes refreshing. Below the surface, I open my eyes, finding the most beautiful coral reef I think I've ever seen. Swimming up to the surface, I take a deep breath, filling my lungs with air before diving back down.

Corals in all different shapes, colors, and sizes make up the large space, with schools of curious fish swimming about. Some are more friendly than others, coming in closer to investigate, while others are skittish. Swimming away at the first sight of Sayshen or I. It's stunning, unlike anything I've ever seen around here. Sayshen wraps his arms around me underwater. His soft fingers trail along my exposed stomach, sending a shockwave through my body. Turning to face him, he kisses me softly before slowly pushing off me and rising to the surface for air. Turning back to the reef, I can't help but feel special knowing Sayshen chose to share this place with me.

Needing air, I follow him to the surface. When I break the surface, I brush my hair from my face, as I inhale deeply. Filling my lungs with the air they need.

"What do you think?" he asks.

"Sayshen—" I breathe. Struggling to find the words to describe just how beautiful I think it is. "It's breathtaking, seriously," I explain. Something brushes past me under the surface of the water, and a gray fin breaks the surface of the water. "Shark!" I shout in a panic as I quickly climb back up onto the jet ski. Sayshen laughs as I sit down on the stern of the jet ski. "Get out of the water, you fucking idiot! Haven't you ever seen jaws!"

He pushes himself up the stern with a cocky grin on his face. Holding the top half of his body out of the water while his lower half stays submerged. "I have,"

"So you want to be fish food, great," I add, rolling my eyes as I lean back against the seat.

"No," he snickers. "But that's just a little reef shark. They're mostly harmless."

"Mostly," I whisper. "Well, I have no intention of being that little guy's lunch," I spit.

"No?" he asks, his eyes darkening as he grabs my hips firmly. "Well, how about mine?" He quickly pulls me down the stern so that my ass barely hangs off the edge. Holding my stare, he runs his flattened tongue across the thin fabric between my legs.

Fuck.

I gasp at the contact. Looking down on him as he uses his thumb to pull my bikini bottoms to the side and does it again. This time, his heated tongue on my chilled flesh sends goosebumps across my skin. My back arches slightly as my hands grip the sides of the jet ski.

My eyes scan the mangrove-filled water around us, praying there's no one around to see.

"Eyes on me, Bex. There's no one around. It's just you and me, and fuck, I am starving for you," he growls before his mouth comes down on my pussy.

"Oh god, Sayshen." I whimper. The heat from his mouth only adds to the sensation as he swirls his tongue around my opening. Teasing and sucking before slowly sliding two of his thick fingers inside me.

"Goddamn, you taste so fucking sweet, baby," he whispers against me. His left hand presses firmly down on my pelvis while his right hand continues its motions, pumping his fingers in and out of me. "Your pussy is so tight. It's fucking squeezing my fingers."

"Fuck. Yes. Right there," I moan. Using one hand, I free my tits from my bikini top and softly pinch my left nipple between my fingers before pulling and struggling gently at my barbell piercing.

"That's it. Play with those pretty fucking tits while you ride my fingers. Fuck. Look at you, baby. So fucking hot."

I can already feel my orgasm building. My head falls back against the seat of the jet ski. I spread my legs wider, allowing him more access. From my knees down is still submerged in the cool ocean water, but with his tongue working its magic around my clit, I've completely forgotten about the shark currently swimming around us.

My free hand finds its way to his hair, and I thread my fingers through it before pulling his face in deeper. "There. Right there. Please," I beg.

Finding my g-spot, Sayshen hooks his fingers inside me and increases his pace. "Greedy fucking girl," he whispers before he spits on my pussy. "I know you're close, Bex, so fucking give it to me. Come for me." Using his arm to pull my thigh up to his face, he sinks his teeth into my soft flesh. My back arches, and I cry out as my orgasm hits me.

Like a tidal wave rocking through me, my body trembles. Sayshen doesn't let up. Holding me down as he fucks me with his fingers the entire time I ride out my orgasm.

"Fuck yeah, baby. That's it. So fucking pretty," he grunts with panted breaths. When I think I can't take anymore and my body begins to go limp, he pulls his fingers out and holds my stare as he licks them clean. "Fuck you taste like mine. All fucking mine," he adds before lowering his mouth to my pussy.

"Oh fuck," I squeal and squirm at the sensitive contact as he licks and sucks up every drop of my release like a starved animal.

Like a shark.

He smiles at me coyly as he gently fixes my bikini bottoms.

Fucking hell, this boy is trouble.

Sitting up, I smile before grabbing him by the chin and forcing his lips to mine. I can taste myself on them. He groans against my lip before abruptly breaking the kiss.

"Fuck, Bex. Let's get back to the house before I can't stop myself from bending you over the fucking ski." Sayshen climbs onto the jet ski, causing it to bob back and forth under his weight. Carefully, he climbs over me, taking the driver's seat before offering me a hand.

"Well, that could be fun," I add, knowing full well the experience would most likely leave me unable to walk for the remainder of the day. Taking my seat behind him, he passes me my life vest, and I quickly slide into it.

"Oh, don't worry, I have plans for tonight," he replies. He starts up the jet ski. Looking over my shoulder, I take in the beauty of this hidden gem one more time before wrapping my arms around his waist. He slowly takes one of my hands in his, lifting it to his mouth, and he kisses my fingers before he takes off across the water and heads back to the beach house.

CHAPTER 25

BEXLEY

Danza Kuduro - Don Omar, Lucenzo

When we get back to the beach house, I help Sayshen dock the jet ski next to the other before we make our way up to the beach house. The rest of the team had beaten us here and are all already hanging out on the deck. I can smell the food cooking on the barbeque as we climb the narrow stairs from the driveway. Sayshen's hand is wrapped tightly around mine as he guides me to where the team awaits us.

"Damn, bruv. Tell me you didn't get your girl lost the first time you took her out?" Thorne jokes from his spot on the wicker lounge. Next to him, Cece silently eyes me. The smirk on her face tells me she suspects some shit happened, but she'll wait for me to give her the details.

"Oh, please. I don't get lost, idiot," Sayshen replies as he plops down on the other side of Thorne. Just when I'm about to take a seat on his lap, Talon scoops me up in his arms and whisks me away. A small scream slips from my lips. "Really, bro? You couldn't wait?"

"Wait? You've had her all day. It's my turn now fucker," Talon replies as he sits me down softly on the railing of the deck. He wraps his arms around my hips, ensuring I don't fall off. "Hey, Princess. How was your ride?"

"Yeah, Princess," Sayshen mocks playfully as he opens a beer. "Tell Big Bro all about how good your ride was," he winks. I roll my eyes before wrapping my arms around Talon's neck and lowering my lips to his. I kiss him softly before running my hands through his still-damp hair. His gorgeous blue eyes lock with mine, and he pulls my hips closer toward him as he buries his face in my chest.

"It was great, but I could use another one," I reply cheekily, shifting my eyes to Sayshen's.

"Oh damn," Wolfe adds, spitting out some of his drink. Around the deck, the rest of the guys and Cece all join in, poking fun at Sayshen as they laugh and joke around.

"Well, in that case, I'd be happy to oblige,' Talon adds, nuzzling his head between my tits. A laugh erupts through me at the gesture. Reign tosses a pillow from the patio set at Sayshen, who whips it back.

"Food is done, fuckers," Draygon announces as he closes the lid to the oversized barbeque. Talon lifts his head from my tits and rubs his nose softly against mine.

"You hungry, Princess?" he asks softly as he lifts his eyes to mine. This new and sensitive side to Talon intrigues me, especially because I know how rough and cold he can be. Though I haven't seen that side of him again. Not since he fell to his knees apologizing and opening up to me about everything he was feeling.

Since then, things have been really good between us. He still struggles with the guilt he feels. He doesn't mention it, but I can tell. Hopefully, in time, he'll be able to move past it all and see that none of what's happened is his fault.

It's Christian's.

"Actually, I am," I reply as I watch the team all get up and gather around the food. Wolfe and Thorne follow behind Cece. Checking out the way her ass jiggles in her black thong bikini. Cece is a fucking gorgeous girl. She's a bit thicker than me, with the curves of a goddamn Kardashian, so I can't even blame them. Cece is my best friend, and I'm so thankful for all her support, especially lately. It's been so nice having another female around. My thoughts find their way to another girl I'd recently grown close to, Lena, and how I haven't seen her much since Cruz's death. "Has anyone talked to Lena?" I ask Talon, "I—I don't think I've seen her since the funeral."

He sighs, clearly distraught with the question, "No one has. She's dodging everyone's calls. Doesn't respond to texts either. She's gone AWOL," he explains. We all knew Lena was struggling. How could she not be? Cruz was everything to her, but knowing she's shutting everyone else out only makes me feel for her more. The pain she must be feeling with his death, I can't even imagine trying to handle that, let alone doing it alone.

"Oh," I reply softly.

"Don't worry. She'll come around when she's ready. We can't and won't push her. Everyone grieves in their own way, and Lena knows we're here for her when she's ready," he explains. Though I don't like that Lena is secluding herself, I know Talon's right. We all grieve in our own way, and while we might not like that Lena chooses to do it alone, we do have to respect her and allow her the time she needs to let go of Cruz.

"Now, let's get some food in this belly before those fuckers eat it all," Talon adds playfully as he picks me up. He presses a kiss to my stomach before throwing me over his shoulder like a barbarian and smacking my ass. I laugh as he runs across the deck, carrying me along with him.

Sayshen was right. Today, this time with all of the team and friends was exactly what we all needed. Rinsing the last dish, I hand it off to Talon, who dries it before putting it away in the cupboard. Sayshen is finishing up sweeping the floor in the large open living space between the kitchen and living room. Talon leans against the island and pulls his phone from his pocket. I watch them closely, wondering how I got so lucky to have not just one guy in my life who gets me and wants to make me happy but two.

To sit and look at how much my life has changed in the short time I've been with them, I sometimes still struggle to believe it's all real and that this isn't a dream.

Having finished, Sayshen dumps the dustpan in the garbage before propping the broom up against the wall. Lifting his eyes from the floor, he shoots me a flirty smile and runs his hand through his hair.

"Fuck, you are fucking perfect," he whispers softly as he steps toward me, wrapping his arms around my waist; he leans against the counter and pulls my back against his chest. Talon places his phone on the island behind him and watches as his brother kisses my neck, slowly working his way down to my shoulder. Softly, he pushes the strap from my dress off my shoulder. It glides down my arm until half my chest is exposed. Lifting his eyes back to his brother, Sayshen whispers against my skin, "Bro, have you had a chance to taste our girl yet?"

Talon's eyes darken as he takes in the sight of my exposed breast. Sayshen's hand firmly cups it, pinching and twisting gently at the piercing through my nipple, "Damn right I have, and there's nothing that tastes sweeter than her," he explains as he slowly steps toward me. He drops to his knees in front of me, pushing up my summer dress's fabric until he is face to face with my powder blue thong. Sayshen hooks his arm under my leg before taking my dress's bunched fabric in his hand, holding them both up and out of his brother's way.

My stomach catches in my throat as I watch him pull my panties to the side. He runs his tongue slowly across the sensitive flesh while holding my stare, sending a tremor through me. "So fucking sweet," he whispers again before his mouth comes down on my pussy. Talon licks me like he's never tasted anything sweeter. Like my juices are his favorite fucking dessert. He laps up every drop of my arousal, spreading it around my swollen flesh with his tongue.

Sayshen's fingers work my nipple as we both watch his brother devour me. My body goes limp against his chest, and he's forced to support my weight as I melt in the sheer pleasure of Talon's tongue as it fucks me. He sucks at my clit, gently pulling it between his teeth.

"Oh my god," I moan. My head falls back against Sayshen's shoulder. My hips desperately grind and roll against Talon's mouth in search of more friction.

Standing here, between them, with one at my back and one on his knees before me, I can't remember a time when I ever felt safer. I feel like a goddamn goddess. The way Talon praises me with his unholy tongue, and Sayshen holds me upright, teasing and twisting my nipple. Together, they have me riding the perfect fine line of pleasure and pain, and I am quickly becoming addicted.

"Fuck, bro. You've had enough. Let me have a taste, greedy fucker," Sayshen asks as he watches his brother run his flattened tongue through my folds.

"You fucking better get down here then because I don't think I can stop myself," Talon whispers with heated breath against my inner thigh. His hooded eyes find their way to mine. The intensity of his stare makes it hard to look away as he licks his lips, savoring the taste of me. Sayshen groans, slowly lowering my leg to slide out from behind me.

"Look how fucking perfect she is." His eyes roam my body before he pushes down the other strap of my dress, sending it to a pile on the floor at my feet. They both gasp. Sayshen bites down on his lips as he takes in the sight of me naked. My skin flushes. My own arousal begins to trail down my thigh as I watch them, unsure of what's going to happen next.

Talon slowly helps me step out of it before tossing it across the room with a smirk.

"We don't fucking deserve her," he admits, shaking his head at his brother. "But fuck if I'm not prepared to spend every goddamn day on my knees for her, tasting her, and fucking her whenever she demands it if that's what it takes."

Before I know it, both of them are on their knees before on the kitchen floor. My back leaned against the cupboard behind me. Their hungry eyes fixated on mine as they look up at me. Sayshen hooks his fingers in the waistband of my panties, pulling them down to my ankles and helping me step out of them.

Talon takes my right leg in his hands and lifts my foot to his mouth. Goosebumps prickle along my skin. Gripping the countertop behind me, I watch as he kisses my foot, working his way up my calf. He nips and sucks at my flesh hungrily before gently placing my foot back down on the cool tile floor.

Sayshen rises the tiniest bit, bringing his mouth to my pussy. He runs his tongue across it the same way Talon did. Using his hands, he spreads my lips and licks again.

"Fuck you were right. Our girl tastes so fucking good," Sayshen explains as his mouth lowers to my inner thigh, licking up the trail of juices as it drips down my leg. My eyes roll back in my head. *Holy fuck.*

One on their knees before me was hard enough to handle, but both? I don't know how long I can handle this.

"Such a sweet fucking pussy she has. Tell me, who's fucking pussy is this?" Talon asks before gliding his tongue across me again. He flicks it over my clit, and my body trembles as he sucks my sensitive flesh into his mouth.

“Yours,” I breathe, “Only yours.”

“That’s right, baby,” Sayshen cuts in. “You and this tight cunt, belong to us now,” he adds before his mouth comes down on my clit. My back arches at the contact as he thrusts his tongue inside me, swirling around as he moans against me. My eyes roll into my head, and my orgasm begins to build, but just when my release is about to come, he stops. Pulling his tongue from me, he licks and laps up all the juices before whipping his mouth on his arm.

His lips pull into a cocky grin, as my eyes lower to his.

“Aw, look at how wound up she is,” Talon laughs, elbowing his brother. “Such a greedy fucking girl.”

“Fucking right she is. Don’t worry, Bex. You’ll come, when we’re ready to let you,” he smirks.

Rising from their knees, they exchange a look before taking one of my hands in each of theirs, and leading me out of the kitchen and through the hallway up to Talon’s bedroom.

Closing the door behind us, Talon turns his hungry eyes on me, “So, Princess, whose dick do you want to sit on first? Mine, or my brother’s? Or maybe we should see how pretty you scream with both your holes filled with Shaw cock.”

Fuck.

My eyes bounce from one brother to the next. Landing on Sayshen as he slides his sweatpants down. He holds my gaze as he climbs up onto Talon’s bed. Resting on his knees in the middle of the bed, he uses his fingers to call me over. Snapping my eyes to Talon, he nods at me with approval before slowly lifting his shirt over his head and sliding his own pants down.

My mouth waters as I take in the site of both of them in the dim bedroom lighting. Fuck I am so fucked. So much about what we’re about to do probably wrong, and yet, I can’t fucking stop myself. I want this. I want them. If ruining me together is what they want, what they need, then I will willingly crumble until nothing remains but a pile of sweat coated bodies.

Slowly climbing up onto the bed, I find myself feeling nervous. I've never been with more than one person at a time, and though I've been with both of them separately, I can't even begin to imagine how intense it will be having both of them at once.

Sayshen takes my hand in his, wrapping his other around my body as he steadies me so that I'm on my knees on the bed. The mattress dips as Talon comes up behind me, sandwiching me between them. Looking back over my shoulder, he kisses my temple softly before brushing my hair over my shoulder.

Suddenly feeling insecure, my eyes drop to the onyx silk sheets of the bed. Releasing my hand, he cups my face softly and forces my eyes to his, "Relax. We have you, baby. It's just us, and we will take care of you," he explains softly before tilting my chin and pressing his lips against mine.

The moment his lips touch mine, all my worries melt away, and when Talon's hands wrap around my torso and pull my back firmly against his chest, I find myself completely consumed in them.

The Shaw brothers.

Sayshen continues to kiss me as Talon's lips press soft, tender kisses along my shoulder. Taking his cock in his hand, Sayshen lines himself up at my pussy, circling the tip around the opening before slowly pushing inside me.

He hisses against my lips and swallows my moans as he pushes himself in deeper and slowly begins to roll his hips. Breaking the kiss, my head falls back against Talon. With his free hand, he tilts my face to his, bringing his lips down on mine before biting down on my bottom lip. I cry out at the sting as the metallic taste of my blood fills my mouth. Bringing his hand to my lips, he brushes his thumb along my lips.

"Suck on it for me, Princess," he commands. I do as I'm told, wrapping my lips around his thumb and swirling my tongue around it. He pulls it out with a sheen coating of saliva and slams his lips down on mine again before he brings his thumb to my ass. "Just relax. You'll enjoy it," he whispers against the shell of my ear.

His thumb circles my puckered hole slowly before he gently pushes it inside me. Sayshen lifts my leg with his arm, holding it up with his forearm as he thrusts up and inside me deeper. They alternate, Sayshen pumping his cock inside me and Talon's working and stretching my ass to accommodate him.

A soft moan escapes my lips. "F—Fuck," The pressure from Talon's thumb working my ass adds to the pleasure of Sayshen's cock inside me. My body stiffens as my orgasm builds, but before I can fall over the edge, Talon's other hand comes down on my clit, hard and fast. Slapping me.

The impact causes me to cry out, "Ow. Fuck."

"Not yet. Not until we say so," Sayshen groans. "Fuck, Bex. God, your pussy feels so fucking good around my cock. Look at it stretching for me. It fucking loves my cock inside it, doesn't it? It knows who it belongs to."

"Fucking right, it does. Look how fucking pretty it looks, swallowing my little brother's dick," Talon adds with a husky tone as he pushes his thumb in deeper before quickly pulling it out. My body quivers with their praise. I want this. I want to please them. I want them to use me however they wish as long as it makes them feel good.

Talon spits on his hand and spreads the saliva around the swollen head of his cock, "I can't wait to hear you sing for us, Princess," he whispers. He nips at my ear lobe, pulling on it before slowly pushing his cock into my ass.

Fuck me. I can't think straight.

The pressure and pure fullness radiating through my body as they take turns thrusting up and into me has me seeing stars. My clit hums with hunger as Sayshen's thumb begins to swirl around it.

"Jesus. Fuck. I can't," I moan.

Sayshen's lips crash down on mine. Swallowing down my cries of pleasure. "Good. Don't. Let go, baby," he whispers.

Their cocks throb inside me. Pumping in and out of me in sync. Each thrust filling me deeper, bringing my orgasm closer. "Come for us, Princess," Talon grunts as he slams into me. His balls smack off my ass cheeks as he sinks his cock inside me, stretching me. "Squeeze our fucking cocks with your tight goddamn holes, and come for us," he adds.

Both of them together is so much. Fuck it's so much. I never would've thought I could handle both of them at once, but fuck I need it. I need more of them. Sayshen pinches my clit between his thumb and finger, rubbing it quickly as they fuck me. Behind me Talon's sweat slicked chest clings to my back. He carefully peels my damp hair from my skin, before sinking his teeth into my shoulder.

I can't do it anymore. My orgasm hits me like a euphoric tidal wave and I can feel myself beginning to clamp down around them.

"Fucking hell, Princess. You're choking my fucking cock," Talon shouts. The sound of our wet bodies coming together echoes around the room.

"Oh. God. Oh, f—fuck." My body starts to convulse as I wrap my arms around each of their necks for support. Sayshen's thumb vigorously circles my clit, and they both ravage my holes with their cocks, pumping in and out of me like they intend to fuck every last drop from me.

"Fuck yeah! Give it to us," Sayshen groans as he fucks me. "That's it, Bex. Fucking hell, you are so goddamn beautiful when you let go," he adds as he finds his own release. His cock swells, and his pace slows as he slams into me hard, filling me with his warm release.

Talon's isn't far behind, his thrusting becoming more frantic as ruthless as he pounds into me. "Goddamn, Princess. You make the sweetest fucking sounds for us, don't you? Such a good fucking girl, taking both our cocks like you are. Who's fucking holes are these?" he growls as he slams into me again. Wrapping his hand around my throat, he pulls my head back against him, "Who's fucking holes, Bexley?"

"Yours," I mutter. "All fucking yours," Sayshen pulls his still semi-hard cock from my pussy, and wipes the trail of come with his fingers before bringing them to my lips.

"Clean them, Bex. I want you to come to my brother's cock, while you taste me on your lips," he whispers, shoving his fingers past my lips. Eagerly I take them into my mouth, sucking and lapping the sweet, salty taste of them.

"Fuck!" Talon moans. "And we fill them so fucking well, don't we, Princess."

"Oh. Fuck. Yes," I mew. Gripping my hips, he slams into me one last time and freezes as his cock empties itself, and he finds his own release.

"Goddamn—" he groans as his cock pulses inside me. His warm cum fills every crevice of my ass before he slowly pulls himself out. "Fucking hell," he whispers. We all collapse with exhaustion on the black silk sheets, with me in the middle of them. My eyes find their way to the ceiling. The room falls silent, with nothing more than the sound of our heavy, panted breaths.

"You're ours, Bex," Sayshen explains, breaking the silence. "Fucking ours."

"Forever," Talon adds, and a smile forms on my lips.

Theirs, forever? I think I can live with that.

CHAPTER 26

BEXLEY

Weekend - Dxvn

Sitting at the island in the kitchen, my eyes are glued to the counter on the other side as I relive the night before in my head. Sipping the coffee Sayshen made me before his shower, I still feel in awe of the entire experience. Talon rounds the corner in a pair of basketball shorts and no shirt, with a greasy white rag draped over his shoulder.

His eyes find mine, and he smirks before coming up behind me. He wraps an arm around my stomach, pulling my back into his chest before pressing a soft kiss to the top of my head. Smiling, I look up at him, offering him a sip of my coffee.

"Ew, what the hell is that?" he spits with disgust as he wipes his mouth on his arm. "Fucking nasty. How do you drink that?"

A laugh erupts through me. "Easy, it tastes great," I retort, placing the mug down on the counter next to my sketch pad. It's been a few weeks since I spent time on my designs, and today felt like the perfect day to jump back into it. Looking down at the design I started this morning, something in me feels different. I love all my designs, and though they're all unique, each one is special in its own way. Each one symbolizes the emotions I felt when I created it, and today's is no exception.

It's stunning.

"Well, what is this?" Talon adds, peering over my shoulder. Panicked, I slam the book shut, hiding my current work in progress from his prying eyes. "Hey!" he shouts playfully as he pokes at my sides.

"It's not done yet," I giggle.

Cocking his brow, he crosses his arms over his chest in question, "So?"

"So it's not ready to be seen—not yet anyway," I explain in a soft tone.

Pulling the rag off his shoulder, he whips me gently with it, "Fine, but I get to see it before my brother. I call dibs."

"Dibs?" I laugh, "What are we, nine?"

"No, but dibs is dibs, and I called it," he replies as he makes his way around the island and opens the door to the large fridge. He pulls out a bottle of water and chugs half the bottle down before turning his eyes back to mine. "I have to head back to the track tomorrow. It's the last race weekend of the season, meaning I won't be able to head back and check on things until Sunday night. Will you be okay here with Sayshen? I don't really want to leave him alone. I don't really know how he's going to handle not being able to race."

"Of course, I'll be fine," I reply. Sayshen seems fine with not being able to race, but truthfully, none of us believe it. The doctors have cleared him to race, but we all thought it best if he sat it out, especially with Christian on the track. It's his first race back since Cruz's death, and none of us know what to expect from him.

"You should get out tonight, go spend some time with Cece or something, do something fun for you. Before being cooped up in here all weekend with this idiot," he adds, tilting his chin to Sayshen as he enters the kitchen behind me.

"This idiot is fine with not racing," Sayshen replies. Reaching me, he wraps his arms around my waist from behind and kisses my neck. "Especially because while you're at the track, I'll be here, finding all the ways to make our girl scream."

"Fuck you," Talon spits playfully as he points his finger toward Sayshen.

"He's right, though," Sayshen adds. "Give Cece a shout, see what she's up to. Go have some girl time, I'm sure you could use a break from both of us."

Not that I agree with them, but I have to admit having some girl time with my best friend does sound rather enticing. It's been way too long, and now that Chrisitan isn't in the picture, I don't have to walk on eggshells when it comes to hanging out with her. I'm free to do whatever, whenever.

"Okay, I will," I smile, pulling out my cell. Sayshen and Talon get to talking about their bikes, and track stuff while I fire off a text to Cece.

Plans tonight? I could use a girls' night.

Rising from the chair, I round the island, placing my mug in the sink. Talon's ass in his shorts is goddamn mouth-watering, and I can't help myself.

SLAP!

My hand smacks down on it hard. He jumps, startled by the contact. Quickly he spins around, and his lips pull into a coy grin.

"Hey, what the shit, where's mine?" Sayshen shouts playfully. "You can't leave me feeling jealous all day," He adds, pointing his round ass toward me. Rolling my eyes, I cross the small space between us, and pat him on the ass.

"There you go, Baby Shaw," I reply with a playful and mocking tone.

My phone vibrates in my hand. Looking at my screen, I see a message from Cece.

Of course, Puta. Sounds great. Mom is making Tamales for dinner; she'll be so happy to see you! Besides, you owe me a shit ton of deets on these boys…

Wrapping his arms around my waist, Sayshen pulls me into him, "Oh fuck no. You don't get to call me that, ever," he retorts with a smile. "It's Daddy to you," he winks.

"Ew," I cringe, placing my hand flat on his chest as I push him back to get by him. "I will never," I laugh as I head down the hall. I text out a quick reply to Cece.

Girl, you wait. The tea is going to blow your mind.

"Aww, where are you going? You can't just hit and quit it, babe," he shouts after me. The sound of Talon's laugh follows me upstairs, echoing down the hall until I close the bathroom door and start to fill up the bath. I dump in the rest of my bubble bath, making a mental note to stop by the pharmacy on the way home tonight and pick up some more.

Tonight will be a great night. I can feel it.

"You dirty, Puta!" Cece laughs loudly with the news of how I spent last night. She's the one person I know will never judge me. She never has. When I made the choice to leave home, with no money and no support, and pursue my dream of being in Fashion, she supported me. Despite everything that could've gone wrong or how silly it might've seemed to her or anyone else, she knew it made me happy, and that was good enough for her.

"Cecilia!" Mrs Mendez scowls from the kitchen, where she's washing up the dinner dishes. We offered to help her, but she refused to let us, saying we hadn't gotten together in so long that we should spend the time catching up. When I left my family, she became a second mother to me, and it's something I was always thankful for. Christian was quick to cut off anyone he could from my life, and though I didn't see it then, I see it now. That's why, as I sit here, laughing with my best friend, I feel so thankful to Talon and Sayshen for recommending that I drive Talon's truck into the city to do this tonight.

It's just what I needed.

Checking the time on my phone, I clear my throat, "I should be getting home, it's getting late."

"Mhmm," Cece smirks. "It has nothing to do with you being in a rush to go home and get fucked by *both* brothers again!" Her comment makes me smile as I fidget with the white denim fabric of the skirt I wore tonight.

"Oh, stop," I laugh. "Trust me, after last night, my body needs the break tonight. Besides, the guys aren't even home. They went riding with the team. I do, however, have to make a pit stop on the way home for a couple of things."

"Alright then," she sighs, rising from the chair. Cece walks me to the door, and Mrs Mendez hugs me goodbye before I head out to the driveway where Talon's truck is parked. Climbing in, I start up the engine and wave goodbye to my best friend and her mom as they watch me back out of the driveway and take off down the quiet suburban street toward the highway.

Thankfully, my late-night trip to Farm Stores is uneventful. Besides myself and the two cashiers, I don't see a single person in here, making shopping quick and easy. After cashing out, I grab the brown paper bag with my stuff tightly in my arms and make my way out to the truck. It's a humid night. The thick and hot air causes each breath to leave my lungs feeling half-filled.

Something about the short walk to the truck is eerie. The hair on the back of my neck is standing up, and I can't shake this feeling of being watched. I pull the key fob out of my pocket and unlock the doors, but when I'm just a few feet away, I notice the tires have been slashed. All four.

What the actual fuck?

Before I can even investigate the damage done to the truck, someone's hands grab the back of my head roughly from behind. I scream as the paperback slips from my arms, and I reach behind me in a panic. Another hand crashes down over my mouth, muffling my screams before the force drags me backward and down a dark alleyway. My heart races as my widened eyes scan the area around us in search of someone. Anyone, who can help me.

But there's no one.

Not a single fucking person.

The sound of the heels of my checkered Vans being dragged along the pavement echoes around the empty parking lot and down the alley. So many thoughts play out in my head, and I wonder if this is it. Is this when I die? Will this be how I leave this world? In some dark alleyway in downtown Tampa. The victim of a random late-night attack.

Fashion College student found dead in an alleyway.

That's what my headline will say.

Suddenly, the person dragging me stops, and I'm slammed up against the wall of a small red brick walk-up apartment. The hand covering my mouth quickly moves to my throat, wrapping around it as it holds me where he wants me.

My head smashes against the brick, sending a stabbing pain across the back of my skull. Holding me against the wall, I can feel the weight of his hate-filled gaze as he looks down on me.

Lifting my eyes, it becomes clear that my attacker is hidden by the shadows in the alley. With his hood up, it's impossible to make out what he looks like.

The pain along the back of my head increases, "Who are you?" I force out through tightly clenched teeth. "What do you want?"

A dark and devious laugh builds in his chest, "Stupid bitch. Don't act like you don't know who the fuck I am."

I freeze in place the moment the words slip from his lips. Knowing full well who that voice belongs to.

Christian.

"C—Christian..." I stutter with trembling lips.

"Thought you could disrespect me and just walk away unscathed, did you?" he laughs. "You never were very smart, Bex, but fuck, I thought even you knew better than that," he spits as his hold on my throat tightens. "Did you learn nothing from all the lessons I taught you? Fucking slut."

"Fuck you!" I spit, doing my best to fight him off.

"Oh, baby," he replies, lowering his lips to ghost over mine. "I don't normally fuck whores, but for you, I'll make an exception," he snickers with warm whiskey-scented breath. He reaches for something on his belt as he runs his tongue along the side of my face, leaving a trail of his disgusting saliva in its wake. I try to turn my face away from him as tonight's dinner threatens to make a reappearance, but his hold on me is too tight.

Slowly, he pulls out a gun and presses it against my cheek. My eyes widen with fear, "Christian—" I stammer, "What are you doing?"

"Isn't it obvious, bitch. I can see the fear in your eyes, Bex. You're scared, and you should be," he whispers. His cock is hard as a rock, and he presses it against my upper thigh as he leans in closer to me, "I'm going to fucking ruin you." Slowly, he trails the barrel of the gun across my skin, moving it down my body before gliding it across my pelvis. "Tell me, how does it feel to be so close to death? To know that I hold your life in my fucking hands. Hmm?" he adds.

Without thinking, I lift my knee, hitting him right in the balls. Catching him off guard, the gun slips from his hand, and he releases his hold on me. I don't waste a single second. I take off running down the alley, back toward Talon's truck, only to remember the tires have been slashed.

Shit, I forgot.

"Help!" I shout. My voice echoes off the buildings around me. "Someone, please!"

Pulling out my cell, I dial Sayshen's number, but it doesn't go through. I find no service bars at the top of my phone screen.

Fuck.

Looking back at the shop, the windows are all dark. The neon *open* sign in the window turned off. They're closed.

I have no other option.

I type out a quick message to Sayshen and hit send.

"You fucking bitch! You're fucking dead," Christian shouts from behind me. Looking over my shoulder, I find him catching up. So I take off running again, heading down Main Street, toward where I told Sayshen to meet me.

Hopefully, my text will go through.

SAYSHEN

It's the perfect night for a ride, and I have to admit, being on the bike again after my crash feels fucking fantastic. One of the perks to racing professionally, is having the best repair team in the country at my beck and call. Didn't take them long to get my R1 back up and running, and fuck am I thankful for it.

I can't stand going too long without riding. It feels unnatural to me. Pulled over on the side of the road in the middle of fucking nowhere so Thorne can take a piss, I decide to check in with Bex seeing as I haven't heard from her for a few hours.

I miss her, what can I say.

Pulling my phone from my pocket, I unlock it and find a text from her.

I NEED YOUR HELP. MEET ME AT CORSA.
IT'S CHRISTIAN.

Fuck.

"Yo, we need to go. Now!" I shout over my shoulder to the guys.

"Bruv, just let me finish," Thorne adds with annoyance. Sensing something in my tone, Talon eyes me.

"What's going on?"

Sliding my phone back in my jacket, I kick up the kickstand on my bike. "He found her. We need to go, *now*."

CHAPTER 27

BEXLEY

Pain - Phix

Taking off down the empty side streets, I run as fast as my legs carry me. I don't have to look over my shoulder to know Christian is behind me. I can hear his feet as they slam down on the pavement in his pursuit.

My heart is racing in my chest. A fear unlike anything I've ever felt before radiates through me as I turn the corner onto Enterprise Rd toward Corsa Moto Works, where I told Sayshen to meet me. I can only hope that somewhere between there and the shop where Christian first attacked me, my phone will pick up service again, and the text will go through. I don't know what will happen if not, but I know it won't be good.

"You can't run forever, whore," Christian shouts behind me. Cars zip past us, and though I scream and shout at them, waving my arms in the air to draw their attention, none of them notice. None of them care.

Reaching the parking lot at Corsa, I head toward the back of the shop, but the moment I round the corner, I realize my mistake—a dead end. I freeze and spin around to backtrack, but it's too late. I come face to face with Christian. His large frame blocks my only way out, and what's worse, is there's no sign of Sayshen or Talon. I'm all alone. I don't even know if my message went through.

His strong hand grabs me by my hair, roughly pulling me to him. My hands snap over his as I frantically try to pry him off me.

"Stupid whore," he laughs, "Where is your precious white knight now?"

"Fuck you!" I spit back as my fists slam into his chest. "Let me go or I swear to fucking god."

"Well, well. Look who is all brave and feisty now," he replies with a menacing snicker. "What will you do? Hmm? You're nothing but a weak and useless bitch. We both know the only thing you're good for is laying on your back and getting fucked, and even then, I've had better." He pulls me along with him to a small grassy area beside the shop.

An uncontrollable laugh erupts through me, "To you, maybe. But I fucked both of them all night long. They had their way with me, filling and fucking both my tight holes. I fucked them so goddamn good, Christian, and you know what? I loved every goddamn second of it." He backhands me in the face, snapping my face to the side. The impact on my skin stings, and I cry out in pain. Tears brimming along my lashes as I continue to fight back. Kicking and pushing, anything to free myself, but it's no use. The hold he has on my hair is too strong, and he's too big.

"If you fucking touch her again, you're dead." My eyes widen as Sayshen's voice draws our attention. Christian's hand quickly drops its hold on my hair, and his arm wraps around my neck, pulling my back tightly against his chest. Lifting my tear-filled eyes to Sayshen, I find him slowly stepping toward us with his own gun pointed directly at Christian. His dark eyes lock with mine as the cool metal of Christian's gun presses firmly against my temple. His chest vibrates behind me as he laughs.

"Well, if it isn't Baby Shaw. Thought I took care of you already, but I guess not."

Sayshen smirks cockily, "Yeah, well, I didn't spend every day of my childhood training for nothing. Takes more than a little love tap to do me in."

"Shame, the same couldn't be said about your friend. Shit, I can still see the way his body was thrown around like a fucking rag doll down the track, and then to have his bike fucking land on him, well, that's gotta be some bad fucking karma. Now that I think about it, what was his name again? Conner? Cohen?" Christian spits, his tone snarky and disrespectful. "Meh, doesn't matter. He's dead now. A Demon feast for the fucking worms." Sayshen's jaw clicks with Christian's cold and careless remark.

My chest rises and falls with quick breaths. Being afraid of Christian isn't anything new to me, and I can handle it. But right now, even with a gun pressed against my head, I'm more afraid for Sayshen than myself. I'm afraid to lose one of the men who owns a piece of my heart, and though I have yet to see Talon, I know he can't be far behind. I can handle Christian hurting me. I'll take it like I have a million other times, but I don't think I will ever recover from something happening to them.

"It's been brought to my attention that you and your brother seem to need a lesson in how to train a bitch, and well, since you're here now, perhaps class should begin," he explains. Holding me tightly against him, he trails the gun's barrel down my body. Sayshen's eyes don't fall for it. He holds Christian's stare, unwilling to break it as he takes another step forward.

"Let her go before I put a fucking bullet in your head. I won't tell you again," Sayshen commands, taking another step toward us. Christian's arm around my throat tightens, cutting off my air supply. My hands grip his arm firmly, desperate to pull him off me as he runs the gun across my pussy over my skirt.

"What's wrong, Baby Shaw? I hear you like watching her get fucked. I can't even blame you, shit I know how pretty this little pussy is," he spits, tapping the barrel against me. "Don't you want to see how pretty it looks wrapped around my barrel? I'll thrust it up into this tight little cunt so fucking deep, and then, bam. Bust my gun's fucking load sending her brains all over the place," he mocks as he acts out, pulling the trigger with the gun buried inside me.

"Bruv, the only brains about to be scattered tonight are yours," Thorne cuts in from behind us. Catching Christian off guard, Christian spins around, giving me an opportunity to escape. Lifting my arm, I bring my elbow down, digging it into his ribs hard and fast. The impact causes him to release his hold on my neck, and he throws me to the ground.

Christian hisses, and goes after Thorne first. Blows are exchanged before Christian nails him good in the jaw with an uppercut. Dazed, Thorne loses his footing and Christian smashes him over the head with the handle of his gun, knocking him out. Thorne's body drops to the ground with a thud. A thin trail of blood leaks from a wound on his head, but I can see his chest rising and falling. He's still alive.

"You're a fucking dead man," Sayshen retorts in a low menacing voice. Within seconds, he crosses the small space between us, but instead of coming to me, he passes me and heads right for Christian behind me.

"No, Sayshen. Don't—" My words are cut off by the sound of Chrisitan's laugh. I watch, unable to bring myself to move or help. Christian raises his hands in the air like he's won. Snapping his eyes to me, he winks cockily before Sayshen tackles him to the ground.

The world around me seems to darken and blur as I inhale deeply. Filling my lungs with the air they so desperately need. My body is numb as I'm forced to watch them battle it out.

Talon. Where the fuck is Talon.

One of their guns is tossed to the ground in the chaos of things. It skids by me before stopping a few feet away. Looking over my shoulder, I find Sayshen and Christian going at it. Fists are flying as they roll about on the ground. Christian gets an advantage and has Sayshen pinned to the ground as he pummels him with his fists.

Pushing myself up on shaky legs, I grab the gun. The weight of it in my hands is heavier than I expected. Holding it up, I try to aim, but it's nearly impossible due to the shock my body is feeling. My arm and hand trembles uncontrollably. Sayshen's face is covered in blood as Christian's fist slams into him again. Closing my eyes, I hook my finger around the trigger. A shot rings out through the night air, and I collapse.

TALON

My bullet hits its mark.

Christian's body collapses on my brother's. Blood quickly soaked through his shirt from the wound, right through the heart. Rushing over to Bexley, I cautiously take the gun from her trembling hands and empty the bullets from the chamber, dropping them to the ground before I tuck it into the waist of my jeans.

"Princess," I whisper with a hushed tone as I cup her face, forcing her to look at me. Slowly, she opens her eyes. Her face is sickly pale, minus the crimson mark across her cheek. The very sight of it has me wanting to put another bullet in his cooling corpse for fucking touching her.

"Talon?" she replies, her voice barely a whisper. I pull her into my chest, wrapping my arms around her small frame, as I sigh with relief. When Sayshen told me about the text, I was fucking terrified. I was worried we'd be too late, and had she not fought back, there was a good chance we would've been.

But she did. She fucking fought, and she ran for her life. I can't even imagine the terror she must've felt, and yet, she was ready to pull the trigger. She was willing to kill to protect my brother, but there was no way I was letting her.

I knew if his death had to be on anyone, it was going to be me.

Looking up, I see Sayshen shove Christian's body off him to quickly jolt upright. We exchange a silent look, where I let him know she's okay. That I have her, and he nods in acceptance before quickly making his way over to where Thorne is still lying unconscious on the pavement.

"He's good," Sayshen pants before collapsing back down on the pavement next to Thorne. "Just knocked out." I nod in response before turning my eyes back on Bexley.

"It's okay. You're safe," I whisper, running my hand along her soft hair.

Her sobs are muffled against my chest as she wraps her trembling arms around my torso. "I—I killed him..." She stammers. Exhaling, I place a soft kiss on her hair.

"No, Princess. I did," I reply, "and now, he'll never fucking touch you again."

CHAPTER 28
BEXLEY

Grave Shift - Darci

Never in my life did I ever think I had it in me to take a life. But I guess when you love someone, you really are willing to protect them, no matter what it costs. I may have loved Christian at one point in my life, but looking back now, it's clear that the man I loved never really existed. He was a facade. Christian used a fictional persona to reel me in, and once he had me right where he wanted me, like a snake, he shed his skin, revealing the real and venomous monster who lurked within.

I'd never wish someone death, but if anyone I've ever crossed paths with deserved it, it was him. And while I wasn't the one who pulled the trigger, my fear, my hesitation to love or see myself as worthy of being loved, died with him.

It all faded away with his last breath.

Sitting myself up, I lean my back against the headboard to Talon's bed. Grabbing my scrunchie from the nightstand, I pull my hair up into a messy bun on the top of my head. What Talon did for me last night is something I can never repay. To bear the weight of knowing you took someone's life is no easy task, and truthfully I don't think I would've been strong enough for it. Maybe that's why Talon stepped in. Why he pulled the trigger before I could. Whatever the reason, I know it was for me. To protect me, but also for Cruz and Reign. For Sayshen.

What happened after is a bit of a blur. No doubt due to shock. I remember the flashing blue and red lights of the police cars, and Sayshen holding me in his arms on the side of the road as the paramedics treated Thorne's wounds. I remember Talon explaining what had happened to the police, and him being scared they would take him away.

Away from us.

But they didn't. The guys explained everything that had been going on. After Talon called Andre, and he showed up with Draygon and Wolfe, they told the police everything that had happened leading up to this moment. After one look at the footage from the Farms Stores security cameras, it was clear to the police that I was attacked.

Though I didn't pull the trigger myself, they deemed it self-defense. Meaning we were all free to go. The team refused to leave us, and we all headed back to the beach house together. While the rest of the guys took up beds around the house, Talon, Sayshen and I all slept together in Talon's bed. They held me. Consoled me, and wiped my tears until I fell asleep in the middle of them.

I haven't spent much time in Talon's room, but looking around, I still find myself shocked at how different it is from what I would've expected. Slate gray walls, with a few frame bike racing posters. Bamboo shelves with plants and books. It's clean and free of clutter though. Which I can't say is surprising, even though Sayshen's is the opposite.

"I was wondering when you'd wake up," Talon says with a quiet tone as he rounds the corner. He's carrying a plate with some fresh fruit and toast, along with a mug of steaming hot coffee. “She’s up!” he yells back down the hall over his shoulder.

The bright rays of sunshine through the window as he approaches my side of the bed and hands me the plate and mug. His piercing blue eyes seem to glow in the sun as he looks down on me with a gentle smile.

“Morning, Princess,” he says with a soft and calming tone.

My cheeks flush, and my lips pull into a slight smile as I take the mug from him. I blow on the hot liquid while holding his gaze, before bringing it slowly to my lips.

“Morning,” I reply, “what time is it?”

“Nearly three in the afternoon,” he explains. My eyes widen.

“And you didn’t wake me up?”

“Well you were out cold, babe. Besides, you needed the rest,” Sayshen explains as he enters the room. Wearing nothing but a thick cotton white towel wrapped around his waist. Raking my eyes across his toned body, I watch as beads of water drip down his chest from his shaggy wet hair. A familiar need builds between my thighs. Slowly, I pull my lip into my mouth with my teeth, biting down on the tender flesh.

Sayshen laughs, as he crawls across the bed toward me. “As much as I’d love to give you the best morning sex of your life, I can’t. The guys are downstairs, they just got back and there is no way in fuck I’m letting them hear the sweet fucking noises you make,” he whispers before pressing his lips softly on mine. “Those noises are just for me.”

“And me, fucker,” Talon adds, shoving his brother to the side. Sayshen rolls onto his back on the bed. A big cocky grin on his face. His hard cock tenting in the towel around him.

“Yeah, I suppose so,” he laughs.

I smile, as I bring the mug to my lips again. “Where did everyone go?”

“The last race was today, Princess.” Talon explains, as he

takes a seat on the edge of the bed. The mattress dips under his weight. "Wolfe, Thorne and Draygon raced for the Demons."

"Shit," with everything going on, I'd forgotten about the last race of the season, "What do you mean? Why didn't you guys go?" I snap, jolting upright in the bed. If I've learned anything about the Shaw brothers over the summer, it's how important racing, and winning the podium is. To know they missed it, to be here with me as the muscles in my chest constricting with guilt.

"Because, Bex. There was nowhere else we wanted to be, but here, with you. After last night, there was no way we were leaving you, not even to race. Besides, Demons still claimed the first and second spots on the podium," Sayshen adds, as he rolls onto his side. He props his head up with his arm, and lifts his eyes to mine. Placing a gentle hand on the blanket over my leg, he rubs it. "Seriously, we didn't want to go. So don't go beating yourself up over it. Even you couldn't have forced us to leave you, not today."

"He's right," Talon cuts in. Him missing the race is the most shocking to me. Especially after everything he's said about me being a distraction. I never would've expected him to put me above racing.

But I also never expected him to kill for me.

Sayshen smirks, "The guys were fine, and Andre supported it. Dad will be a bit pissed off—"

"Dad will be more than a bit pissed off, but I'll handle it," Talon adds, cutting off Sayshen's words.

"Talon! Baby Shaw!" Draygon shouts as he runs up the stairs.

"In here," Talon replies.

Draygon enters the room. His eyes land on Sayshen first, whose cock is still tented in his towel. His brow furrows, "I'm not even going to fucking ask."

"Probably a good thing," I reply with a giggle.

"What is it?" Talon asks, crossing his arms over his chest as he looks back over his shoulder at his friend. Draygon's expression is unreadable, as he turns his focus to Talon.

"It's, Lena. She's at the strip," he explains.

"Why the fuck would she be at the strip?" Sayshen snaps as he quickly rises from the bed.

"I don't know bro, but she's not alone. She's with some dude, and from what I'm hearing, no one knows who he is," Draygon adds, before tucking his phone into his pocket. "I know Coach said to steer clear of the strip for a bit and let shit die down, but if Lena is there, we need to find her."

"Draygon's right. I'm coming with you, I want to know why she ghosted the team the way she did," Sayshen spits as he takes off down the hall to his room. I knew the guys were worried about her after she went MIA after Cruz's funeral, and I have to admit, I've been worried too. We all handle grief differently, and maybe she just needed some space, but she had to know that the team would worry. They, like me, just want to be there for her through it.

It's what Cruz would've wanted.

"Alright, fine, but we go together. Someone has to make sure you fucking idiots don't get into any shit," Talon adds.

"Fine, I'll go tell the guys," Draygon replies before heading back downstairs.

Turning his sights on me, Talon cups my face gently in his hand, "Princess, you going to be okay to ride?"

I nod in agreement, lifting the mug to my lips and tossing back the rest of the coffee. "I'll be fine."

"She rides with me," Sayshen shouts from his room. Rolling my eyes, I smile, as I place the mug on the nightstand.

Talon's head falls back to rest on his shoulders as he sighs. "Like fuck she does, it's my turn fucker."

I climb from the bed to get ready. As I pass Talon, he smacks my ass, and winks at me cockily. Shaking my head, I smile as I make my way to the hall.

I have no idea what to expect at the strip. Or how Lena will react to us all showing up. But what I do know, is that this family fought for me. Regardless of what it cost them… and Lena, is a part of this family.

So now it's my turn to return the favor.

To fight for my family.

To be continued…

EPILOGUE

LENA

Lose Face - Daniel Di Angelo

Cruz's zx10 purrs to life beneath me as I watch the guys doing wheelies through the crowds up and down the strip. Eighteen days. That's how long it's been since he took his last breath. Since he sat on the very seat I'm seated on now, and yet, it still doesn't feel real. He was my best friend, my other half. Without him, I don't know how I'm supposed to move forward. This bike is all I have left of him, and while it brings me some comfort, it also brings me so much pain.

"Is this the best the guys around here have got?" Revel asks with his usual cocky tone.

Revel St Clair.

Trophy winning asshole with a competitive side that almost always ends in bloodshed, and yet, he's one of the few people I trust with my life. Because it wouldn't be the first time he's saved me.

Revel, and I spent a few years in the same foster home when we were younger. Being four years older than me, he quickly took me under his wing. He was the best big brother a girl could ask for. Things seemed great. For a time, I felt like I had finally found my forever family. My home.

But I was so very wrong.

When I turned thirteen, and my body began to change, I unwillingly began to draw the attention of our foster father. His nightly visits to my bedroom became more frequent. His touching, more aggressive and demanding. At first, I kept it a secret. He knew exactly how to ensure I wouldn't say anything. He told me if I said anything, or made a single noise he'd make sure Revel was taken back to the group home, or worse.

That he'd make sure the big brother I'd grown so attached to, would never see me again. He'd be thrown back into the system. A system where no one would want a kid like him. A kid with a dark past. Because who wants damaged goods?

So, I kept my mouth shut.

I buried my face into the pillows, and swallowed down the sobs that slipped from my lips, because it was all I could do to keep my family together.

That is until Revel walked in one night.

That night, everything changed.

"You good?" His voice pulls me from the dark thoughts, bringing me back to reality.

"Yeah, as good as I can be anyway," I reply.

He eyes me, clearly not buying my bullshit, "You don't have to lie to me. I didn't know him, but I sure as fuck know loss. I know how hard it hits. It doesn't matter how strong someone is, there's some pain that just takes longer to cope with."

Running my thumb over the neon green throttle grip of Cruz's bike, I smile. I can still remember the day he got them. He found them at some random yard sale downtown, and he was so fucking excited about them. They match the Demons colors. His team's colors, and though they're simple grips, they meant something to him.

Since his funeral, I've ignored the team. Not because of

anything they have done, they're all great and I love them all like family, but they don't understand the pain I'm feeling. They don't feel his loss the same way I do. I've read all their texts. Even their emails, and listened to all their voice messages. Talon and Sayshen are worried I blame them. That I'm angry their drama with Christian resulted in Cruz's death. Maybe I should be, but I'm not.

I know they never expected trying to protect Bexley to cost them a team member, and they never would've wanted it. Christian is the only one responsible, and thankfully, he's now lying cold and stiff beneath six feet of dirt. Where he belongs.

"Lena!" Wolfe's familiar voice shouts from behind me. Turning around, I find the rest of the team all pulling up. Draygon in his 02' Toyota Supra MK IV, with Reign in the passenger seat. Reign eyes me as he slowly climbs out of Draygon's car. He's on crutches, which means he must be healing well. Good.

At least he's breathing.

The Demons all make their way toward where Revel and I stand in the crowd, and I sigh. I knew it was only a matter of time before they came looking for me, and I get why, but I'm not ready for them. I'm not ready to face them all, not yet.

"That them?" Revel nods his head in their direction as Thorne, Talon, and Wolfe approach. Sayshen, Bexley, and Draygon all wait behind for Reign.

"What the hell, Lena? Haven't you been getting our texts?" Talon shouts, clearly upset with my ghosting them. "We've been worried. You can't just disappear on us."

"Why?" I snap, finding his commanding tone annoying. "I mean, the reason for me being with you guys so much is gone, right? So why do I owe any of you a reply?" My tone is cold and harsher than I intend, but it gets the point across.

"Fuck that," Wolfe spits. "You're family. You're a Demon. Cruz wouldn't—"

My body stiffens with the sound of his name. "Don't."

The rest of the team reaches us, and they all stand in a group next to Revel and I, watching and waiting for an explanation for my absence. But I don't owe them one.

"Don't say his name. Not now," I whisper, turning my eyes back to the stunt riders as they continue their show.

"We all miss him, Lena. But you're still family, even without Cru—"

"I think she said not to mention his name," Revel snaps, cocking his head to the side interrupting Sayshen mid-sentence.

"Sorry," Thorne adds as he turns to face Revel, "I beg you tell me who this guy is..."

"Who I am doesn't fucking matter. She told you once not to say his name. Don't make her tell you again," Revel threatens.

Thorne laughs, pulling his helmet off his head. "Oh look, we have a fucking comedian in our midst, because you must be joking if you think you can talk to me like that, cuz!"

The veins in Revel's blacked out arm tick with his increasing pulse. He lives for this type of shit. For confrontation. I swear he gets off on it. Revel clicks his tongue, and takes a step toward Thorne.

Quickly climbing off the bike, I cut him off, placing myself between him and the team. It's been years since I've seen or had any contact with Revel. But having heard about Cruz's death, he sought me out. He told me everything. How, even though we were torn apart that night, he never stopped watching out for me. He kept his distance, but that I was happy. I was living the life I deserved, and he didn't want to remind me of shit I'd healed from. So he stayed away.

But even with it having been so long, I can see the same signs I did that night. The same body language and look in his eye. Revel is the type of guy who can snap at any second. You wouldn't even see it coming. He will laugh with you, while envisioning your death in his head, and though I want to keep my distance from the Demons right now, I don't want them hurt.

I love them. All of them. Even Bexley. And I know they just want to be there for me, and support me. But they can't. Not without causing me more pain, anyways.

"Enough," I yell, giving Revel a warning look. "I'm not doing this shit. Not today. Revel, let's go," I add. Gently placing my hand on his chest, I push him backward toward the bike. He huffs with annoyance, but nods his head at me as he walks backward, unwilling to break Thorne's gaze.

Grabbing his helmet, he climbs on Cruz's bike, and starts up the engine. Talon's eyes twitch with anger as he watches Revel rev the engine. The Speed Demons logos are still plastered across the body work of the bike with all the team's sponsor logos. Even Cruz's number is still sitting on the front fender of the bike. It's just like he left it. All of it.

"I'm not gone," I explain, eyeing the team one by one. I know they're angry. Confused even, and I get it. "I just need time. Space. And I need you guys, to respect that."

Draygon crosses his arms over his chest, and Bexley wraps her arms around Sayshen's for support.

Pulling my helmet back over my head, I climb on behind Revel.

"Where are we going?" he asks, looking over his shoulder.

Taking one last look at the team, I can see the hurt and anger in their eyes as they watch us. "Anywhere but here," I reply.

Revel flicks his visor closed, and I wrap my arms around him as he pulls out onto the paved road of the strip, and takes off down Morris Bridge Road headed back into the city.

I know I can't hide from them forever, and I don't want to. One day, I will have to talk to them. To let them back in. But one day, is not today.

ACKNOWLEDGMENTS

This book never would've been what it is, without the people listed here. So much love, support, teamwork, and research went into this one, and being a part of the track and racing community it is so near and dear to my heart. So thank you, to all of you who contributed in any way at all.

Firstly, to my biker boys. Thank you! Your content brought this book to life. Your videos and pictures truly helped bring my characters and the story to life and I am beyond grateful to all of you for allowing me to use it as well as sharing and helping promote! Your support means so much,vand I truly can't wait to work with you all for book two!

If you're not already following these guys on Instagram, make sure you do!
They are a great bunch of guys with epic bike content!

s1krrafa
zx10mezz
duckin_r1
sharkboy_r1
sam.dxb
rwad_r1
sloth_r6
yamahawtie
ap_m0t0

R1mica
true.visionphotography

Lori, where do I begin? From the moment I told you my idea for this book, you were on board. Through all the chaos, the ups & downs, you supported me and helped me! There is no doubt in my mind, that this book and all that comes with it, wouldn't have happened, without it! From late night or early morning rambling, to crying over the rollercoaster of a ride, you were always there, and I know that no one loves these characters or this book as much as me, other than you! Thank you for always cheering for me. For picking me up on the bad days, and supporting me through the tough chapters I had to write. From the bottom of my pitch-black and depraved heart. I love you.

BETAs, Riggs, Ashley, Bria, Justine...BITCHES. Thank you for all of the love, support, and honest feedback along the way. I know it was hectic, and crazy for a while there, but we made it through! Your feedback, love and support helped bring this baby to life. Thank you, for the crazy voice notes, the daily drooling, the shit talking (Wet Wipe), and hyping me up on the days I doubted myself. Most importantly, thank you for taking the time to read, and fall in love with the Shaw brothers, I know it wasn't always easy, (Talon definitely loved to test your patience) But in the end I couldn't be more in love with their story.

Renee, thank you for always supporting and listening to me! For putting up with my madness during the plotting and spending long hours editing the same grammar and punctuation mistakes I make in every single book. Words can't express how thankful I am to you for keeping me on task and checking in daily from the future to make sure I'm alive and doing good! I love you!

Street Team, YOU GUYS KILLED IT! To have people coming to me saying that my street team is slaying, because they're seeing promo for Apex all over socials, is truly an honor! I already knew I had the best fucking team, but I am so proud to have the world seeing it too! You guys made this happen! You took the promo, the Pintrest boards and the info and you ran with it, making some of the most amazing and creative content I've seen in BookTok and I am so fucking grateful. This book and the hype it has gotten would never have happened without you guys and your hard work. You guys should be proud! I know I am! I love each and every one of you! Thank you!

Mom, thank you for always supporting me. No matter what. Whatever crazy idea my brain comes up with, you always listen, with no judgement. You always support and listen to me. My mornings wouldn't have been the same if I didn't have you to bounce ideas off of, and vent to. Thanks for giving me life, I love you!

Eddie, Snowstorm, without you, this book would never have even been a thought. It was your idea to incorporate track racing into a book, and while I had planned for it to be a simple novella, my brain took that thought and ran with it. Thank you for helping me with the bike slang, and the fine tuning of things. For spending hours spraying edges of my books and always doing everything you can to support me. I love you.

Andre Kress, thank you for allowing me to not only include your name as a main part of this story, but your business and foundation as well. (Corsa Moto Works) I am so thankful to have the opportunity to work with you and I hope that Apex, and the Full Send Series help bring some attention to you and all the things you do for the bike community.

The CAANE Foundation
Found on FB and to donate send via PayPal at
caanefoundation@gmail.com

MEET THE AUTHOR

Nova Kane is a Canadian stay-at-home mom who loves bringing dark and depraved men to life. When she isn't writing, she can be found hiding in a blanket fort with her fifth mug of coffee while binge-watching true crime docs or reading.

Stay up to date with her books by following her socials:

Instagram
Author.Novakane

Facebook Group
Dark And Depraved Readers